The Cafe at
SUGAR SAND INN

SUGAR SAND BEACH
BOOK 3

LEIGH DUNCAN

The Cafe At Sugar Sand Inn
Sugar Sand Beach Series, Book 3

Copyright ©2021 by Leigh D. Duncan

This book is a work of fiction. The characters, events, and places portrayed in this book are products of the author's imagination and are either fictitious or are used fictitiously. Any similarity to real person, living or dead, is purely coincidental and not intended by the author.

Digital ISBN: 978-1-944258-28-3
Print ISBN: 978-1-944258-29-0
Gardenia Street Publishing

Published in the United States of America

Welcome Back to Sugar Sand Beach!

Escape to Sugar Sand Beach with Nina Gray and her best friends for a second chance at all life has to offer.

At forty-five, Chef Nina has all but given up on her dream of having a kitchen of her very own. Once hailed as the fresh, new face on the restaurant scene, she saw her hopes for the future fall like an overbaked soufflé after the man she loved betrayed her and destroyed her reputation. For ten years, Nina has worked hard at regaining the trust of the top chefs in the DC area. But opening a restaurant of her own? That dream went up in a puff of smoke a long time ago.

Or she thought it had…until, thanks to the best friends a girl could ever want, Nina gets one more chance to make her dreams come true. While Michelle, Reggie and Erin concentrate on converting a run-down beach house into an inn, Nina tests out new dishes and recipes for the soon-to-be-opened Cafe at Sugar Sand Inn. But when rumors of Nina's past threaten the Cafe, will diners and guests patronize the beautiful restaurant she's always wanted? Or will history repeat itself?

Join Nina, Michelle, Reggie and Erin as they build new lives in Sugar Sand Beach, where fresh opportunities for life, love and happiness are as limitless as the blue Florida skies.

One

Nina

*L*ate-afternoon sunlight filtered through the leaves of a scrub oak outside the window and threw dappled patterns on the hardwood floor of the stately Queen Anne-style house. In the spacious kitchen, Nina drew in a deep breath. The scent of spicy, cheesy goodness filled the air. Her nose told her the crackers she'd made for tonight's snack were baked to perfection. Seconds before the timer dinged, she removed the cookie sheet from the oversize oven in the massive Aga range. Casting a critical eye over the cheese crisps, she nodded her approval. Her nose hadn't let her down. It rarely did. Flakes of red pepper dotted the orange rounds. The edges had browned beautifully. Experience told her the appetizers would break with a nice snap, exactly what she wanted them to do. She set the pan aside to cool. It was Friday, the night they toasted the end of the work week with something a bit stronger than their usual sweet iced tea. She gathered the ingredients for a large pitcher of Gulf Coast Sunset, the inn's signature punch.

Smiling, she muddled thin peach slices with a few sprigs of mint and basil from the inn's own garden. She'd have to remember to thank Reggie. Her young friend had worked wonders with a plot of ground that had suffered from years of neglect. She'd already been able to use some of Reggie's herbs in various dishes.

As for the rest, the tomatoes and beans were in bloom. The lettuce, melons and cucumbers were maturing nicely. The berries would take longer, but before too many years passed, the strawberries and blackberries she'd serve guests at the inn would be farm-to-table fresh. She could hardly wait. Until that day came, though, a local farmer's market would supply whatever they needed.

When the aroma of the herbs and fresh fruit rose to greet her from the bottom of the pitcher, she took a tray of her special lemonade and rum blend from the freezer. After adding the slushy mix to the fruit, she topped everything off with club soda and gave it a stir. A couple of mint sprigs put the finishing touch on the drink that she and the others would enjoy while they relaxed at the end of another busy week.

A sturdy serving tray sat at one end of the long, granite counter. She plated the crackers, centered the dish atop a small stack of napkins on the tray and arranged four tall glasses and the pitcher around them.

From the hall came the sound of footsteps. The heavy front door opened and closed behind Erin and Michelle, who were, no doubt, heading for the porch and the nightly confab that had become routine in the weeks since the four best friends had arrived at Sugar Sand Beach. She hefted her contribution to the evening's festivities and headed down the main hall toward the front door.

Her shoes whispered against the gleaming hardwood floors, and she couldn't help but take a moment to savor the differences they'd already made in the house Michelle had inherited from her birth mother. Had it only been a month since she and Michelle, Reggie and Erin had pulled up stakes in Northern Virginia and moved, lock, stock and barrel, to Florida's Panhandle? In some ways, it felt like a lifetime ago. In others, like it had just happened yesterday.

As much as she didn't want to admit it, the first time she'd stepped foot inside the shuttered two-story house, it had taken every ounce of courage she owned—and then some—not to run straight back outside and down to the beach. Once the most beautiful home in Sugar Sand Beach, Nancy Simmons's house had sat vacant for at least five years after her death. That first day Nina had left footprints in the dirt that coated the floors. So much dust had accumulated inside that it piled in drifts in the corners. Spiderwebs had adorned every window. They'd dripped from every doorjamb. Heat and humidity had turned the shelves and counters in the kitchen into a filthy, grimy mess.

Yet they'd been lucky. It could have been so much worse. Storm shutters had protected the windows. The roof hadn't sprung a single leak. And thanks to the efforts of Chris Johnson, the handyman who'd continued looking after the place, damage to the property had been kept to the barest of minimums. All she and Erin and Michelle and Reggie had to do was clean.

Which had been quite enough, thank you very much.

The yoga classes she'd taken through the years might have kept her forty-five-year-old body limber and flexible. The long hours on her feet in some of the busiest restaurants in Northern Virginia had built stamina. But nothing had prepared her for the aches and pains that came from spending sunup to sundown sweeping and scrubbing ceilings, walls and floors. She'd lost count of the number of area rugs she'd hauled outside and shaken until her own muscles shook from exhaustion. Or the number of buckets of soapy water she'd filled or the dirty ones she'd emptied. The house boasted twenty-six chandeliers. She knew because she'd helped Michelle lower every one of them. Together, they'd cleaned each precious crystal drop until it sparkled.

But they hadn't worked alone. While she and Michelle tackled the overhead lights, Reggie and Erin had vacuumed five years of dust from thick drapes. They'd treated the salvageable ones to a deep steam cleaning. The rest, they'd tossed. The day Reggie and her older sister had shaken out the drop clothes that had protected the furniture, they'd practically transformed the backyard into a Kansas dust storm.

But their efforts had paid off. By the time the townsfolk of Sugar Sand Beach had gathered at the house to satisfy their curiosity and meet their newest neighbors, she and Reggie and Erin and Michelle had cleaned and polished their way clear across the downstairs of the eight-bedroom house. Now everywhere she looked, wood gleamed and glass sparkled.

Sure, they still had more work to do. Some of the rooms upstairs hadn't been touched. No one had ventured into the tower with a broom and a mop. The apartment attached to the gardener's shed cried out for attention, too. To say nothing of all the hoops she'd have to jump through in order to open a cafe on the premises. But they had time. Time to tackle all of those tasks before the fall, when they planned to welcome their first guests to the Sugar Sand Inn.

Despite all the hard work that lay both behind and ahead of her, she'd never been happier. Her faith that she and her friends could really make this work, that they could take the hundred-year-old home Michelle had inherited and convert it into a first-class inn and cafe, grew a little stronger with each passing day. They could do this. They *needed* to do this. Each one of them had too much at stake for failure to even be an option. They'd given up too much, invested too much of themselves, not to see the project through.

Some mornings, when she woke to her cat making biscuits on the pillow beside her, she could hardly believe she'd walked away from the job she'd spent the last ten years striving to attain. But then she reminded herself that her position as head saucier had gotten as shaky as an aspic. Chad, the new sous chef at the Michelin one-star restaurant in Arlington, had already replaced several of the staff before he took aim at her job. She'd known it was only a matter of time before he gave her the boot.

It was no wonder that she'd jumped at the chance to join forces with Michelle, Reggie and Erin in converting the old house to a beachfront inn. The opportunity to run her own kitchen—even a small cafe—was simply too good to pass up.

Her throat tightened. Deliberately, she shook her head. She'd nurtured the dream of opening her own restaurant from the day her grandmother had put a whisk in her hand and taught her how to make perfectly scrambled eggs. From the beginning, she'd known becoming a chef wouldn't be easy—nothing worth doing ever was. But she'd been convinced she could make it. After all, while the other girls in high school were practically drooling over the captain of the football team, nothing gave her a headier rush than crafting a beautiful crème brûlée. She'd worked her way through college by washing dishes and chopping vegetables in every kitchen that would hire her. Not just to pay the bills but to gain experience. Culinary school had moved her several rungs up the ladder to success. A string of jobs had followed, each enhancing her resume a little bit more.

The chefs she worked under had praised her innovative techniques, the originality she brought to the dishes she prepared. But the years had passed. With each one, her hope of ever getting the chance to run her own kitchen had dimmed a little.

Oh, she'd come close. So close. She'd nearly clutched the brass ring once…until a single mistake had thrown her entire career into disarray.

Her footsteps faltered. Few cooks could afford to open a restaurant on their own, no matter how much they scrimped and saved. To do it right, a smart chef needed investors with deep pockets to back them. She'd thought she'd finally found hers.

Her stomach churned as she recalled the day she'd been prepping for the busy dinner service at work when she'd overheard that *her* investors, the ones who'd wined and dined her for the past six months, had chosen Tobias as their new head chef. To this day, she told herself she could have handled that. After all, she and Tobias been a team for more than two years. Working and—there was no sense in denying it—sleeping together. Standing side by side while they created mouthwatering dishes. Planning for the day when one of them would be handed the keys to their very own restaurant.

She'd thought he was her soul mate. That they'd be together forever. They'd even made a pact, both swearing that whoever got their big break first, they'd make the other their second-in-command. But Tobias had broken that promise—and her heart—when he chose someone else as his sous chef. As if that wasn't enough, he'd claimed all the recipes Nina had helped create were his alone. When she'd dared to protest, he'd accused her of trying to steal his work.

Loudly. Publicly.

That was the straw that had finally broken her. She'd thrown down her apron and walked out.

Which, as it turned out, had been a big mistake. Huge. No one stormed out of one of the most respected kitchens in Arlington in the middle of the hectic dinner service. Not unless they intended to kiss their career goodbye.

She should have known better. She *had* known better. Gushing arterial blood? That might be an excuse for leaving one's station.

Disappointment? A broken heart? Betrayal? Never. No one untied their apron strings over something so trivial. It simply wasn't done. No. Chefs were expected to slap a Band-Aid over whatever ailed them and keep on cooking. Which they did, if they wanted to hang on to their job, their reputations.

Unfortunately, that day, keeping her job had been the last thing on her mind.

She'd been fired, of course. And with Tobias bad-mouthing her to anyone who'd listen, she'd tumbled from the upper rungs of the success ladder all the way to the bottom. She'd spent the next five years taking jobs usually reserved for untrained kitchen help and wondering how she could have ever been so foolish. It was only long after Tobias's kitchen had gone belly-up—like so many new restaurants did—that she'd begun the slow climb to the top again.

By then, though, she'd blown her chance. When she'd finally been promoted to head saucier at Cafe Chez Jacques, she'd known she'd climbed as far back up the ladder as she'd ever go. She'd have remained at that level—maybe not at Jacques's, but at someplace similar—for the rest of her career if it hadn't been for Michelle.

Her friend had offered her the opportunity of

a lifetime. A chance to open the Cafe at Sugar Sand Inn. It had been a dream come true, which was why she'd sunk every dime she owned into the venture. She'd do whatever it took to make the small bistro a success. Both for her and for her friends who'd invested so much of their lives—and their own life savings—in the inn.

Laughter drifted from the front porch. The glasses on the tray rattled as Nina started. She needed to stop woolgathering and join the others. She took a second to make sure everything was balanced before she headed outside. Reggie, ever helpful, sprang to her feet and held the door open.

"What was so funny?" Nina asked as she divided the fruity concoction between the four glasses and handed two to Reggie.

"Erin didn't see Mr. Pibbs curled up on the chair. She nearly sat on him." Her glossy black hair swinging, Michelle giggled. "He wasn't happy." She took one of the drinks from Reggie's outstretched hand.

"How could you miss him?" Nina arched an eyebrow at her tanned and fit friend. Erin had the good grace to blush.

Mr. Pibbs had only been a few days old when Nina had discovered him—alone and mewing pitifully—in the alley behind her apartment.

Back then, he'd been so tiny he'd fit in the palm of her hand with room to spare. Not so, now. The orange-and-white tabby had filled out nicely. Maybe too nicely. The cat definitely had presence. "It's all right, baby," she cooed. "She wouldn't hurt you."

In answer, the big cat twitched one ear and curled into a ball. Nina picked him up and resettled him in her lap. Letting the cares of another busy week drop from her shoulders, she sipped her drink. The rum and peach blended well together, she noted as the icy liquid slid down her throat. As for the mint, it complemented the drink perfectly.

"I like these crackers," Reggie declared.

Nina's smile deepened. Watching people enjoy the food she prepared gave her a sense of satisfaction like no other. "I'm glad," she told Erin's sister and the youngest of their group of fast friends.

"Whatever you do"—Reggie stopped to swallow—"don't lose that recipe." She eyed the plate and the remaining crackers.

"Don't worry. I'll hang on to it," Nina assured her. "It's one of my favorites."

"I don't know how you come up with stuff like this," Reggie said, helping herself to seconds.

"I didn't invent these." While she'd love to claim the credit for the simple snack, the truth was an author had served the treats at a gathering she'd attended several years ago. Nina had liked them so much, she'd asked for the recipe, which she'd kicked up just a notch with added spice.

"Well, they're great," Reggie repeated. Leaning forward, the strawberry blonde passed an envelope to Michelle and quickly explained that she wanted to add the contents to the Sugar Sand Inn fund.

The move caught everyone by surprise. Not that she or Michelle, or even Reggie's sister Erin, thought the younger woman wouldn't gladly contribute to the inn…if she could. But until now, Reggie hadn't had two dimes to rub together. Apparently, though, that had changed after Reggie pointed out the error of his ways to her soon-to-be ex. The man had been a royal pain—walking out on the poor girl on what was probably the worst day of her life, then trying to cheat her out of her fair share of their assets. He'd shown up in Sugar Sand Beach in the middle of their open house where he'd created a world-class scene.

But Reggie had changed in the weeks following the day Sam had demanded a divorce. She wasn't the same woman who'd kowtowed to her husband's every wish and demand. Once he'd realized he was no longer dealing with the timid, browbeaten woman he'd married, the bully had caved. As bullies often did. The result was a generous settlement and a firm commitment to their divorce.

Nina stopped petting Mr. Pibbs long enough to raise her glass in a toast to her friend. "The next six months, until your divorce is final, will fly by," she promised.

"Here, here," Michelle said. Ice clinked as she touched her glass to Reggie's.

"I'm happy for you, sis," Erin said, echoing the sentiments of the others.

For a few minutes, they chatted about nothing of importance while they drank in the beauty of another glorious sunset on the balmy Gulf coast of Florida. The faint sound of the waves lapping the shore drifted over the dunes. A car slowed at the gate on the main road. It sped up again, its headlights cutting through the gathering dusk. Birds called good night as they roosted in the nearby scrub pines. A pair of sandhill cranes winged past, no doubt headed for their nest near the lake at the back of the five-acre property.

When the sun had slipped another inch lower on the horizon, Michelle cleared her throat. "I've ordered sheets and comforters for two of the upstairs bedrooms," she said, diving into the business part of their usual evening get-togethers. "We'll need to get those rooms prepped and painted before too long. This week, if anyone's free to help out."

Nina lifted her hand from Mr. Pibbs's silky fur long enough to signal that she'd pitch in. "I'm pretty handy with a roller," she added.

The cat signaled his displeasure at the interruption by bumping her hand with his head. She quickly resumed stroking the kitty she readily admitted to spoiling rotten.

"Someone from the health department is coming out first thing Tuesday to give us an idea of what changes we'll need to make in the kitchen." Nina had her fingers crossed that he wouldn't demand major renovations. "I posted an opening for kitchen help on a couple of job boards," she said as she ran her fingers down the cat's back. "If we get any good responses, I'll need to chat with the applicants a bit, but that's all I have on my agenda next week." Though it'd be months before the cafe opened for business, training a good assistant might take a while. She wanted to get started as soon as possible.

Michelle nodded. "I think, between the two of us, we can knock those rooms out in a couple of days."

"Sounds good." Her blond hair in its usual ponytail, Erin crossed her ankles. "I spent most of my time checking out the nearby tourist locations this week. Lots of places rent watercraft, but none of them provide the kind of guided tours I have in mind for the inn. The thing is, we'll need more kayaks, a couple of canoes, life jackets and the like. I was thinking I'd make a run down to the Keys to pick up my Jeep and the gear I left there. I was hoping Reggie could come with me."

Nina glanced toward the road. The car that had passed by the entrance to the property a few minutes earlier had doubled back. This time, the driver turned onto the graveled drive that led to the house. She straightened slightly.

"I'm up for a road trip." Reggie set her napkin on the glass-topped wicker table. "This would be a good time for me to take a few days away from the garden."

"Are we expecting company?" Nina asked. Her questioning gaze met with three sets of raised eyebrows.

"Who's that?" Reggie wanted to know as a long, dark sedan crested the small rise that stood between the main road and the gate.

No one answered.

With the others, Nina watched the approaching car. An odd sense of apprehension coursed through her as the vehicle pulled onto the parking pad and stopped. She leaned forward. Her taste for anything sweet suddenly disappeared, and she placed her unfinished drink on the table.

The car door opened. A man stepped out. Tall and heavily built, he'd rolled up the sleeves of the plaid shirt he wore over dark jeans.

Nina froze. Her gaze fell to the man's feet and the pair of brown alligator boots he wore. She sucked in a breath. At the same instant, every fiber of her being went on high alert. Her hands fisted. She stood. In the process, she unceremoniously dumped Mr. Pibbs on the floor.

The cat yowled. Before she could muster her wits or apologize, Mr. Pibbs shot through the open front door and disappeared.

"Nina?" Reggie whispered. "What's wrong?"

She couldn't answer. Her mouth had gone bone dry. Besides, how was she supposed to explain that the man who'd broken her heart, the last man on earth she'd ever expected to see again, was walking toward her?

"How are you this lovely evening, ladies?" Tobias's voice poured like silky smooth chocolate from between full lips that curved into a smile. His nod singled her out. "Nina."

"Toby," she answered, unable to resist using the nickname she knew he hated.

"Ouch!" Tobias struck one fist to his chest. "You wound me." His attention shifted to her friends, who, fully aware of the sudden tension in the air, stared fixedly at him with stony expressions. The lips Nina had once loved to kiss thinned for a split-second before they reassembled into a smile that had charmed countless men and women. "I'm Tobias Wright. Let's see now." He removed dark sunglasses to reveal piercing blue eyes. He focused, one by one, on the women on the porch. "You must be Michelle. I was sorry to hear of your husband's passing. My deepest condolences." He bowed slightly.

Michelle stiffened and gave him a frosty, "Thank you."

Tobias's gaze shifted. "Back from wandering the world, Erin?" he asked. "I'd love to buy you a cup of coffee sometime and have you tell me all about the strange and fascinating foods you encountered in your travels." Perhaps sensing he wouldn't get a response—or at least, not the one he wanted—he moved on to the young woman who sat, coiled like a wire ready to spring, nearest Nina. "This, of course, must be Reggie. Who else could it be? With those pretty eyes, no one could miss the fact that you and Erin are sisters."

Nina ground her back teeth. In the two years she and Tobias had been together, he'd never once found the time to meet her friends. Now he'd shown up on her doorstep having obviously done his homework. No one did that unless they were after something. Her voice surprisingly cool and even, considering how badly her legs shook, she demanded to know what it was. "What do you want?"

"Straight to the point, Nina. That's one thing I could always count on you for." Tobias swung to face her. "You look as beautiful as always, I might add."

Her lips pursed. She didn't need his compliments to bolster her self-confidence. Her daily regimen included yoga sessions, a diet rich in fresh fruits and vegetables and a plethora of skincare products that helped keep her skin soft and supple. He, on the other hand, hadn't done much, if anything, to stave off the effects of middle age. Tobias might think leaving his shirt untucked hid his considerable paunch, but—*Hate to break it to ya, big fella*—it didn't. The heavy golden mane he'd been so proud of had receded a full inch. His once-chiseled features had softened.

"I'd like a word, if you wouldn't mind." When she didn't trot right down the stairs to his side—as if she would—he added, "It's the least you can do considering how much you owe me."

"I owe you?" Her voice climbed an octave. The man was delusional. There was no other explanation. They'd once been a well-oiled team both inside and outside the kitchen. Together, they'd dreamed of the successful restaurant they'd run. But he'd ripped the tablecloth out from under their plans. He'd burned her love for him to a crisp when he'd grabbed the brass ring and left her behind. Worse, the lies he'd spread about her had made it all but impossible for her to find work in any kitchen in Northern Virginia. Okay, so he hadn't destroyed her career—she'd done that herself when she walked off the job— but he'd assembled all the ingredients. A mise en place for disaster. "Seems to me you've got something backwards."

Tobias gave the same beguiling smile that had once made her heart race. Today her pulse didn't so much as skip a beat. She was really and truly over him.

He held up his hands, palms facing her.

20

"Neither of us are blameless. But do you really want to hash out our differences in front of your friends? Can't we"—he glanced around—"go for a walk? Just the two of us?"

Wordlessly, she sought advice from Michelle, Erin and Reggie. The expressions on their faces told her they'd have her back, no matter what she decided. Her desire to go anywhere with Tobias wavered between zero and zilch. But the man was wrong if he considered himself the injured party in their relationship. And she was just the person to straighten him out.

She sucked in a fortifying breath. The sinking sun hovered over the horizon. Although the trees cast long shadows, an hour or so of light remained. "I'll give you twenty minutes," she said as she marched down the front steps with her back held ramrod-straight.

Tobias reached for her, thought better of it and let his hand fall to his side. "Which way?" he asked, falling in beside her.

"We'll take the path to the lake." Without looking at them, she assured her friends she'd be back well before dark. The time limit put Tobias on notice to get to the point while it all but guaranteed the others would send out a search party if she didn't return by the time the frogs sang their nightly chorus.

As they walked, she concentrated on taking deep, calming breaths. She drank in the lemony smell that rose from a patch of moonflower. The light breeze rippled through the tall seagrass on either side of the path. The rhythmic sound of distant waves rolling ashore helped still her jittery nerves.

"I am truly sorry for the way things ended between us," Tobias began once they were well out of earshot from the porch.

"Really?" The opening so surprised Nina that she nearly lost her footing.

"Is that so hard for you to believe? You and I"—he gestured to her—"we had something special." His voice dropped to a near-whisper. "I've missed you."

Good grief. Was he trying to get her to come back to him? He'd destroyed her. It had taken her years to get over his betrayal. He was wrong—so wrong—if he thought he could roll back the clock with a simple apology. "Too little. Too late," she said, summing up all she was feeling in the fewest words possible.

"I tried to explain. I wanted to talk to you that night, but you left the restaurant in such a rush I never had the chance. By the time I finished my shift and had drinks with the investors, you'd cleared all your things out of our apartment.

I didn't know where you'd gone. You wouldn't return my phone calls." Several heartbeats went by before he added, "I never thought you'd be so petty. So jealous."

"I wasn't jealous." The denial escaped her lips before she could stop it. She backtracked. "Okay, maybe I was. A little." She held her thumb and index finger mere centimeters apart. "But that wasn't the real problem."

"No?" Doubt coated Tobias's voice like a finished custard coated the back of a spoon.

"No," she said firmly. "The Hardy brothers were *my* investors. You knew I'd been working with them for months." The wealthy businessmen owned several successful restaurants in the DC area. The minute she'd heard they were looking to expand their holdings, she'd thrown her chef's toque into the proverbial ring. And it had worked. She'd been in talks with them for six months when they invited her to bring a date to dinner one night. In one of the dumber moves she'd ever made, she'd taken Tobias. Who had poured on the charm, overwhelming her own personality. Within a week, the Hardys' interest in her had dried up. Before a second week passed, they'd named her boyfriend as their new chef. "You pulled the chance for me to have a kitchen of my own right out from under me."

"It wasn't my choice, Nina," Tobias protested. "It was theirs. Their market analysis told them a male chef would fit the image they wanted for a restaurant that served mostly meat and potatoes. Nicely prepared meat and potatoes." He bared his teeth in a toothy grin. "But meat and potatoes all the same."

"That's sexist!" She kicked at a stone in the path.

"True. But it's also the way the world works." Tobias hooked his thumbs onto the pockets of his jeans. "What was I supposed to say when they asked me to run their kitchen? No? They made it clear you were no longer in the running."

"Did you at least try to make them reconsider?"

"What good would that have done?" He shrugged. "Their minds were made up. If I had turned them down, they'd have simply found another chef—a male chef—to lead their staff. I couldn't do that. You wouldn't have wanted me to do that."

Tobias at least had the decency to tell the truth about what he'd done, she thought. That didn't make it right or make her feel one bit better about it, but it was something. And he wasn't wrong about one thing. No chef in their right mind turned down the opportunity to run their own kitchen.

Too bad he hadn't bothered to talk to her about it. As his friend, as his lover, hadn't she deserved that much consideration? If he'd come to her ahead of time and told her what he was doing and why, she'd never have asked him to walk away from such a great opportunity. But he hadn't. Instead, he'd let the news blindside her. Worse, he hadn't fulfilled his promise.

Why was that?

"We had a pact, you and me. Whichever one of us made it, they were supposed to make the other one their second-in-command," she reminded him. "I was going to be your sous chef. Or you were going to be mine. But you picked some novice fresh out of culinary school." She'd only been able to think of one reason he'd do that. "You were sleeping with her, weren't you?"

"With Sophia?" His brows slammed together. "No!" he said with more vehemence than she expected of him. "She's John Hardy's daughter. He made it clear that making her my sous chef wasn't negotiable. He didn't leave me any choice. I had to play by their rules."

She worried a hangnail. The situation sounded eerily similar to the one she'd encountered at her last job. One of the owners had strong-armed the head chef at Cafe Chez Jacques into giving his nephew the job of sous chef. It hadn't mattered that Chad possessed neither the experience nor the temperament the position required. He'd been given free rein over the staff.

Had she misjudged Tobias?

She shook her head. For whatever reason, the investors had chosen him over her. Now he claimed John Hardy had insisted on naming his daughter as the second-in-command for the restaurant. That still left the not-so-little matter of the work her former lover had stolen. Try as she might, she couldn't think of a single good reason to explain away that bad act.

"And the recipes?" she asked, refusing to let him off the hook. She pressed one hand to her chest. "You know good and well those didn't belong to you. I created most of them. You might have added a sprinkle of salt, a pinch of spice. That didn't make those dishes yours. You had no right to say they were. Or to accuse me of stealing from you. Do you have any idea what that did to my reputation, my career?"

Grass rustled and a twig snapped as something moved through a clump of nearby bushes. Tobias halted. He scanned the tall grass on either side of the path through wide eyes. "Is it safe for us to be out here? Are there bears?"

"Probably. But what you really need to worry

about are the wild hogs. And the gators. One of them might take offense to your choice of footwear." She pointed a finger at his feet. When it came to shoes, most chefs chose comfort and support over fashion. Not Tobias. For as long as she'd known him, he'd insisted on wearing alligator boots for both work and play. His choice of footwear was so much a part of his identity, her stomach had knotted the moment he'd stepped from his car and she'd taken her first good look at what he was wearing.

"Let's, um, let's not go any farther," Tobias murmured.

"Whatever you say," she said. In public, Tobias looked and acted the part of a man's man. But she'd seen the real figure behind his carefully crafted image. In reality, Tobias was a bit of a wimp. She should know. She'd listened to him moan and groan often enough when he hobbled into their apartment after a long shift. It didn't matter that she'd worked equally long hours—he expected her to fetch and carry without complaint while he relaxed, his feet soaking in an icy footbath.

Another twig snapped. Tobias swung his head toward the sound. "Maybe, now that we've cleared the air between us, we should head back."

"Not so fast." She planted her feet. As far as she was concerned, the air between them remained just as murky as it had been before his arrival. "You still haven't answered my question about the recipes. Why did you accuse me of stealing them when you know good and well I created them?"

"Nina, darling. You can't still be holding on to that grudge."

It was her turn for total honesty. "I can. And I do."

Tobias expelled a long-suffering sigh. "I had to say I created those recipes on my own. Don't you understand? I needed every advantage with the Hardys. You would have done the same thing."

She doubted it and let that show in her expression.

Tobias's focus shifted this way and that, everywhere, in fact, except straight at her. "It was only supposed to be temporary. If you hadn't raised such a ruckus about those silly recipes, I could have hired you. Not as my right hand but as a line cook. We'd have continued working together, creating new dishes for the restaurant."

New recipes he'd claim as his own, she thought when he paused to take a breath.

"In a few years, when the Hardys were ready to open their next restaurant—something that was more bistro and less chophouse—I would've insisted you were perfect for the spot. But you ruined any chance of that happening when you let your temper get the best of you. And that, my dear, ruined me."

This should be interesting.

She folded her arms across her chest. "How—exactly—was any of that my fault?"

Unable to stop herself, she'd read every review of Tobias's restaurant on Yelp. For the first year, patrons had raved about the citrus butter finish on their steaks, the spicy sauce that came with their pork chops—both her recipes—and seemed willing to overlook long delays in getting their orders. But as time passed and the food service continued at a glacial pace, the reports focused more on two- and three-hour waits and poor management. In less than two years, the restaurant had closed, buried under a deluge of bad reviews.

Tobias wagged a finger in her direction. "You created doubt. After you stormed out of the kitchen that day, the Hardys said they believed me when I swore those recipes were mine alone."

"Which they weren't," she put in.

"To-ma-to, to-mah-to. Café, cafe," he said,

putting his own spin on the facts. "But the minute reservations started to drop off and I suggested changes, I saw the doubt in their eyes. They blamed every dissatisfied customer on me. When I developed a new menu, they said it didn't have enough spark, that my new dishes lacked the originality. All because of the accusations you'd made."

And they'd circled back to the point where it was all her fault. Why was she not surprised? That was one thing she hadn't missed about Tobias, that whenever things went wrong, he looked for someone else to blame. Since she worked and slept at his side, he'd heaped most of it on her.

Tired of his mind games, she turned to him. "So why now? Why seek me out now?" Slower, she repeated her original question. "What do you want, Toby?"

He pressed his hands together, his fingers steepled under his chin. "I'm opening a new restaurant soon. With new backers. The Happy Dolphin. It's smaller. Not at all on the same scale as the one in Arlington. But it's taken me a long time to get to this point. I don't want you to ruin it for me."

"Don't be ridiculous. No one in Virginia cares what I think or say down here in Florida.

Unless…" Her heart thudded. She eyed him carefully. "Where is this new restaurant of yours?"

"In Panama City."

Her heart sank. Panama City was less than an hour east of Sugar Sand Beach. She licked her lips. "And your specialty?"

"Seafood, of course." He answered with a careless shrug. "With the abundance of fish and shellfish fresh from the Gulf, why choose anything else?"

She trapped a groan behind closed lips. Though her cafe's offerings would be limited to breakfast and lunch at first, she hoped to add a dinner service before the year was out. In keeping with the farm-to-table theme, she'd planned on taking advantage of the freshest food available by including two seafood options each night. A move that would put her in direct competition with Tobias's new place.

She scuffed one foot through the sand. "That brings us back to my original question. What do you want, To—"

"Nothing," he said, cutting her off before she used the dreaded nickname. "I mean that in the most literal sense. You open your cafe. I'll run the Happy Dolphin. We'll bury the hatchet between us and go our separate ways."

She mulled the suggestion over for a long ten seconds. As much as the world seemed to thrive on conflict these days, an ongoing feud between two chefs with similar restaurants a few miles apart was bad for business. She and Tobias were bound to attend some of the same civic functions, bid on the same catering events, run into each other at trade shows and the like. "We'll agree not to say a word about the other?"

"Yes." Tobias nodded. "That's all I'm asking."

She swallowed. A truce could work in both their favors. As long as he held up his end of the bargain. She eyed him cautiously. Could she trust him to do that much?

Two

Reggie

"He's getting into his car," Reggie called from her post by the front door. The rattle of silverware and dishes told her Michelle was setting the table in the breakfast nook. Water ran in the kitchen sink where Erin washed greens for a salad.

Reggie peered through the glass panel. In the red glow of Tobias's taillights, she spotted Nina standing at the edge of the parking area. Her friend remained there until the black sedan crested the small hill and disappeared down the other side. The instant Nina started toward the house, Reggie ducked away from the door. "They didn't kiss," she announced on her way to the kitchen.

"Well, that's good," Michelle said, sounding relieved. "I'd hate to have to shake some sense into her. She was devastated the last time."

Erin, who'd been out of town when Tobias and Nina's past relationship blew up, put the lettuce in the spinner and gave it a whirl. "Hard to imagine our solid, stable Nina losing her head over someone who'd treat her so badly."

"She told me she'd been involved with someone a lot like Sam." Reggie's soon-to-be ex had undermined her self-confidence at every opportunity. "That whenever anything went wrong in his life, it was always her fault. I guess she was talking about Tobias?" Ten years younger than Michelle, Nina and Erin, Reggie hadn't really been considered one of the close-knit group until she married Sam five years ago. By then, Tobias had fallen into the he-who-will-not-be-named category.

"None other," Michelle confirmed. "The man ruined her. Both emotionally and professionally."

Crossing to a small nook, Reggie ducked into the butler's pantry. A rack over the granite counter held bottles of wine. Most of them were hostess gifts their neighbors had brought to the open house. Drawers on either side of a built-in cabinet held an assortment of bottle openers and other supplies. Recalling the discussion she'd had with Nina the day she'd heard the news about Sam's secret bank account, Reggie selected two bottles of red. She opened both.

The front door squeaked open and closed. Footsteps echoed down the hall. A few seconds later, Nina stood in the kitchen doorway looking frumpled. Far different from her usual graceful elegance.

"You're cooking?" she asked. Surprise registered in her dark eyes. By unspoken agreement, the kitchen had become her domain.

"We all managed to survive before we had a full-time chef." An excellent cook in her own right, Michelle tried and failed to look indignant. When Nina pinned her with a skeptical look, she caved. "Okay, you got me. I'm warming," she admitted. "I have no idea what it is, but I grabbed the casserole you had in the fridge and stuck it in the oven."

"Your guess is as good as mine," Nina said. "I took it out of the freezer. It's one of the mystery dishes the women from the Ladies' Auxiliary brought to the open house. They were all very careful to tape their names to the bottom of the pans so we could return them. But we have to guess what's in them."

"I made a salad in case whatever it is turns

out to be dreadful." Erin carried a wooden bowl to the table. She'd piled tomatoes, carrots and cucumbers atop the lettuce.

Nina sniffed. "The casserole can't be too bad. It smells decent."

Reggie emerged from the butler's pantry with the wine. "Just in case both the salad and the casserole go into the compost heap, we have this." At the table, she poured generous servings into each of the four glasses.

Nina sidled closer. When Reggie finished, the cook took the bottle and added another splash to her own glass. "I think I'm going to need that tonight," she explained.

"Things didn't go well with Tobias?" Michelle asked, wearing kitchen mitts as she removed the casserole from the oven.

"Yeah, what did he want?" Erin asked over her shoulder while she grabbed a selection of salad dressings from the door of the Sub-Zero they'd inherited along with the fully furnished house.

"Let's fix our plates," Nina suggested. She downed several gulps of wine. "I'd better eat something soon, or the next thing you know, I'll be passed out on the couch."

"Everyone's entitled to overindulge once in a while. If having an old boyfriend show up without warning doesn't qualify as a good reason, I don't know what does." Erin added a bowl of croutons to the table.

"Don't worry. If you fall asleep, we'll throw a blanket over you on our way upstairs," Reggie assured her friend.

"Nice to know you've got my back." Nina issued the dry retort as she slid onto the bench seat while the others took their usual spots at the table.

It was Michelle's turn to say the blessing. Tonight, she kept the prayer short and sweet, and within seconds they were filling their plates. The casserole, as it turned out, featured chunks of chicken, loads of veggies and a respectable sauce beneath a crunchy, cornbread crust.

"Not bad," Nina pronounced after sampling the topping, chicken and sauce separately. "I would've added some thyme and cut back on the salt a bit, but for potluck, I've had a lot worse."

"Reminds me of a dish my grandmother used to make." Reggie glanced across the table at Erin. "Remember? She used to serve it whenever the preacher came to Sunday dinner." Their grandparents had owned a hardscrabble farm in West Virginia, not far from the retirement community where Reggie and Erin's parents now lived. All through grade school and junior high, both girls had spent a month each summer helping their grandfather tend his small herd of dairy cows.

"Yes." Erin rolled her eyes. "Hers had slices of hard-boiled egg across the top. That was a definite turn-off for me."

Reggie speared a chunk of chicken and chewed thoughtfully. "Oh, yeah. I'd forgotten the eggs. Rubbery, overcooked, dried-out, hard-boiled eggs. No wonder the preacher didn't come to dinner all that often."

"Our grandmother wasn't exactly a world-class cook," Erin explained to Nina.

"So I gather," Nina nodded.

"Not like you…or Tobias?" Reggie hinted.

At the mention of her former lover, Nina took another fortifying sip of wine. "He has an interesting take on our breakup," she said. Her hand on the stem, she slowly rotated the glass.

"How so?"

"None of it was his fault, naturally. No surprise there. He's a competent chef. Definitely not Michelin material." Earning a star in the well-known ranking system was something most chefs only dreamed of. "But when it comes to shifting blame, he's in a class all by himself."

Reggie thought her ex might qualify for a spot in that group, but she wisely held her tongue. Her friends and her sister had rallied around her when Sam had walked out on their marriage. Tonight, she'd help them do the same for Nina.

Wine sloshed against the sides of her glass when Nina stopped spinning it in circles. "To hear Tobias tell it, the investors I'd been working with for several months suddenly decided—without any influence from him, mind you—that they'd be better off with a man as their head chef."

Across the table, Erin glared daggers. "Tell me he didn't say that."

"Yep. That's his story, and he's sticking to it." Nina took another swallow. "It's been a minute, so you might not remember that Toby and I had sworn we were a package deal. If I found backers for my restaurant, I'd make him my sous chef. And vice versa."

"Only he didn't live up to his end of the bargain." Michelle added a bit more balsamic vinaigrette to her salad. "There was another girl. Sally or Susan—something like that. Did you ever find out if they were fooling around together?"

"Sophia," Nina clarified. "I had these two investors—the Hardy brothers," she told the others. "They own several restaurants in the DC area. All top-notch places. Any chef would want to throw in with them. Anyway, Sophia, she's John Hardy's daughter. Toby swears John insisted on making her the sous chef. Funny thing, though, that never came up—not once—in all the time the Hardys were in talks with me."

"So what was that crack he made about you owing him?" Erin wanted to know.

Nina chased a lettuce leaf around her plate with her fork. "The restaurant he and the Hardy brothers opened—The Arlington Grille—it failed in less than two years."

"Whew!" Reggie whistled. Nina was such an excellent cook that Reggie had once asked her friend why she didn't have her own restaurant. When she learned it could cost upwards of three grand per place setting, she cringed. It made her want to order the most expensive thing on the menu at her favorite mom-and-pop diner, just to help the owners break even. As for Tobias's Grille, it had been out of her price range, but she'd peeked in the window once. The place was huge, with seating for hundreds. "That's a lot of money not to get any return on their investment."

Nina shrugged. "The Hardys gave the place a fresh look and reopened six months later with a new chef and a new name—Tapas Galore. I think it's still around."

"It is." Michelle chewed thoughtfully. "I've been there a time or two. Good food. Great atmosphere."

"Anyway, Toby blames me for the failure of his restaurant." Nina pushed her nearly untouched meal away. "He says when I raised a stink over the recipes we created, recipes he claimed sole credit for, his backers lost faith in him. Without their trust, he says he couldn't turn things around when the Grille went through the usual ups and downs." She snorted. "In the restaurant biz, you're lucky when a single week goes by without hitting a rough patch."

"Arlington Grille had a lot more wrong with it than a couple of rough patches," Michelle said softly.

Nina zeroed in on her friend. "You went there?"

"Once." Michelle sipped from her water glass. "One of Allen's co-workers had heard of a new place, so we met them at the Grille for dinner. It was an unmitigated disaster from the moment we walked through the door."

"Tell me more," the chef demanded.

Reggie chortled when interest flickered in Nina's eyes.

Michelle ticked off a list of grievances on her fingers. "They'd lost our reservation. We sat in

41

the bar for two hours before the hostess showed us to a table, and then it was right next to the kitchen." Michelle shook her head. "It was noisy. A constant stream of wait staff passed within inches. None of them stopped at our table, though. Service was positively glacial. The staff treated it as if it were par for the course. After someone finally took our order, we waited another hour for our food. When it came, the steaks were overcooked. By then, steam was rolling out of Allan's ears."

Reggie clamped one hand over her mouth. Everyone at the table knew Michelle's late husband didn't tolerate poor service well.

"He asked to speak with the manager," Michelle said. "Instead, Tobias stopped by our table. I didn't know he was the chef until then. He basically accused us of trying to scam the restaurant for a couple of free meals. He said if we didn't like the food, we didn't have to come back."

Nina gasped. "With an attitude like that, no wonder the restaurant folded. The customer is always right. Always." She buried her face in her hands.

"That was the last straw," Michelle continued. "Allan asked for the check, and we left. I think that's the only time I've ever walked out of a restaurant without leaving a tip. If Tobias had been the least bit apologetic, we would have given the place another chance. But the way he treated us? Yeah, no."

"That's Toby for you," Nina said with a sigh. "Nothing is ever his fault. It's always someone else's. Break your promise? 'The investors made me do it.' Steal your girlfriend's work? Blame that on the investors, too. Restaurant fails? It's all the customers' fault…unless somehow it was mine." She pointed to her chest.

"You're not buyin' any of his garbage, are you?" Reggie asked. She was still trying to crawl out from under the damage her soon-to-be-ex had inflicted to her self-esteem. But Nina was stronger than that, wasn't she?

The soft touch of Nina's hand on hers offered reassurance. "Don't worry. I know Tobias is wrong. Like Michelle pointed out, there were a lot of problems with Arlington Grille, not the least of which was Toby himself."

Reggie swallowed. "Just don't let him make you feel guilty for his mistakes. You had every right to be angry over the things he did."

"Got it," Nina nodded. She swirled what was left of her wine and downed it. "Here's the thing, though. Toby is opening a new restaurant in Panama City. The Happy Dolphin. That's why

43

he came here this evening, to ask me"—she made air quotes—"not to spread lies about him. In return, he promised not to say anything negative about me. He wants us to put the past behind us. Start over with a clean slate."

"I'm sensing a 'but,'" Erin said. Grabbing the second bottle of red, she topped off everyone's glasses.

"You know me too well," Nina said with a weak smile. "Yeah, there's a but. I don't know if I can trust him to keep his word. I think looking for a scapegoat is the way he operates. He says he's changed, but I wouldn't put it past him to let his version of our past slip out the first time he loses a catering gig. Or when something goes wrong at his new place." She mopped her face with her hands.

"Hey. It'll be all right," Erin soothed. "People will see Tobias for what he is. His own hubris will bring him down."

Nina gave her head a sad shake. "I don't think we can take that chance. If it was just me, I'd deal with it. But it's not. The cafe will be part of Sugar Sand Inn." She held up two intertwined fingers. "Damaging one will hurt the other." She sent a pleading look around the table. "We have so much at stake here. All the money we've sunk into the Inn. The work we've done. He could destroy all that by spreading rumors about us, about me."

Erin waved a dismissive hand. "No one around here will put any stock in what Tobias says. You saw how wonderfully everyone treated us at the open house and how they supported our plan to open an inn at the town council meeting."

"She's right," Reggie said with a nod to her older sister. "The people in Sugar Sand Beach like us and want to see us succeed. They aren't going to believe Tobias's lies."

"I wish it was that simple. But I saw firsthand how much harm he can do," Nina said. "It took years for people to forget the lies he spread about me in Virginia. I can't help worrying he'll do the same thing here."

"When does his new place open?" Michelle leaned forward.

"In a few weeks. That gives him a huge head start since our cafe won't open till the fall." Nina shook her head. "I wish there was some way I could get ahead of the curve so that when he makes his move—whatever it is—people will already be familiar with our menu."

Reggie rubbed her chin between her index finger and her thumb. "There might be a way," she said slowly.

"What is it?" Erin prodded.

Her friends had been so encouraging that she was finding it easier and easier to speak up. Still, she took a beat to gather her courage. "I stopped by the hardware store the other day to pick up some lumber and nails for a small toolshed I'm building out by the garden. Hauling the hoes and clippers out there every time I want to pull weeds gets—" One glance around the table let her know her friends didn't need to hear the entire story. "Never mind why," she said. "That's not important. What's important is the Fourth of July weekend. Apparently Sugar Sand Beach throws an old-fashioned celebration. I saw a flyer at the hardware store. There'll be a parade with a grand marshal and a marching band. Some floats. Fireworks at night."

Nina ran a hand through her hair. "What's all this got to do with the cafe? Or any of us?"

Suddenly aware that three sets of eyes had focused on her, Reggie felt her cheeks heat. "Right." She cut to the chase. "There's a craft fair. I asked Ronnie Pruitt about it." Ronnie and her brother, Frank, owned the only hardware store in the small, coastal town. "He said people come from miles around to spend the day in Sugar Sand Beach. I was thinking the inn could get a booth. Nina could serve food. Michelle could give out information about the inn…" She left it to the others to fill in the blanks.

Erin's eyes widened. "Reggie, you are a bloody genius," she swore softly.

Nina leaned over and gave her a squeeze. "Reggie, my dear, you've missed your calling. You should be in a think tank somewhere. You came up with that brilliant suggestion of holding an open house. And now this craft fair idea. If this pans out, we'll owe you big time."

Reggie sat back to catch her breath while excitement rippled through the room. Six months ago, she'd been content to stay in her lane, stick to her role as gardener and leave coming up with good ideas to the older, supposedly wiser, members of their little group. Her friends and her sister had seen her as more than a follower, however, and they'd encouraged her to speak her mind. She'd been working on that lately. Without Sam around to shoot holes in every suggestion she made, she was making progress. Sometimes, though, she still had to pinch herself when Michelle or Nina took one of her suggestions and ran with it.

"Sugar Sand Inn could rent a booth," Michelle agreed. "We'd set up a small table with pictures of the inn, some of the finished bedrooms. We could have stacks of brochures and a signup sheet for anyone who was interested in making a reservation."

"I'd be happy to chat with folks about some of the kayak tours and leisure activities we'll offer," Erin added.

"On the other side of the booth, I could serve small plates. A variety of dishes. All items I'm planning to have on the cafe's menu. Shrimp salad in lettuce cups. Pasta salad. Those bison meatballs people raved about at the open house—I've been tinkering with that recipe. Wait till you taste my next batch. You'll love them!" Nina's excitement grew with every word. "For dessert, we can have lots of miniatures—tiny éclairs, bite-size cupcakes, crème brûlée."

"Don't forget the cookies," Reggie put in. People had fallen in love with Nina's lemon cookies and bars at the open house.

"Yes, yes!" exclaimed Michelle.

Nina drummed her fingers on the tabletop. "This could work. It would definitely introduce the kinds of things we'll be serving in the cafe to a broader audience than we had at the open house."

"Okay. What do we have to do to pull this off?" Always the organizer, Michelle began answering her own question. "Let's see. First thing Monday morning, I'll head into town and sign us up for a booth. The bigger, the better."

"Tuesday," Erin corrected. "Monday is a holiday—Memorial Day. Nothing will be open."

"Memorial Day already?" Michelle blinked. "I guess it is. We've been so busy. First with the open house and then the town council meeting. Lately, one day runs right into the next. But you're right. Summer is right around the corner."

"I'll be tied up with the health inspector Tuesday," Nina said. "Between now and Wednesday, I'll rough out a menu. Then we'll have to make sure we have everything we need on hand. Plasticware, plates, napkins—the works. That'll mean at least one, probably two trips to the big box store in Destin. After that, I'll do several dry runs. I have to warn you all— there will be taste tests."

Reggie faked a groan and held her stomach. "Oh, the hardships we must endure!" She grinned and dropped the act. "Any time you need a judge, call on me."

"This makes it more important than ever for me to bring my gear up from Key West. We'll want everyone to see that we have plenty of equipment for our guests." Erin turned to her. "Reggie, are you still able to go this week?"

"Definitely. I'd like to make that trip as soon as possible," she agreed. "Once things start ripening in the garden, that'll take up more of my time."

"And the closer we get to the Fourth of July, the more hectic things will get in the kitchen." Nina clamped one hand over her mouth. "Oh, wait. I forgot." She turned to Michelle. "I promised to help you paint."

Michelle's dark hair brushed her cheek as she shook her head. "Listen. Much as I want to prep the rooms upstairs, we have plenty of time to do that. This is more important. Besides, we'll only have a month to get ready, and there's a lot to do."

Reggie leaned back, glad she'd been able to help out. Not so long ago, she'd felt like she was just tagging along on her sister's and their friends' venture to convert Michelle's inheritance into an inn. Freshly separated from her husband of five years, she'd barely had enough money to help with the groceries. She certainly hadn't had the kind of funds Erin, Nina and Michelle had sunk into their project. But thanks to an astute divorce attorney and a newfound sense of her own self-worth, she'd been able to help out financially after Sam turned over her fair share of their marital assets. She wouldn't deny it, though—making suggestions and having people actually listen to her ideas gave her the biggest thrill.

She tapped her chin as a new thought occurred to her. She'd spent the last month trimming and taming the bushes and plants that had grown wild while the house sat vacant. With that out of the way, the yard and grounds wouldn't require more than a weekly trim. And until the garden began to produce, she'd have a little extra time on her hands. Time she could put to good use painting those rooms Michelle was so keen on fixing up.

As ideas went, this one felt right. Of course, an extra set of hands would make the work go faster, and she knew just the person to help her. She and Chris had worked well together on several projects lately. Unless he was tied up doing something else, they could knock those bedrooms out in a day or two. It didn't hurt that the tall single dad was as easy to talk to as he was easy on the eyes, either. Not that she wanted anything more out of their relationship. Until her divorce was final, friendship was all she could offer the man. All she wanted from him, too.

For now.

Three

Nina

Nina finished loading the dishwasher and checked her watch. An hour remained before her appointment with the health inspector. Just enough time to give the counters a final wipe-down and, if she was lucky, help herself to a calming cup of tea. She thought she might need it, though why she felt as nervous as Mr. Pibbs when his food bowl was empty, she didn't know. It wasn't like the health department could shut down the cafe. After all, it was kind of hard to close a place that was months away from serving its first cup of coffee.

But what if the inspector uncovered some fatal flaw in her plans? What then? She'd spent her entire life preparing for the moment when she could finally open her own restaurant. Now that the goal was within reach, what if something went terribly wrong?

The questions made her fingers tremble. Trying to ignore them, she lit the flame under the teapot that sat in its usual place on one of the six burners on the Aga range. While she waited for the water to boil, she grabbed the bottle of disinfectant. After liberally spraying the counters, she went over each one with a handful of clean paper towels. Not so much as a single crumb or smudge dotted the glossy surfaces by the time she finished.

The pot whistled a cheery note that let her know the water had reached the right temperature for tea. She reached for the porcelain handle just as someone rapped sharply on the back door. Her eyes narrowed. She wasn't expecting company. No one else was home, either. Intent on signing up for a booth at the craft fair, Michelle had headed into the tiny town of Sugar Sand Beach nearly an hour ago. The distant sound of an engine told Nina that Reggie was mowing the lawn a final time before she and Erin left for the Keys in the morning. The last time she'd seen Erin, the blonde was dressed for a run and disappearing down the path that led to the beach. She wouldn't be back for at least another hour.

Nina gulped. Had the health inspector shown up early?

"Of course, he did," she answered.

She knew from experience how much inspectors loved to spring their little surprises. When she'd worked at Cafe Chez Jacques, neither the staff nor the owners had ever known when someone from the Health Department might show up. But when they did, oh boy. The moment a man in a lab coat walked through the door, an edgy tension sped up and down the line. Everyone, from the lead cooks to the dishwashers, started to sweat. They checked their workstations, making sure there were no signs of cross-contamination. Frowns deepened into scowls as people second-guessed themselves.

Did I store that last batch of sauce correctly? The steak on my cutting board—has it been sitting out too long? Are my uniform and hair net neat and tidy? Am I going to be the reason everyone gets sent home today?

Even though she'd asked for this visit, even though she was in no danger of getting a citation, the familiar sense of trepidation coursed through her. Relinquishing her hold on the handle of the teapot, she shut off the flame with a twist of one of the stove's knobs. Her breath shuddered. She gave the kitchen a final check. Reassured that everything was just as it should be, she hurried to the sun porch.

Sure enough, the man standing on the other side of the screen door wore a lab coat. At her approach, he flashed a set of credentials like some sort of FBI agent. "Lance Parker, Health Department," he announced.

"Chef Gray." Nina's clogs whispered across the tiled floor. She tugged on the hem of her chef's whites. Had she sounded too formal? Her stomach muscles tightened. "Nina," she corrected. She held the door open for the inspector.

While Lance typed a few notes into an electronic tablet, she studied the man who might very well hold the fate of her restaurant in his hands. Sandy-colored hair worn in a crew cut and a square-shouldered posture spoke of a military background. Crow's-feet radiating from a pair of smallish brown eyes put him in his mid-fifties. If the crisp creases down the legs of his pants and his recently shined shoes were any indication, Lance was a stickler for details. Which made him a perfect fit for a position where uncovering hidden problems was part of the job description.

Lance finished typing and looked up. His

gaze slid over her shoulder to the spacious kitchen. "Let's get started, shall we?"

"Of course," she said smoothly. "Welcome to the Sugar Sand Inn and Cafe. We're still a few months away from…"

"Yes. Yes. That's all in my notes." Lance brushed past her. He pulled a pair of thin gloves from his pocket. Stretching the latex over his fingers, he headed into the heart of the kitchen. His rubber-soled shoes squeaked when he came to a halt in the middle of the room. Without saying a word, he surveyed the granite counters, the glossy white cabinets, the massive Aga stove that sat across from the built-in refrigerator and freezer. "Where's your hand-washing station?" he asked, making the question sound like an accusation.

"It hasn't been installed yet." She stifled a flare of irritation. "You know this is just a preliminary visit, right? We're not open yet."

Lance shook his head. "That's not what they told me. Says here"—he tapped the screen of the handheld device—"General Inspection."

"I'm sorry," she said, although she wasn't sure why she was apologizing. "I made it very clear when I called. I asked for someone to come out early so I can make sure to purchase the right equipment and avoid problems later."

"You did?" Lance's long-suffering sigh let her know this wasn't the first time he'd been sent into the field with the wrong information. His stiff demeanor thawed a bit. A small smile transformed his expression from that of a stern tyrant to a man of reason. "All right, Chef Nina. I'm glad you asked for my input on the ground floor, as it were. You wouldn't believe how many times I've walked into a fully operational restaurant where the owners didn't ask for advice ahead of time and made costly mistakes."

"That's exactly what I'm hoping to avoid." Now that the inspector had warmed up a bit, some of the stiffness in her own shoulders eased.

Lance gave her attire a quick glance while she resisted the urge to smooth the white chef's jacket she wore over black slacks. "Do you have any experience in the food service industry?"

"A bit," she assured him with a smile. "After obtaining a degree in business management from the University of Virginia, I studied at the CIA," she said, referring to the well-respected Culinary Institute of America. "I've worked as a professional cook for over twenty years. Mostly in Northern Virginia. My last position was as the head saucier at a Michelin-ranked restaurant in Arlington."

"Impressive," Lance nodded. "Sounds like

you know your way around a commercial kitchen. I tell you what." He tucked his tablet in the deep pocket of his lab coat. "As long as I'm here, let's go through a regular inspection. I'll point out any discrepancies and problem areas. Since you're not open for business, I won't issue citations or warnings. Sound good?"

"That works," she said agreeably. What Lance had proposed was exactly what she'd hoped for. She picked up the small clipboard and pencil she'd left on the counter.

"So the first thing is, you'll need a dedicated hand-washing station. It should have a hands-free paper towel dispenser and a soap dispenser. Make sure the sink has both hot and cold running water."

"Will do." Even though she was well aware of the need for sanitizing equipment, she jotted a careful note. Done, she pointed to a spot at the end of the counter. "I thought I'd locate it right over there." The position was out of the way of the food prep area while still convenient for frequent use.

"That's a good place for it." Lance nodded. Crossing to the empty kitchen sink, he ran hot water over a thermometer he took from the pocket of his lab coat. "What are your plans for dishwashing? You know you'll need separate compartments for washing, rinsing and disinfecting."

"We have a built-in dishwasher that reaches the required temperature." She patted the appliance that ran quietly under the counter. "I've also ordered a small, commercial dishwasher."

"Will it handle pots and pans?"

She gulped. Nancy Simmons had had the kitchen completely remodeled a short time before her death. A beautiful farm sink had been one of many upgrades, which included side-by-side Sub-Zero appliances as well as a gorgeous Aga stove that most cooks only dreamed of having. She'd hoped to hang on to most of the fixtures, but it sounded like the sink, as pretty as it was, wasn't practical for a commercial setting. "I'll talk with our handyman. I suppose we could replace it with one that has three compartments."

Lance gave the matter a second thought. "You could get away with three plastic tubs," he suggested. "It would minimize your initial costs. If and when you outgrow that system, you can replace it later."

"Thanks," she murmured. Lance's plan would save her a bundle of money.

She followed him into the large, walk-in pantry, where she held her breath as the man in the white coat singled out one shelf. He pulled every box and storage container on it away from the wall. Taking a flashlight from a pocket, he played the beam down the now-bare surface. "No problems here," he announced to her immense relief. Shorter than her own five feet ten inches, Lance stood on his tiptoes to reach the top shelf. He ran one finger along the edge and held his gloved hand up to the light. "Can't get much cleaner than that." He rubbed his fingers together.

Stepping from the pantry, he nodded. "Everything looks good. Just make sure you follow proper storage guidelines."

She nodded. From raw meat to boxed pasta, everything had its place in a well-run kitchen. Not only had she followed all the rules, she'd nagged Reggie, Michelle and Erin into following them, too.

Continuing with his inspection, Lance checked the temperature in both the refrigerator and the freezer, tested every burner on the gas range, and examined the dishes that had been stored in the cupboards.

"Well," he said at last, "everything looks good here. How long before you plan to open?"

Relief rippled through her midsection. "I haven't set an exact date yet. Late September or early October. We'll probably hold a soft opening shortly before the first guests arrive at the Inn. At first, we'll be open for breakfast and lunch only. Once that's running smoothly, we'll offer dinner, too."

"Good. I've seen too many owners dive into full service right off the bat. Next thing you know, they're cutting corners. A lot of times, we have to shut them down. How about staff? How many will you have?"

"I'm looking for an assistant now. Eventually, I'll add two part-time prep cooks." She pictured a bustling kitchen, plates filled with food that not only looked good but tasted amazing. "I'm not sure about the front of the house, yet. One or two wait staff and someone to bus the tables, I suppose."

Lance's eyes narrowed. "That's a lot of help for such a small place." He scanned the breakfast nook. "There's not much room for seating."

"Oh, no." She laughed lightly. "This area will be off-limits to our guests. They'll eat in the dining room. Would you like to see it?" When Lance gave a quick nod, she led the way past the entrance to the back parlor and through a hall that had been widened at some point to make it wheelchair accessible.

The inspector pulled up short at the entrance

to the room, which was airy and light, with picture windows overlooking the grounds. His gaze swept past the immense dining table that sat twelve. A large sideboard ran along one wall. "Not very big, is it?"

At his words, a warning bell went off in her head. She'd always thought the dining room was a little on the small side for a house that boasted multiple sitting rooms and parlors, a fully-stocked library and a large family room. But she'd worked in many restaurants where space was at a premium.

"Um, we want to maintain a cozy atmosphere. We'll take out all the existing furniture and replace it with six four-tops." The small, round tables would fit comfortably, and she'd done the math. With seating for twenty-four, she could turn a modest profit on a dinner service.

But Lance only shook his head, a move that made those warning bells ring louder.

"You'll need to speak with the fire marshal— his office determines maximum occupancy." Despite the inspector's words, he whipped a tape measure out of a pocket that she was beginning to think held everything but the kitchen sink. "Here, hold this end."

She pressed the free end of the tape measure to the wall while Lance scooted around the table to the other side of the room.

"Sixteen feet," he called out. "Now let's get the length."

Moving to the adjacent walls, they repeated the process.

"Twenty," he announced. The tape measure rolled smoothly into the dispenser. "According to my calculations, you'll have a maximum occupancy of twenty-one."

Ouch! She winced. "Are you sure?" At Cafe Chez Jacques, they'd squeezed twice as many diners into a much smaller space.

"Like I said, you'll have to check with the fire marshal to be sure. In the past, he's been pretty insistent on requiring fifteen square feet per person." Lance slowly turned in a circle. "He's not going to be happy about only having one entrance, either."

Her heart sank. She could knock a hole in the wall to provide more access, but that would take more floor space away from the already tight accommodations. Sighing, she fought an urge to tug on her hair. Figuring she might as well find out all the bad news now rather than later, she asked, "Is there anything else?"

Lance stepped into the hallway. "You'll need to put down rubber matting out here to prevent slips and falls."

She clenched her teeth. She hated the idea of hiding the century-old hardwood floors under thick, absorbent padding.

"To be honest," the inspector continued, "I'm not a fan of carrying heavy trays from the kitchen and down the hall to the dining room. That'll get old in a hurry."

"There's not much choice, though, is there?" The Queen Anne-style house had been built at a time when servants thought nothing of ferrying heavy silver trays loaded with dishes back and forth from the kitchen to the dining room.

"Well, no. Not really. I hate to be negative—you've done such a great job prepping this place—but I don't see this working as a restaurant with a full dinner service. What you want to do will require twice as much square footage. My official recommendation is that you look for something larger. You wouldn't have to go far—maybe Panama City or closer to Destin," he said, mentioning the two closest towns.

Lance was missing the point. The restaurant had to be located on the premises. The inn and the cafe were a package deal. Whether the inspector liked it or not, she'd thrown her lot in with Michelle, Erin and Reggie.

"And if I wanted to open for breakfast and lunch, you wouldn't have any problem with that?" She slid one hand behind her back and crossed her fingers. Not being able to serve dinner was heartbreaking enough. If he shot down her plans completely, she'd be devastated.

"For a cafe with limited options for breakfast and lunch and seating for twenty, twenty-one in a pinch? Certainly. My office would be happy to grant your application once you make the improvements we discussed—the hand-wash area, rubber mats in high-traffic areas." Lance shook his head. "For anything more than that, though, I'm afraid not."

Tears stung the back of her throat as her dreams of preparing elegant dinners for a houseful of guests faded. She blinked rapidly, fighting back the urge to cry. She lagged behind Lance long enough to calm herself with the deep, pranayama breathing she used in her daily yoga sessions. By the time she made it to the door, the hand she extended no longer shook.

"I appreciate your visit today," she told the inspector.

"Well," Lance said as he tucked his tablet beneath one arm. "I hope I've saved you from making a costly mistake. I look forward to visiting again when you open the cafe."

If that even happens.

Her shoulders slumped beneath a heavy

layer of defeat as she watched him walk toward the government vehicle he'd left in the graveled parking area. She'd managed to put on a happy face during the health inspector's visit, but his news had been beyond disheartening. Devastating was more like it. Not only had Lance rejected her plans for a dinner service, but if he was right about the maximum occupancy, the cafe wouldn't accommodate enough guests at breakfast and lunch to make it profitable, either.

How was she going to break the news to Michelle, Erin and Reggie? She shook her head while tears gathered in her eyes and her dreams of running her own kitchen faded.

Four

Michelle

"Hey, Sug!"

Sally called the greeting as soon as Michelle stepped across the threshold into Maggie's Diner, where the good smells of bacon and toast floated in the air. "Good timin'. Take a seat anywheres you'd like. I'll be right with ya."

Michelle's warm smile deepened at the thick accent that dripped like molasses from the waitress's lips. She had to admit, the Southern drawl had taken her by surprise on her first visit to the diner. As had the friendliness of almost everyone she'd met in Sugar Sand Beach. Here, in this laid-back community where the warm Gulf breezes blew, people cared about their neighbors to an extent she hadn't experienced in Northern Virginia.

"Thanks, Sally," Michelle answered. She headed for a booth by the large picture window overlooking the nearly vacant parking lot. She'd hoped to arrive after the breakfast rush and before the start of the busy lunch hour. From the looks of the sparsely filled tables and chairs, she'd hit her mark.

Almost before she settled her purse on the bench seat, her favorite waitress appeared at the end of the table, two empty mugs in one hand, a carafe of hot coffee in the other. "You meetin' anybody?" A thick, brown curl had escaped Sally's messy updo. She set one of the white cups on the table and tucked the errant strand behind one ear. "Maybe that handsome lawyer you been keepin' time with?"

"Dave?" Michelle arched a brow as if she didn't know exactly who the waitress meant. "He's just a friend. And no, he won't be joining me today."

Although she wouldn't mind seeing him again. And soon. Dave Rollins had been instrumental in fulfilling her birth mother's wish that she inherit Nancy Simmons's property. Over the course of the past two months, Michelle had come to think of him as a friend. A good friend. One day, that friendship might deepen into something more, but for now, neither of them was in any rush.

"That's a pity, sure 'nuf. He's fi-ine." Sally stretched the final word into two syllables. "Coffee then? You want a menu?"

"Definitely coffee." Knowing she'd have some at the diner, Michelle had skipped her usual second cup this morning. "Is Maggie around?" The savvy owner was usually holed up in her office, either tending to her official duties as mayor of Sugar Sand Beach or handling the business end of running the only restaurant in town.

A rare frown creased Sally's forehead. "She's been on a tear all morning. Our regular delivery man was out sick, so some fool truck driver took his place. He dropped off a pallet of dry goods in the middle of the night last night—can you believe it?" Sally didn't wait for an answer. "Why he'd do that, I have no idea. He had to see we were closed." The brunette shook her head. "When Maggie came in this morning, raccoons had had a feast! Marshmallows and cereal all over the loading dock. They smashed jars of peanut butter and chocolate sauce, too."

Laughter bubbled up from Michelle's midsection. She clamped one hand over her mouth to suppress it. She shouldn't laugh. But the image of the mess the raccoons had made was too much. A tiny giggle escaped.

Sally grinned. "It was quite the sight, all right." Pouring coffee, she said, "Maggie, she's been on the phone with the company all morning, getting them to adjust our bill." She nodded as if there was no doubt whatsoever that her boss would succeed in her mission. "But that leaves us short for the week. Someone's gonna hafta make a run to Destin."

That sounded about right. According to Nina, the big box store in Destin carried most of the products a restaurant might need at only slightly higher prices than the food distributors. Which definitely came in handy whenever a weekly delivery fell through.

"Sounds like Maggie's already had a full day." Michelle sighed. "I was hoping to talk to her about a booth for the Fourth of July festivities." The task was at the top of her list of things to do today. She slept better at night when she crossed off every item before she turned in. "But I'm good here." She stirred her coffee. "I'll just wait till she's free."

The waitress's usual smile returned. "You'll finally have time to try those cheese grits I been tellin' you 'bout."

"I guess you're right." Michelle gave in to Sally's well-intentioned pestering at last. The first day she'd visited the diner, the waitress had told her their cheese grits would "change her life." She'd repeated the advice every chance she got. The problem was, Michelle didn't particularly like the dish made from finely ground corn. The few times she'd had it, it had reminded her of Cream of Wheat—without the sugar and milk that made the breakfast cereal almost palatable.

"I'll put your order in and tell Maggie you'd like to see her. Back in two shakes."

When Sally spun toward the kitchen that filled one corner of the diner, Michelle pulled her cell phone from her purse. Her stomach sank a bit when no little red dot appeared on the calls icon. Hoping Aaron or Ashley had at least emailed, she scrolled through a dozen ads from fabric and body-care suppliers, a couple of sale notices from her favorite department stores back in Virginia, and one offer that promised a wealth of riches...if she'd only provide a supposed diplomat in a country on the other side of the world with full access to her personal data.

"Thanks, but no thanks," she murmured and hit the delete key.

Her eyes watered. She hadn't heard from either of the twins in over a week. Both juniors at the University of Virginia—Michelle's alma mater—they'd promised to come for a visit this summer. So far, though, neither of them had

71

scheduled a flight. Wondering if her children would ever forgive her for moving to Florida, she put the phone to sleep.

Granted, Aaron and Ashley had learned of her plans to relocate under less than ideal circumstances. But geez. The least they could do was give her a chance to talk it over with them. It wasn't like she'd been biding her time, waiting for them to turn their backs long enough for her to sell the only house they'd ever lived in. She knew how much they loved their home in Fairfax. She'd loved it, too. She would have been perfectly content to live out the rest of her life there.

Only she hadn't had a choice. The death of her husband—the father of her children—had left her practically penniless. If it hadn't been for Nancy Simmons and three of the best friends anyone could ever ask for, she'd have lost that house to foreclosure. She'd probably be working at some dead-end job, the best a woman of her age with no work experience could hope for. Worse, she'd be living paycheck to paycheck in the cheapest apartment she could find.

She wanted to explain all that to the twins. She *needed* to explain it to them. And she would. As soon as they cooled down enough to remember that she was their mother, someone they should call once in a while.

"Here you go."

She blinked and turned away from the window when Sally slid a bowl in front of her. "Sorry. Lost in thought, I guess."

"Whatever's on your mind, you eat them there grits and everythin'll be right as rain. You'll see. They'll change your life." Sally topped off Michelle's coffee and left her to her thoughts.

Michelle doubtfully eyed the dish the waitress had sworn would make everything right in her world. The yellowish concoction sure didn't look like a miracle cure. Nor did the thin layer of melted cheese that floated on top. She spooned up a small bite.

Okay, I'll admit when I'm wrong.

"Mmmm," she murmured when yummy cheese and a hint of smoky spice hit her tongue. The grits she'd had in the past had the texture of, well, grit. These were smooth and creamy and loaded with flavor. They were so good, in fact, they threatened to become her new, personal favorite breakfast food.

Which might not change her life, but a steady diet of corn, butter and cheese would certainly force her to change her wardrobe. As she ate her way toward the bottom of the bowl, she pictured having to replace the fitted pants and tops she favored with loose caftans and shapeless shifts.

She polished off one last spoonful. The rest of the grits cried out for her to eat them, too. It required more self-control than she expected to push the bowl aside.

"You didn't like them?" Sally reappeared at her table a minute later.

"I liked them too much." Michelle patted her tummy. Not so long ago she'd carried an extra fifteen pounds on her five-foot-six frame. She'd worked off the extra weight during the move. She didn't want it to pay a return visit.

"I hear ya!" Sally said. "But you gotta admit, they're amazing."

"That they are," she agreed. A warmth that only good carbs could generate radiated from her midsection.

"Tol' ya you'd like 'em. Oh, here comes Maggie now." In a practiced move, Sally removed the half-full dish with one hand and re-filled Michelle's coffee cup with the other. Turning, she sped off toward the kitchen.

Michelle watched as a tiny woman stopped midway down the hall that led to offices and restrooms. Maggie's short, white hair curled around her face like a halo. Wearing her trademark black polo over black slacks, she traded a few words with the cooks in the kitchen before she continued toward the dining area.

She paused by the cash register long enough to hold a finger up to Michelle. "Just a second," she mouthed.

Michelle nodded and sipped her coffee. In addition to serving good food, Maggie had a knack for making each of her guests feel right at home. It was an excellent trait for a restaurant owner to have. Otherwise, most people would simply cook for themselves.

This time of day, only a few customers lingered over coffee or hurriedly finished eating before they dashed off to work or play. Maggie stopped at each table, where she made sure her customers were satisfied with their meals. More than that, though, she expressed genuine concern about family members or friends. She even lingered at one table where a young family sat and cracked jokes with the kids long enough for a harried-looking mother to finish her biscuit.

Four retirees dressed in overalls and faded jeans occupied a table near Michelle's. Here Maggie leaned in to give one grizzled old-timer a quick hug.

"Uncle Jack," she said warmly. "Good to see you this morning. Did you have a good night?"

Jack reached up with an age-spotted hand to pat the one his niece left on his shoulder. "Aw, you know. 'Bout as good as a man my age can."

He reached for his coffee mug with shaky fingers. "Think we can get some high-test?" He eyed his cronies with a sly smile.

"Now, Uncle Jack. You know the doctor said caffeine was bad for you. But you can have all the decaf you want." Maggie's tone held just the right blend of sympathy and firmness. She signaled a waitress Michelle didn't recognize. The young woman rushed over with an orange-topped carafe.

"Y'all planning to stay for a while today?" Maggie asked the men at the table while the girl with dark eyes and darker hair refilled cups.

"Where else we got to go, Maggie?" asked the grizzled old-timer who sat across from Jack.

"The community center opens at noon," Maggie suggested.

"For bingo." Jack's garrulous reply made it clear to everyone within listening distance that the older man didn't think much of the game.

"They don't serve no coffee there. Nothin' to eat, neither," complained another one of Jack's friends.

"All right. Stay here," Maggie said. "Long as you remember the rules. Don't cause any of my girls trouble, especially Tamara. She's new, and I don't want her to quit. And only one dessert each. Can't have you boys eating up all my profits," she cautioned with a good-natured smile.

Michelle had heard similar versions of the conversation during past visits to the diner. The part about the dessert was new, though, and she suspected Maggie had added it as much for Tamara's benefit as Uncle Jack's. Mentally, she added an item onto her to-do list. She'd planned to transform one of the side parlors into a gathering spot for people like Maggie's uncle and his pals, senior citizens who had lots of time on their hands. It sounded like the need for such a place was real, and she vowed to put her plan into action soon.

Before Michelle's coffee had time to get cold, Maggie slipped onto the bench opposite her. "Whew! I've been on the go since four this morning. It feels good to take a break. How've you been, Michelle?"

"Sally told me you had a busy morning." An image of marauding raccoons formed in her mind. "Everything work out okay?"

Maggie frowned. "I swear. I was on the phone with that trucking company for over an hour. They were sure givin' me the runaround. Said it wasn't their fault; I should'a had someone there to accept the delivery. I finally sent 'em a picture of the big sign by the back door. The one that clearly states, 'No deliveries after 9 p.m.' That did it." Her frown deepened, and she shook her head so hard her white curls bounced. "Never go into business for yourself. It's one headache after another."

"I'm afraid you're a little late with that advice," Michelle said with a grin. Maggie knew full well that she and her friends had poured their life savings into converting Nancy Simmons's house into a first-class inn.

"Everything moving forward? No problems?" Maggie wanted to know. As mayor, she'd been a driving force in getting the town council to approve Michelle's zoning request a week earlier.

"I—we—can't thank you enough for letting me speak at the council meeting. I'm still pinching myself about that. I didn't expect our request to sail through like it did." Michelle had thanked the woman before, but gratefulness always bore repeating.

Maggie waved a hand. "I was just doing my job. You're the one who made the impassioned speech. That's what swayed everyone to your side."

"Everyone but Orson," Michelle reminded the mayor. One of Sugar Sand Beach's favorite sons, Orson Danner and his investors had had big plans for the tiny seaside town.

"Don't worry about Orson. If there's one thing I've learned about that young man, it's that he always lands on his feet. I swear, he's like a cat. I heard he and his cronies already put in a bid on a larger property in St. James."

"Oh?" Michelle cringed. Was some other small town going to get plowed under by Orson and his plans for a large development aimed at winter visitors?

"Relax." Maggie sipped her coffee. "St. James is actually a much better choice for everyone concerned. Not as many family-owned businesses for Orson and his investment team to contend with. About twenty years ago, some big developer bought up all the land around there. They were going to turn it into the next Seaside," she explained. One of the best resort areas in the state, Seaside catered to tourists and winter residents. "But the housing market flattened, and that developer went belly-up. Bad for him, but good for Orson."

"He was pretty upset at the council meeting. I'd hate to have hard feelings between us." Although nearly everyone in Sugar Sand Beach had gone out of their way to make Michelle and her friends feel welcome, Orson had chosen a different path. "Maybe if this new deal goes through for him, we can put the past behind us."

"I'm sure he'll be fine." Maggie added a teaspoon of sugar to her coffee. "Orson's heart was in the right place. He honestly believed he was doing a good thing by building here in Sugar Sand Beach. I tried to tell him people around these parts don't like change, but he had to learn for himself. Folks were willing to hear him out—we're polite like that—but when it came time to vote, I'm certain he would have walked away empty-handed."

This tidbit was something Michelle hadn't heard before, and the news sent a ripple of relief coursing through her. "I appreciate your telling me that, Maggie. It helps to know I wasn't solely responsible for making him change his plans."

"I'm sure you didn't come here to talk about Orson. Sally said you needed a minute. What's up?" The busy owner checked her watch.

Aware that Maggie could be called away any second, Michelle didn't waste any more time. "I'm hoping there are still some booths available for the craft fair."

"As a matter of fact, we have several spaces left." Maggie's smile brightened. "They're a hundred dollars apiece, plus ten percent of your gross sales."

Huh. Having to fork over a percentage of the sales complicated matters.

Nina hadn't mentioned charging for her samples, had she?

"The problem is, I don't think we were planning to sell anything." Her hair had fallen forward, and Michelle brushed it out of her face.

"Hmmm." Maggie tapped her spoon lightly against the tabletop while she pondered this new dilemma. "Okay," she said after a minute. "The hundred dollars covers the town's expenses— trash pickup, electric, that sort of thing. We can't waive it. But the ten percent goes into a fund for Robert Phelps. He's a Sugar Sand Beach boy. Lost one leg and an arm to an IUD while he was serving his country. He's been in rehab ever since. We've been working with a specialist to build a house for him when he comes home. One that's fully accessible. Ramps instead of steps or stairs. Extra wide doorways. Anything to make life easier for him. If you could see your way clear to making a donation, that would be an acceptable substitute."

"Of course." Michelle didn't even have to give the idea a second thought.

"Well, then, it's settled. I'm sure everyone will be glad to visit your booth. Polly Denton— you know her, don't you?" Without waiting for an answer, Maggie said, "Of course, you do. You met her at the council meeting. Polly's the one who's actually in charge of the craft fair. She has a handout that lists all the rules. Swing by her shop and pick one up."

Michelle nodded. In keeping with a desire to support local businesses as much as possible, she'd planned to stop by Polly's Posies anyway to look at dried floral arrangements for the inn.

Maggie drummed her fingers lightly against the table. "You've never been to one of our Fourth of July celebrations. I think you're in for a treat." Small-town pride glimmered in the mayor's eyes. "People from miles around polish up their antique cars for the car show and parade on Friday. This year our grand marshal is Agnes Spivey. She's been playing the organ at the First Baptist Church for thirty years. The Moose Club has a briefcase drill team that's a hoot and a half. The Shriners put on a show with their little bikes. That night, there'll be fireworks. But the real draw is the craft fair on Saturday and Sunday. We have over a hundred and fifty vendors lined up, and the cutoff date isn't for two weeks yet. We usually get a couple of thousand people in town that weekend."

Michelle whistled softly. When Reggie had first mentioned the craft fair, she'd assumed a few hundred would attend. Apparently, she'd been wrong about that.

They chatted until a crisis in the kitchen demanded Maggie's attention. Not long after she left the table, Michelle paid the check and left Sally a generous tip. Heading for the car she'd parked under the towering oak tree in the center of the diner's parking lot, she fumbled in her purse for her phone. After checking for messages from her twins—there weren't any—she sent a group text to Nina, Reggie and Erin. In it, she gave her friends a heads-up about the larger-than-anticipated crowds at the craft fair and promised more information when they got together this evening.

Within minutes of leaving the diner, Michelle pulled into one of the slanted parking spots that lined the business district of Sugar Sand Beach. She smiled to herself as she shook her head. Calling the single street a business district really was a stretch. Maggie, as well as other mayors who'd served the small community in the past, had prevented national franchises from sinking their teeth into the town. As a result, mom-and-pop stores sat on either side of a divided road that ran a couple of football fields in length. Gus looked after the small, family-owned grocery store at one end of town. A brother and sister team, the Pruitts, ran a hardware store that anchored the other. In the middle of the block, the First Baptist Church stood opposite the Community Center. Souvenir shops, a barber-shop, a hair salon, and a couple of other stores, including Polly's Posies, peppered the rest of the street.

After checking the side-view mirror for cars, Michelle stepped from her vehicle into the heat and humidity of a late spring day. Despite the warm temperature, wood smoke drifted heavily in the air. Her eyes crinkled as she recalled the council meeting where Jimbo Dutton had complained in jest about plans to expand the smokehouse behind the grocery store. As if anyone would vote against the proposal. She might be a relative newcomer to the area, but even she knew Gus and his family produced the best smoked sausage in the state. Maybe in the entire South. Why, if her tummy wasn't already full of tasty cheese grits, she'd swing by the grocery store and pick up a sausage dog for lunch.

As it was, though, she had places to go and people to see.

She'd no sooner gotten herself moving again

when the display in the flower shop's window caught her eye. In a nod to the approaching wedding season, Polly had dressed a headless mannequin in a bridal gown. The figure's clasped hands held a bouquet of fuchsia and cream-colored hydrangeas paired with double roses of the softest pink. Mauve-colored satin draped a stand that held a centerpiece featuring the same flowers.

The effect was stunning and, as she studied it, Michelle imagined the day her own daughter would walk down the aisle. She whispered a prayer that by the time that day came, she and Ashley would have put their difficulties behind them. She wanted to be seated in the front pew of the church when the organist played the "Wedding March."

Ideas filled her head like bubbles in a glass of champagne while she took a closer look at the display. Could they host weddings at the Inn? The property certainly offered plenty of room for large, outdoor ceremonies. The parlors, with their beautiful woodwork, would make excellent settings for smaller, more intimate wedding parties. Or what about turning the turret into a honeymoon suite? The space was a blank slate, just waiting for a special purpose. She pictured plush pillows, airy curtains at windows overlooking the Gulf, sumptuous bedding. A beautiful, private retreat.

It was definitely something to consider, she told herself. Of course, she wouldn't act on the idea until the others weighed in. Erin, Nina or Reggie might have different plans for the turret, and she'd meant it when she said they'd all have an equal say in decisions concerning the inn. Sure, she'd inherited the property from her birth mother, but without her best friends' help, she'd still be floundering. She owed them, and as soon as Dave finished the paperwork, she'd repay her debt by officially making the four of them equal partners in their venture.

Tucking thoughts of the future aside for the moment, she headed into Polly's Posies. A bell jingled cheerily when she opened the door. The heady scent of flowers and greenery enveloped her. Miss Polly wasn't in her usual space behind the counter, so she browsed while she waited to say hello.

Her goal for today's shopping trip was to find a dried floral arrangement for the Manatee suite. She'd painted the bedroom and the adjoining sitting room a pale gray as a tribute to the large, gentle mammals. Crisp white linens with navy piping, luscious white comforters and scads of navy and white pillows gave the suite a light, refreshing look. As soon as she added a few finishing touches—including the floral arrangement—the suite would be ready for its first guests. A giddy thrill passed through her at the thought of hanging the Open for Business sign on the front gate.

She wandered through the shop, admiring Miss Polly's talented design work, checking out discreetly placed price tags, soaking in the oxygen-rich atmosphere. Before long she spotted an arrangement that met her needs perfectly. She had just held the distressed wooden box filled with blue roses, gray tulips and creamy white carnations up to the light to get a better look at it when a man's voice came from somewhere in the back of the shop. Michelle turned toward the sound in time to see the owner push through the swinging doors that separated the sales floor from the workroom.

"Hey, Miss Polly," she called.

"Oh, my stars!" The older woman gasped, and her blue eyes went wide. She placed a wrinkled hand over her heart. "You startled me. I didn't know anyone was out here."

"I'm sorry." Realizing she still held the floral arrangement in the air, Michelle lowered her hands. "I thought you'd hear the bell, but I guess you were busy with another customer?" She glanced expectantly toward the swinging doors. Where was the owner of the voice she'd heard?

"Oh, pshaw." Polly pressed one finger to her ear. "I had my AirPods in while I was working on an order. The dang thing fell out a minute ago. Speakers must'a come on." She removed a tiny device from one ear and slipped it into a pocket. Apparently over her initial fright, Polly leaned forward. "Do you like audiobooks? They're perfect for when I'm working here by myself. I can't get enough of them."

"I haven't really tried them," Michelle admitted. "I'm more of a print book gal." She read a few chapters every night before she turned in.

"My eyes aren't as good as they once were. Old age, you know. I still love me a good murder mystery. The more twisted, the better. I only listen to 'em while I'm workin' though. Never at home in the dead of the night. That'd be foolish. I wouldn't get a wink's worth of sleep." Polly loosed a soft feminine laugh that was almost girlish.

Michelle took a beat to sort out this new insight into Polly's character. The woman was well into her eighties. Michelle would have pegged the shop owner for a fan of women's fiction. She might have even bet money that Maggie Miller or Amy Ashley topped the older woman's list of favorite authors. But no. The spry octogenarian liked gruesome whodunits. Which she listened to through state-of-the-art AirPods, no less. Polly was chock full of surprises.

"So what brings you in today, dear? Can I help you with something?" Polly stepped around the counter.

Michelle held out the arrangement she'd found. "I've flat fallen in love with this."

"Ooooh, you've picked out a good one. It's one of my favorites." Polly took the arrangement and fussed over it a minute, straightening a leaf here, tucking in a bit of loose moss there. "These are sola blossoms," she said, running her fingers lightly over the paper-thin petals. "They're all handmade from sliced tapioca root. They'll last practically forever."

"They are lovely," Michelle agreed. "I've used them in wreaths before and been very happy with how well they hold up."

"Oh?" Polly squinted. "You craft?"

"Only a little. For my own enjoyment more than anything else. In Virginia, I made a wreath for our front door every holiday. Some years I'd get real ambitious and decorate the Christmas tree with homemade ornaments. I had more time on my hands after the twins went off to college than I do now," she confessed.

"Twins? Oh, my goodness. I didn't know you had twins." Polly plunked the arrangement down on the counter behind her. She turned to face Michelle. "Now, see? That's the sort of thing neighbors should know about one another. We're overdue for a nice, long chat, you and me. Why don't you tell me more about yourself."

"Ooooh!" Michelle fanned her face with her fingers. She'd heard through the rumor mill that Polly could ferret out facts better than an FBI agent. "I feel like I walked into the middle of an episode of that old game show *This Is Your Life*. Do you remember it? I used to watch it with my parents when I was just a little girl."

Polly's eyes brightened. "I used to *love* that show. That Ralph Edwards—he was so clever!" Her focus narrowed. She tipped an imaginary mike to Michelle. "So, Michelle Robinson, this is your life! Spill it, girl."

"Yes, ma'am." She went along with the game. After all, Polly hadn't given her much choice. She gave the owner the same stringently abbreviated version of her life she gave anyone in Sugar Sand Beach. One that eliminated any mention of her adoptive parents or her birth mother. Only Dave Rollins knew the full story of her relationship with Nancy Simmons. As Nancy's attorney of record, he'd been sworn to secrecy.

"You know," Polly said when Michelle finished, "there's one thing I still don't understand."

Instinctively, Michelle braced.

"I knew Nancy her entire life. Knew her parents, too, though they were quite a bit older. In all that time, none of them ever once mentioned you. So how is it she left you her estate?"

Michelle had to give Polly credit. The woman might be getting up there in years, but she hadn't lost a single step. Polly served on the town council, ran her own flower shop. She might not drive at night anymore, but she could still get straight to the heart of a matter. She took a breath, prepared to share as much as she could of the real story of how she'd landed in Sugar Sand Beach.

"It was as much of a surprise to me as it was to everyone else," she answered truthfully. "Nancy and I are related on my mother's side, but our two families were, um, estranged." Which, she supposed, was the kindest possible way of explaining how adoption laws had prevented her birth mother from reuniting with the child she'd put up for adoption. "It's a pity. By all accounts, Nancy was a wonderful person, a true pillar of the community. I only hope I can do right by her."

She crossed her fingers and hoped her

answer would put an end to Polly's questions. Someone else might not quibble over sharing Nancy's story. Michelle supposed that would be their right. But her birth mother had gone to great lengths to keep anyone from learning she'd gotten pregnant out of wedlock. Much less that she'd signed over all parental rights to her child. Nancy had, however, left a letter behind for her daughter. In it, she'd explained all the trauma and turmoil she'd suffered. After a sleepless night in which Michelle had read the letter over and over again, protecting her birth mother's secrets had become just as important to her as it had been to Nancy.

"I'm sure Nancy would have loved to see the old house filled with people and laughter. You're doing a good thing, honey," Polly said at last.

Relieved that the inquisition had drawn to a close, Michelle exhaled slowly while the shop owner returned to her usual place behind the sales counter.

"Let me ring you up, then." Polly peered across the counter. "Unless there's something else you needed?"

"How'd you guess?" Michelle asked lightly. "I spoke with Maggie this morning. She said you're the person to talk to about getting a booth for next month's craft fair."

"That I am." Polly pressed the enter key on the laptop she'd left open at the end of the counter. The keyboard emitted soft clicks as the owner logged in and scrolled through several screens. "Here we go," she said less than a minute later. "This is the layout."

When Polly angled the computer so they both could see the display, Michelle stared at lines of red boxes and a few green ones arranged in neat rows.

"Here's the entrance, just beyond the hardware store," Polly said, pointing to the first line of boxes. "The blocks in red are already spoken for. The green ones are still available." Her finger hovered over a row at the back of the lot. "Most of the food vendors are here. We'll have picnic benches set up under a big tent there. You'll probably want to steer clear of the kiddie area off to the left. That's where we'll have face painting, pony rides and a petting zoo. Wood carvers and a man who makes tiki poles from palm trees usually set up in this corner." Polly tapped a spot close to the entrance. "We try to have something for everyone."

Michelle studied the map. "I'm not sure which area would be best for us. Nina's hoping to drum up business for the cafe by giving out little samples. Small plates, she calls them. But we'll also have a display for the inn. Plus, Erin will be there with information about the outdoor activities she's planning for our guests."

"Sort of a mixed bag, then." Polly pointed to a green box one row over from the food booths. "What about here? It's close to the picnic benches and on the outside ring." She leaned forward as if she were sharing a secret. "Those spots have a little more room than the others, and with all you're offering, it sounds like you'll need it."

"Excellent," she agreed.

Polly tapped a few keys on the computer, and the green square turned red. "Okay, it's yours." She pulled a handout from under the counter. "This lays out all the particulars, but I'll go over the basics. For a fee of one hundred dollars, we're renting you a 15x15 plot with access to electricity. The rest is up to you. Most vendors set up canvas tents, open on one end. Others opt for canopies. The booths sit back-to-back with electric feeds running in between them. You'll need to supply your own heavy-duty extension cords, tables, chairs, et cetera. Got it?"

"Will do," Michelle said. One of her friends in Virginia had been an avid photographer who sold framed prints of her work at craft fairs. She'd filled in for her regular helper a time or two, and the rules sounded much the same as those they'd followed up north.

"So you're trying to drum up business for the inn, are you?" Polly wanted to know.

"Yes, ma'am. We want to give everyone a taste of some of the items Nina will be serving in the cafe. So they'll come and eat there once we're open for business."

"She going to have them yummy meatballs she had at the open house?" Polly's fingers flew over the keys as she prepared Michelle's invoice.

"Pretty sure she will." She'd make sure of it.

"Me and my son'll be sure to stop by then. He always comes home for the Fourth." Polly hit a button, and somewhere nearby, a printer hummed.

Surprise shifted in Michelle's midsection. "Miss Polly, I didn't know you had children." She gave herself a mental kick in the pants for not shining the *This Is Your Life* spotlight on the store owner.

"Just the one. Wally. Well, Walter to everybody but me. He's fifty-two."

"Does he live nearby?"

"Practically right next door. He's on the other side of Panama City. Got him a big ol' place right on the beach." She leaned forward, her voice dropping to a whisper. "All glass and chrome, his place is. He's always trying to get me to retire and move in with him, but his house is a little too

95

fancy for me." She sighed. "That's what these young folks like these days, I suppose."

"What's he do for a living?" Michelle asked. Beachfront property didn't come cheap, as she'd recently learned.

"He's always had a head for numbers, that boy. Put it to work buying an' sellin' businesses. He does all right for himself."

Michelle recognized understated bragging when she heard it. She occasionally indulged in it herself when she talked about Aaron and Ashley. "Is he married?" She asked the question more for politeness's sake than any other.

"You're not looking for a new beau, are ya? Or any of your friends lookin'?" A speculative gleam came into Polly's eyes. "'Cause my Wally, he's quite the catch. I'm not just sayin' that because I'm his mother. You want to see his picture?"

"Doing a little matchmaking, are you, Miss Polly?" Michelle imagined a younger, more masculine version of one of Sugar Sand Beach's movers and shakers.

The older woman's pale cheeks pinked. "Can't blame a mom for tryin', can you? I'd like to have one grandchild before I die."

"Let's hope that day doesn't come for a long, long time." Smiling, she paid her bill and, within minutes, she stood on the sidewalk.

She'd have to warn the rest of the girls, Michelle told herself as she carried the pretty floral arrangement to her car. She could well imagine the tiny shop owner—with her son in tow—cornering Nina or Erin at the craft fair. Her friends would have to tread carefully. Otherwise, Miss Polly would strong-arm one or both of them into going on a date with Wally before they even knew what was happening.

Five

Nina

Nina's legs felt like they could give out at any moment. She propped her hands on the kitchen counter and leaned forward, her arms bearing the full weight of her upper body. Loosed from its usual tidy chignon, her long hair formed a dark curtain around her face. Her shoulders shook. Tears ran down her cheeks. One drop fell from her jaw and splashed onto the counter.

It's over.

Her hopes, her dreams of running her own kitchen had crashed around her. It had happened once before when Tobias betrayed her. When he told lies about her. She'd survived then, but she wouldn't bounce back this time. It had taken years of hard work—answering every request with a snappy, "Yes, Chef," never taking a day off, always being the first in and the last to leave wherever she was working. But eventually, she'd rebuilt her reputation, even achieved a small amount of success as the head saucier at a Michelin-rated restaurant.

All with the hope that somehow, someday, she'd have a kitchen of her own.

She should have known it would never happen.

And it wouldn't. She'd lost everything this time. She hadn't had much other than her savings, but she'd given up her tiny apartment with its hand-me-down furniture. She'd left friends and co-workers behind. She'd sunk every dime she had in the Sugar Sand Inn and Cafe.

And for what? Her dream had disappeared like a puff of smoke.

She shook her head. A few more tears joined the others on the counter.

There'd be no coming back this time. No striving to be the best, to make a name for herself. Why bother, when she'd never hang her name over the door? She might as well take a job slinging hash at the local diner. She had no one but herself to blame this time. Somehow, that made it hurt worse. She moaned.

"Hey, everybody! I'm home!" The front door

snicked shut. "Nina? Was that the health inspector's car I saw on the way in?"

Nina jerked upright. Grabbing a napkin from the dispenser on the end of the counter, she mopped the small puddle her tears had formed. She hurriedly ran her hands over her face, wiping away the dampness. Not that it did any good. Her eyes continued to leak. She spun toward the sink so Michelle wouldn't see her cry.

Michelle's voice grew louder as hurried footsteps came down the hallway. "Tell me everything! I bet he lo—" Michelle's voice cut off. The soft scuff of shoes against the hardwood floors halted. "Nina?"

"It's okay. I'm okay. I just need a minute." Her words came out muffled. Her nose dripped.

Plastic crackled as Michelle dropped whatever she'd been holding on the table. Two seconds later, Nina felt the comforting weight of her friend's hand on her shoulder.

"What's wrong? Were the changes he wanted more expensive than we expected? We knew we couldn't just open a restaurant without spending some money. Whatever it is, I'm sure we can come up with a solution," Michelle soothed.

Nina only shook her head. This was one problem money couldn't fix. The dining room simply wouldn't hold enough tables to make the cafe profitable. Unless a kitchen turned a tidy profit, it couldn't stay in business.

"Talk to me, honey. You have to tell me what's wrong so we can fix it."

Nina practiced her yoga breathing until she could inhale and exhale smoothly. "It's worse than I ever imagined. There's simply not enough room."

"In this huge house?" Michelle's voice climbed. "Impossible."

Nina shook her head. Turning away from Michelle, she grabbed a handful of napkins and pressed them to her face. "Lance Parker—he's the health inspector—he said we could only seat twenty in the dining room. That's not enough. We need six tables—twenty-four diners—to break even. Eight would be better."

"Lance Parker?" Michelle snorted. "Sounds like a character in a romance novel."

"He doesn't look like one." Words tumbled from Nina's lips. "Trust me, he's more wing man than hero. All spit-and-polish. A stickler for details. Don't get me wrong—he's exactly the kind of person you want for a health inspector. I respect that, and everything was going great until I showed him where we plan to serve our guests. It went downhill after that. Fast. He took one look at the dining room, said it was too small, and then found a dozen other reasons why we shouldn't open."

"Maybe he was wrong. He's just one man. With just one opinion. I'm sure the next guy will—"

"No," Nina interrupted with a sigh. "I checked with the fire marshal after Lance left. He said the same thing. We need fifteen square feet per person, minimum. The dining room simply doesn't have that much. We'd need another door, too. Two separate ways in and out. Which would use up even more floor space. Plus, I've worked with enough health inspectors in the past to know this one is going to get real finicky if we go ahead with our plans."

She supposed they could open for takeout only. But what would be the point? Half her joy in being a chef came from watching the happy faces of her customers while they ate the food she'd prepared.

"I know we wanted six tables, but what if we cut back and only had three?" Michelle asked.

"We wouldn't break even, much less turn a profit. Besides, the inspector absolutely hates the idea of servers sharing the same hallway as customers."

"Well, he has a point there," Michelle conceded. "It would be, um, messy."

"In a perfect world, the wait staff would never bump into a guest or spill anything." Nina gave a grudging nod. "We don't live in a perfect world."

"Did your friend Lance have any suggestions?"

"Yeah." Nina barked a laugh and fought more tears. "He thinks we should find another location. Something with two or three times the square footage. Maybe on the main drag in Sugar Sand Beach." She shook her head. "Not gonna happen."

"I agree," Michelle said firmly. "We can't call this the Sugar Sand Inn *and Cafe* if people have to get in their cars to grab breakfast. Plus, much as Maggie supported us at the town council meeting, I'd hate to think how she'd react if we opened a restaurant across the street from her diner. So where else do we have space?"

The soft whir of the overhead fan was the only sound for a few minutes while Nina considered and discarded a couple of ideas.

"What if we remodeled the gardener's shed? Opened the cafe there?" Michelle asked when Reggie drove the noisy tractor past the window.

Could they? Nina quickly calculated the improvements they'd need to make. "Do you know how expensive that would be?" Her shoulders slumped. "We'd have to gut that beautiful little apartment out there. Even then, I'm pretty sure we'd still run into a space problem—the square footage might be even less than the kitchen and dining room combined. To say nothing of the logistics. Guests here at the inn would have to dress and cross the yard in order to get a cup of coffee. That's fine on days like today, but what if it's raining?"

"We have had some incredible storms," Michelle admitted.

"And they say we haven't seen anything until we've lived through a hurricane or two."

Michelle visibly shuddered. "Okay. Not the gardener's shed, then. What about here in the house? Instead of moving the cafe someplace else, can we expand the dining room?"

Nina closed her eyes to let a bird's-eye view of the first floor play against the backs of her lids. The house had been built in the 1920s, when the focus was more on function than flow. As a result, doors and rooms branched off a long hallway that extended from the back of the house to the front. The kitchen and living room sat on one side of the hall. Across from them were the front and back parlors with the dining room sandwiched between them. She looked up from the spot on the floor she'd been studying. "Expand it how?"

"What if we turned the back parlor into another dining area?" Michelle asked. Her tone said she was simply trying the idea on for size.

"You're talking about knocking down walls and losing a room." Nina tugged on a loose strand of hair while the tiniest bit of hope flickered in her chest. "That's an awfully big change."

"True. But it would double the square footage of the dining area. C'mon, let's take a look."

Michelle led the way out of the kitchen, across the hall and into the small sitting room at the rear of the house. Light filtered through a stained-glass window overlooking the backyard. Two other large windows flooded the room with sunshine. The sparse furnishings included a settee and several uncomfortable tufted armchairs.

"Whatever we do, we have to preserve that stained glass," Nina murmured.

"Definitely," Michelle agreed. She spun in a slow circle. "You know, I think this room is even larger than the dining room." She gestured toward the wall that divided them. "If we knocked a hole right there, we could create one large dining area. And since there's already a separate door leading to the hall, it would solve your egress problem."

"This might work." Nina sniffed as her tears dried up. The tiny flicker of hope grew a bit larger. She pictured their guests entering and exiting from the door closest to the front of the house while servers carried plates and trays from the kitchen straight across the hall and into the dining area. "We should probably have someone take a look at what we're thinking," she cautioned. "Someone more knowledgeable about construction than we are. What if we knocked down the wall and the whole second floor came crashing down?"

"Right." Michelle nodded. "We'll need to run the whole idea by Reggie and Erin, too. We can do that tonight. Before that, though, let's ask Chris." The handyman had recently repaired all the railings around the front porch. Currently he was prepping the exterior of the house for the painters who would give the whole place a fresh new look. "He should be able to tell us if what we're proposing is even feasible."

Doubts rolled in, clouding the rosy image that had begun to form in Nina's mind. She hadn't considered that Reggie or Erin might give the idea a big ol' thumbs down. "Do you think they'll go for it?"

Michelle shrugged. "I don't see why not. We need the cafe. This seems like the best solution."

"I'd want to get Lance's buy-in before anyone grabs a sledgehammer. I'd hate to go to all the effort and expense only to find out he's still opposed to the idea." Nina managed a tremulous smile when Michelle squeezed her upper arm.

"Smart thinking. We'll measure everything out, make sure we have enough space for—how many tables did you say you needed?"

"Six. Eight would be better." Once word of the new restaurant spread, they could turn a tidy profit with eight tables.

"Eight, then." Michelle gave the room a second hard look. Crossing her fingers, she held them up. "Maybe more, but we'll plan on eight. At least."

Two hours later, Chris climbed onto the stepladder he'd erected in the back parlor. His expression serious, he ran a stud finder along the wall near the ceiling, repeating a process he'd performed at several different heights. The device chirped softly. "My best guess is that this wall is not load-bearing. There's only one way to tell for sure, though, and that's to open 'er up and find out."

"We're not quite ready to break out the safety goggles," Nina warned. "But that's very good news." A few minutes earlier, Michelle had raced out of the room, her phone pressed to one ear. Now Nina balanced Michelle's spiral notebook on the back of the settee and jotted down Chris's findings so she'd have the facts at her fingertips when she and her friends gathered for their nightly get-together on the front porch.

"I have a little bit more for you." Chris climbed down from the ladder. "This here room is the same width as the dining room, but it's another two feet longer. That's gonna give you a whole lot more space."

Nina's heart leaped. Quickly, she ran the calculations in her head. The answer boggled her mind. Could they really have room for eleven tables? Or ten, with a coffee station so the wait staff wouldn't have to run back and forth to the kitchen every time someone wanted a refill? That was more than she'd even dared to hope for. She pressed a hand to her mouth. She could practically see servers clad in black pants and white shirts waiting on satisfied customers.

"There's just one thing." Chris folded his arms across his chest.

Why? Why was there always "just one thing"? Nina held her breath and waited. After all this,

Chris wasn't going to let her down, was he?

A thick lock of blond hair fell onto his forehead as the broad-shouldered handyman shook his head. "The thing is, you're talking a bigger job than I'm comfortable taking on. I mean, I'll be glad to help out. But there's electric wiring to deal with, air-conditioning vents to consider." He pointed down to the bottom of the wall they'd proposed removing. "The wood floor ends at the baseboards and picks up on the other side. In between, there's probably nothing but bare plywood. That'll have to be patched. Finding a match to these ol' hardwoods ain't gonna be easy. You'll also need drywall and a host of other things. Some I might not even know about."

"So you're saying you don't want the job?" Nina asked. Disappointment made her heart sink.

"Not exactly." Chris brushed his hair out of his eyes. "I'm saying it's too big a job for one man. You need a crew and a crew boss. A contractor. Someone who'll know what to do if he runs into a problem in the middle of the project."

"That sounds ominous. Like what?" In one of the detective shows she'd watched, the heroine had discovered a dead body hidden behind a wall in her house. That wasn't going to happen here, was it?

"Termites," Chris said, eliminating one problem and doling out another. "That's the biggest concern." He tapped a spot on the ladder. The hinged strip folded in the middle. "I've punched holes in walls before only to find there was nothing left of the two-by-fours but sawdust."

"Oh, dear!" Nina scanned the ceiling. Was the whole house about to dissolve around them? She cast a desperate look at Chris. "Tell me that's not something we have to worry about."

"Whoa, there." Concern etched Chris's face. He held up one hand like a stop sign. "No need to get worked up."

Nina pressed a hand over her racing heart. What was wrong with her? She didn't normally go off the deep end, yet here she was, assuming the absolute worst at every turn. Deliberately, she cleared her mind, calmed her breathing, shook the tension from her hands. "Sorry," she murmured to Chris when she felt more like herself again. "It's been a day. I feel like I've been on an emotional roller coaster ever since I got up this morning."

Chris turned thoughtful. "My mom gets like that sometimes. Feels like the world is closing in on her. You want me to get ya a glass of water or something?"

"No, thanks. I'll be all right." She took another deep, calming breath. "Now what were you saying about termites?"

"I'm just sayin' you never know what you're gonna find when you open up a wall. But I haven't seen any sign of termites, and I looked the house over from top to bottom before you moved in. Didn't spot a single pile of wings or sawdust anywheres. That's what ya gotta look out for." He scuffed one shoe against the floor as if he was reluctant to bring up another problem. At last, he rolled one shoulder and said, "The other thing to consider is how fast you want the job done. It'd take me a good six months to do all this on my lonesome."

"Six months," Nina whispered. They'd have to delay opening the inn. Instead of September, October at the latest, it'd be Christmas before they could welcome their first guests. Worse, she imagined months of listening to saws buzz and hammers pound. Of plastic tarps hung across every opening to keep the sawdust from spreading. She groaned. Those tarps never worked. She couldn't imagine trying to prepare dishes for the craft fair with all that dust and dirt floating in the air. Ugh. She and Michelle and

Erin and Reggie would be sweeping and dusting for weeks on end.

She corralled her wayward thoughts. Okay, they'd just have to hire someone else to do the job. Still, a contractor and a crew sounded awfully expensive, and she said as much.

"Anything worth doing is worth doing right, isn't it? I know a guy who'd do this for you, and he won't charge you an arm and a leg." Chris finished folding the stepladder and leaned it against the wall.

"I guess it can't do any harm to find out all we can." The more information she had at her fingertips tonight when she reported on the health inspector's visit to Reggie and Erin, the better. "Could you talk to him, see if he's available?"

"Sure thing." Chris whipped his phone out of a back pocket.

Seconds later, Nina crossed to the window, where she studied the sparse traffic on the distant road while she tried not to listen in on the one-sided conversation taking place behind her. A task that was nearly impossible, considering she and Chris were standing not ten feet apart.

"Hey, man. Catch you at a good time?" Chris's voice shifted to a lower register. He paused, presumably to give the person on the other end of the line a chance to respond before he spoke again. "Yeah, she's fine. Growing like a weed. How are the girls?"

Chris's side of the conversation ebbed and flowed. "Good. Good." After a pause, he said, "Nah, man. Been too busy to take the boat out. How 'bout you?" He whistled. "Twenty-six pounds. That's a he—" He stopped short. "A heck of a redfish. Work must be slow if you're able to get out on the water that much." Another pause, then, "Oh, really?" A grin spread across the lower half of his face. "I hear ya. Listen, if you're free, I have a job for you out at the Simmons place. You know it, right?" After the briefest of pauses, he continued. "The new owners want to knock down a wall so they can turn two rooms into one big one. You interested?" Chris fell silent except for a few yes or no answers while the person on the other end of the line probably asked for additional information. At last, he said, "Yeah? Thanks, man. I'll let 'em know." There was a final pause before he nodded. "Sure thing. We'll grab a beer real soon."

Nina turned away from the window as Chris ended the call and returned the phone to his back pocket. She looked at him expectantly.

Chris hefted the ladder. "Well, good news," he announced. "Zeke'll be here first thing tomorrow. He'll look everything over and give you a quote."

"That soon?" Nina ran a hand through her hair. They hadn't even decided if they wanted to do this yet.

"Zeke's usually booked solid, but he had another job that fell through this month. I'd take advantage of it if I were you. He and his crew are fast, too. Probably knock this out in a week." Carrying the ladder, Chris started for the door.

A week?

Goosebumps raced down Nina's arms. The chance to double the space for the cafe and have the work finished in time to open on schedule was too good to pass up, wasn't it? If this guy Zeke could do the job, they should follow Chris's advice and take advantage of the opportunity. Her usual confident air returning, she squared her shoulders and smoothed a hand over her white chef's jacket. Expanding the dining area should resolve her problems with the health inspector, but she'd give Lance a call this afternoon. Once he heard their solution to the issues he'd raised, she was sure he'd give his okay. That left Reggie and Erin—she'd bring them up to speed tonight and pray the sisters gave her their blessing.

Six

Erin

T rotting up the front steps to the house, Erin checked to see if anyone else had arrived for their usual evening get-together. A tiny ball of tension uncurled in her midsection when Michelle wasn't already waiting on the white rattan furniture. When Nina hadn't left a tray loaded with glasses on the table while she ducked back inside for a pitcher of iced tea. When her sister was nowhere in sight.

Excellent!

She had the entire porch to herself. She could use a few minutes alone to recharge before the rest of the crew arrived. For most of her adult life, she'd gone where she wanted when she wanted without having to answer to anyone else. She didn't have that luxury in Sugar Sand Beach, and the change was taking some getting used to. She eased onto one of the comfy cushions, kicked off her sandals, and propped her feet up on the glass-topped coffee table.

Ahhh. Bliss.

In the west, the sun slowly sank toward the horizon. Shadows lengthened. Birds flocked to their nests. Crickets chirped, and a warm, welcome feeling of fulfillment stole over her. Her eyes dropped to half-mast while memories of the past few weeks played across the backs of her eyelids. Whether she was delivering gift baskets to business owners with Michelle or helping Nina wash the kitchen shelves or exploring the local waterways, she'd never felt more at home than she had ever since she arrived in Sugar Sand Beach.

And then there was Reggie. She and her sister had forged deeper bonds than Erin could have ever imagined during the move and the weeks that had followed. Mostly because she'd been at Reggie's side when that slimeball of a husband had walked out on her sister. Or when he'd tried to lure her back into a loveless marriage. She'd always be grateful that she hadn't been off climbing a mountain somewhere or trekking across the desert when Reggie's world fell apart.

It had happened before—all those failed

attempts to have a baby—and she'd been so disconnected, she hadn't even known. This time she'd been close enough to offer a shoulder and some sisterly advice. In the process, she'd discovered she liked—really liked—her sister. She'd always loved Reggie, of course. That had been a given from the moment she'd come home from school one day and learned she was no longer the only star at the center of her parents' universe.

But *like* her sister? How could she when they'd barely known each other? Which, she supposed, was only natural considering the ten-year gap in their ages. They'd never been at the same stage in their lives together. Never attended school together. Never shared the same interests.

Until now.

Now they worked and played together. They had goals in common. They even bickered like, well, like sisters. She'd discovered Reggie was as bright as she was witty, as hardworking as she was teasing, an all-around good person. The discovery was almost enough to make her regret all the years they'd spent apart.

Metal rattled behind her. The front door slid open. Erin started and blinked, realizing that she'd dozed off while she was staring off into space. She uncrossed her ankles and stretched.

Reggie, dressed in shorts and a summery top, her strawberry-blond hair in a messy topknot, slipped through the door and out onto the porch. In her arms she carried a purring Mr. Pibbs.

"Look who's decided to join us tonight." Reggie rubbed the big cat's head. She eyed the empty seats. "Oh, good. I caught you alone. I wanted to touch base with you about tomorrow. We're still leaving in the morning, aren't we?"

"That's the plan." Erin yawned. "It's a twelve- or thirteen-hour drive, depending on traffic. I'd like to be on the road by six. Does that work for you?"

"Yeah. My bag is packed. As long as I can grab a cup of coffee on the way out the door, I'm all set."

"I took your truck down to Jimbo's after my run this morning. He checked the fluids and the belts. Kicked the tires." Breaking down on the side of the road was never fun. Not even in the US, where tow trucks and roadside assistance were plentiful. "It's all gassed up and ready to go."

"Wup. There goes my excuse to stop for breakfast. I thought we'd fill up while we, you know, filled up." Reggie grinned.

Erin shook her head. Her sister was

perpetually in motion, a calorie-burning machine who was always hungry. "Don't worry. I won't let you starve. There's lots of fast-food places along the way."

"I don't suppose we'll have much time for sightseeing while we're there."

Erin had planned on having Reggie empty out the storage unit while she took care of other business, but the hopeful note in her sister's voice forced her to shift gears. "I made an appointment at the property management office for first thing Thursday. I'll be there a couple of hours. You could take one of the beach bikes and ride around the island while I'm gone."

"I'd like that. I've never been to the Keys before."

Erin smiled. "This is the best time of year to go. Not too hot, and the crowds have thinned out. You'll love it. Quaint shops. Beautiful beaches. It's a little slice of paradise."

Which was why she needed to visit the management company. She'd never seen much sense in letting the cottage sit vacant over the summers while she was guiding tourists on kayak trips in Alaska. Or when she was off on one of her many travels. Especially when the income from summer rentals alone paid the mortgage for the entire year. Now that she'd be staying in Sugar Sand Beach for the foreseeable future, she could generate a nice cash flow by renting out the place year-round.

Of course, that begged the question of whether or not she planned to stay in Sugar Sand Beach. She'd been here for a month already. Before that, she'd spent several weeks helping Michelle prepare for the move. Usually a restless yearning to hit the road struck her after only a short while in one place. That feeling normally grew until she finally packed her bag, threw a dart at a map pinned to the wall, and set out for wherever the dart landed. Which hadn't happened so far. In fact, as much as she wanted, needed, to retrieve her gear from Key West, she dreaded the idea of getting in the truck tomorrow. She liked it right where she was, thank you very much, and if the truth were known, she'd rather stay put.

Except the sound of footsteps coming from inside the house told her she needed to get up off her duff and lend Nina a hand. She sprang to her feet and held the door wide. The tall brunette emerged seconds later carrying a tray that looked much too heavy for her thin frame.

"Here, let me help you with that," Erin said. She grabbed an icy platter filled with peeled shrimp.

From Reggie's lap, Mr. Pibbs mewed just loud enough to let everyone know he'd detected the scent of his favorite food.

Erin waited while Nina settled her burden on the table before she added the platter to the array of glasses and napkins around the pitcher of iced tea. She snagged a shrimp as her payment for helping out and swished it through a small bowl of some kind of tasty-looking sauce. Popping the morsel in her mouth, she sank into her chair while she savored the spicy goodness of remoulade and cold seafood.

"Nina, I swear," she said, "you're killing us with kindness here. I'm going to get as big as a cow if you keep feeding us like this."

"As hard as we're working these days, we deserve good food." Nina anchored the napkins with a couple of spoons. "Besides, shrimp aren't fattening."

"I'd point out that the sauce is definitely not calorie-free, but I'm afraid you won't let me have any more. It's soooo good."

"Thanks." Nina turned away, her cheeks pink. "I see Mr. Pibbs has found a new friend this evening. You can make him get down if you want," she said to Reggie.

"He followed me downstairs. I think he's figured out we have snacks at our little get-togethers and he wants in on the action." Reggie raised the cat to her face and buried her head in his fur.

"You all are going to spoil him rotten," Nina groused with a forgiving smile. "There'll be no living with him."

Mr. Pibbs squirmed out of Reggie's grasp. Without moving from her lap, the big cat eyed the platter while his tail swished back and forth. His tongue darted between his lips.

"Uh, uh, uh," Nina warned. She shook one finger at her fur baby. "No shrimp for you yet. You have to wait like everyone else. Except for a certain rude person whose name I won't mention."

"Ooops. Sorry." Erin laughed at the stern look Nina cast her way. She always stole a taste of whatever treat the chef had fixed for them that night, and Nina always gave her grief about it.

Reggie ran a hand down Mr. Pibbs's back. The big cat responded by curling into a ball on her lap. "I'm bushed. Weeds grow like crazy around here. After I mowed this morning, I spent most of the day..."

"Hold up." Erin held out a hand. "Let's wait till Michelle gets here. Otherwise, we'll have to repeat everything."

"Good point. Where is our illustrious leader?" Reggie asked.

"She'll be along in a minute," Nina said. "She was putting away a bucket of cleaning supplies when I left the kitchen." Her voice dropped to a whisper. "She got a phone call earlier and bolted out of the room. I think it might have been one of the kids."

"I hope so," Erin said. "I'm going to have to disown them if they don't start treating their mother better." At Ashley and Aaron's christening, she'd promised to be her godchildren's spiritual guide. A task she'd obviously failed, considering how selfish the twins were acting.

She would have said more, but Michelle eased the front door open just then and joined the others on the porch. "Another beautiful night," she sighed as she took her usual seat.

"Everyone says how hot it is in Florida, but I can't complain." Leaning over Mr. Pibbs's plump body, Reggie filled a glass of tea from the pitcher.

"We're lucky. We're right on the Gulf. All that water and the sea breezes help keep temperatures about ten degrees cooler than it is farther inland." Erin filled her own glass. "You'll see what I mean when we head south tomorrow. By the time we get to Orlando, stepping out of the car will feel like stepping into a hot, damp oven."

"Lovely. Can't wait." Reggie sipped her iced tea and smacked her lips. "I swear, Nina, you've nailed this perfectly."

"It took a while, but I finally found the secret," Nina said as she filled two glasses. She handed one to Michelle.

"Oh?" Erin raised an eyebrow.

"Yeah, you just treat it like you do your hair." Nina folded her legs until she sat cross-legged in her chair.

Erin scratched her head. That wasn't the answer she'd expected. "Say, what?"

"Well, you know. Our hair gets oily, so we wet it down, add soap to wash it and get it clean. No one goes around with a soapy head, so we rinse it to get rid of the soap. Then we dry it, right? But before that, we treat it with conditioner to make it lie smooth and mousse to give it lift. Finally, we add a little bit of oil for shine. But since no one likes oily hair, we have to repeat the whole process the next day."

Reggie grinned. "And tea?"

"We boil the water to get it hot, add ice to make it cold, sweeten it with sugar and then squeeze lemon juice into it to make it sour."

"Then we drink it all up so you have to start over again tomorrow." Reggie raised her glass. "Cheers!"

Laughter flowed and glasses clinked as Erin and the others settled in to catch up on one another's activities of the day. Erin was eager to hear how things had gone with the health inspector, but Michelle nodded to Reggie instead of Nina.

Her sister reported on the status of the garden—which was thriving. "Everything's freshly mowed or weeded. Both ATVs are up and running now, in case anyone wants to ride down to the lake while Erin and I are in the Keys."

Erin had begun clearing space in the garage for the equipment she'd bring with her on the return trip from her cottage. "I'll store all the life vests and other gear in the empty apartment for now, but we probably ought to pick a more permanent spot soon." She had a couple of ideas that might work. "Right now, I'm more concerned about the big stuff. In addition to the kayaks and a canoe, I need room for the trailer." The one she kept in the Keys was specially outfitted for hauling her watercraft. They'd tow it back with them. "I could use some more space in the garage. What are we doing with Nancy's sedan or the van?" The two vehicles hadn't been used since Nancy's death five years earlier. "Can we get rid of them?"

"Let's circle back to the van in a minute." Michelle leaned forward as she updated everyone on the status of their booth at the craft fair. She turned to Nina. "I know you didn't plan to charge for the small plates, but I think we're going to have to." When the brunette's lips turned down at the corners, Michelle hurriedly explained. "We were thinking somewhere around five hundred attendees, right?

"Ye-es," Nina said tentatively.

"Maggie told me we should expect between fifteen hundred and two thousand, as long as the weather holds."

"Seriously?" A mix of panic and excitement swirled in Nina's brown eyes. "That's a lot of potential customers, but assuming we give everyone who visits our booth just a tidbit, that's still a ton of food. I'm going to need to double— no, triple—what I was planning to make."

"Right." Michelle swirled the iced tea in her glass. "That's one reason I thought we should charge a little something. Not much. Just enough to recoup our expenses. Maybe a dollar a plate?"

Nina thought for a second before she nodded. "I can definitely keep the costs around a dollar. But with that big a crowd, I might need some help. What if we hired a couple of kids from the Culinary Arts program at South Walton High?"

"That's a good idea," Reggie said. "It'd be a great experience for them." Her eyes narrowing, she focused on Michelle. "You said 'one reason.' Was there another one?"

"Actually, yes. Glad you asked." Michelle aimed a smile at Reggie. "In addition to a very modest fee for the booth, the town collects ten percent of the proceeds from our sales for a local charity. This year, all that money goes into a building fund for a wounded soldier from right here in Sugar Sand Beach. I was thinking…"

"What?" Anticipation stirred in Erin's gut.

"Well, since you mentioned the van"— Michelle's gaze sought Reggie's—"do you have any idea whether it's drivable?"

Reggie scooted forward until she perched on the edge of her chair. "I haven't even tried to start it, but I can as soon as we get back from the Keys. The other vehicles Chris put into storage started without too much trouble. Why, what are you thinking?"

Michelle traced one finger across the hem of her shorts. "That wheelchair lift makes it a mighty good gift for our veteran, don't you think?"

"I thought you were going to say that!" Mr. Pibbs batted at Reggie's hand as her fist sliced through the air. "Yes, baby," Reggie cooed to the cat. Still focused on the kitty, she addressed the others. "We can definitely spare the van. We already have Michelle's SUV, my truck and Nancy's old pickup. There's also a really sweet sedan that has about fifty thousand miles on it."

"And my Jeep. We'll bring that back with us," Erin put in.

"Plus, the two ATVs," Reggie added. "For a woman who rarely left the house, Nancy sure kept a lot of vehicles. But the van, it was practically brand-new when she passed. She couldn't have had it more than a couple of months."

"What do you think?" Michelle turned to the others.

Erin felt pressured to agree when her friend pinned her with an expectant look. She didn't want to be the only naysayer, but she thought there were a few other things to consider. "I wouldn't want to donate the van and then find out it needs a ton of expensive work the recipient can't afford," she suggested.

Michelle bit her lower lip. "True. I guess we'd have to have it thoroughly checked out."

"We could ask Jimbo to give it a good going-over," Reggie suggested. Most people in town took their cars his garage when they needed service.

Michelle tapped her chin. "Assuming the

van's in good shape, we should look for ways to get the town involved."

"So it's not just 'our' project but something from everyone in Sugar Sand Beach?" Nina asked, making air quotes.

"Yeah," Michelle agreed. "What if we asked kids at the day care to make signs and banners for it? Then someone could drive it in the Fourth of July parade."

"I like that idea," Nina nodded. "What else?"

"This is just a thought off the top of my head," Erin said. "But once word spreads—and if you get Jimbo involved, word will spread—we could ask for donations. We could put any money we collect toward a year's supply of gas and maintenance."

"Whoa!" Michelle fanned her face. "This turned into a much bigger deal than I thought it would. Not that giving away a wheelchair-accessible van is a *small* deal." Her eyes sparkled with tears.

Erin reached over and squeezed her friend's hand. Though none of them had served in the military personally, Michelle's adoptive father and her own dad had done a stint or two in Vietnam. Nina had lost an uncle to another conflict, as well. As a result, the four of them shared an utmost respect for anyone who risked life and limb for their country.

Michelle brushed her eyes and drew in a ragged breath. "Okay, I'll pass the torch to Nina now. We saved her for last 'cause she has a lot to tell us."

All eyes shifted expectantly toward the chef. Rather than brimming over with excitement, though, Nina twisted a napkin between her fingers until it formed a tight spiral.

Erin recognized the move as a sign that their resident cook had bad news to share. Some big issue to resolve, no doubt. Otherwise, Nina would have filled them in on the health inspector's report the instant she stepped onto the porch. Hoping to break the ice while letting Nina know they were firmly on her side, Erin tossed out an easy question. "So what hoops did our distinguished visitor want us to jump through?"

Nina managed a wry smile. "To make a very long, sad story short, both Mr. Parker—he's the health inspector—and the fire marshal say if we want to use the dining room for the cafe, we can't open. There's only one way in and out, and the room's too small."

Erin's stomach dropped like it had when she bungee-jumped off the Bloukrans Bridge in South Africa. She and Nina had been friends forever. When they were just little kids playing in the dirt, Nina had baked mud pies that Erin would dutifully pretend to eat. In school, Nina had opted for every class even remotely associated with food or restaurants. She'd aced her degree in college and spent the next twenty years preparing to open her own place. Seeing her hopes dashed now that she was so close to fulfilling her dream would hurt like the Dickens. But they weren't going to throw in the towel. They'd make whatever changes they needed… for Nina.

"And the solution is?" Erin prompted. There had to be one.

Nina's smile turned wistful. "Michelle and I have looked at it from several different angles. We rejected Mr. Parker's suggestion that we look for a different space in town. That means we have to do some remodeling. One option would be to gut the entire back end of the house and create a good-size dining area right off the kitchen."

"But we'd lose both the living room and the library in the process, and it'd be a major undertaking," Michelle put in.

"The other idea—and this is the one we like the best—is to open the wall between the dining room and the back parlor—make that all one big dining area. It would give us the square footage we need. It would also resolve the entrance/exit issue since both rooms already open onto the hallway."

Erin gulped. She'd harbored the notion of using the back parlor as an office for the inn's leisure activities. The room was big enough for a counter where people could sign up for various activities—bike riding, guided wildlife tours, fishing expeditions or, her personal favorites, kayaking along the coast or through the labyrinth of freshwater ribbons in the Topsail Hill Preserve. She'd thought of hanging pictures on the walls of happy guests enjoying all the inn had to offer. And yet… The big house had plenty of other rooms she could use, but it sounded like there was only one good solution to the cafe's space problem.

"Works for me," she said before anyone else chimed in.

When Michelle and Reggie shook their heads in agreement, tears seeped from the corners of Nina's eyes.

"Really, you guys? You'd give up a whole room? Just like that?"

"Just like that." Reggie snapped her fingers.

"So when do we start knocking down walls?" Erin interlaced her fingers and stretched. "I've never swung a sledgehammer, but I've always wanted to."

"Sorry. Can't help you there." Nina laughed. "I thought Chris might handle the work for us. But he said we need a contractor to do the job right. He recommended someone. The guy—Zeke—is coming out first thing tomorrow to give us an estimate. If it's reasonable, he and his crew can do the work next week."

"I love it when a plan comes together." Erin grinned.

The business of the day handled, they dug into the tasty shrimp appetizer. Everyone pretended not to see it when Reggie slipped Mr. Pibbs a shrimp. Or was it two? Nevertheless, the kitty jumped from Reggie's lap to his human mom's. There he made a pest of himself until Nina finally gave in and fed him her last bit of seafood.

"Dinner in about forty-five minutes?" the chef asked when they'd picked the platter clean. She gathered Mr. Pibbs in her arms and stood. "It'll take about that long for the quiche to bake if I slip it in the oven now. The salad's already made."

"That works." Reggie stood and began loading glasses and napkins on the tray. "I'll carry this in and lock up the outbuildings for the night. The keys will be on the rack by the back door if anyone needs to get into the garage or the gardener's shed while we're gone." She hefted the tray and followed Nina.

When the door closed behind the others, Erin leaned closer to Michelle. "Nina said you got a phone call earlier," she said, carefully testing the waters. Ever since the move, her friend had been on tenterhooks where her children were concerned. "One of the kids?"

"Aaron." Michelle nodded.

"Has he booked a flight to Florida yet?" A trip to see his mom would be a sure sign that Aaron had seen the error of his ways.

"Unfortunately, no. But I understand. He's only a month into his internship with CJX. He won't get any time off until just before school starts again. But he's beginning to see that acting like a spoiled brat won't get him where he wants to go in life."

You think? Not wanting to make Michelle feel any worse than she already did, Erin kept the thought to herself.

"We talked for over an hour. I wasn't going to say anything about the move, but he actually brought it up. How'd he put it?" Michelle thought for a moment. "He said he knew moving down here hadn't been an easy decision for me to make. Just knowing he recognizes that was, like, major progress. I told him how plans for the

inn were coming together. And—bottom line—
he offered to build a website for us."

"Whoa!" Erin felt her eyes go wide. She
clenched her fingers together and traded fist-
bumps with Michelle. "You could have led with
that—that's huge!"

"Yeah, I guess it is. We need a website, and I
sure can't do it. I tried." Some of the concern that
had etched Michelle's face of late faded. A fresh
measure of happiness replaced it. "I was so
relieved after talking to him. For the first time
since I found out I wasn't going to be able to
hang on to the house, I feel like things are
actually going to be okay. Now, if only Ashley
would get her act together, too."

"She'll come around," Erin said with more far
assurance than she felt. "She just needs a little
more time."

"Let's hope those words go straight from
your lips to my stubborn daughter's ears."

Michelle wouldn't pressure her children into
behaving better. After all, her children were over
twenty-one. Young, impressionable, and with a
sense of entitlement that was hard to overlook.
But adults all the same. As their mother, she had
to tread carefully.

Erin, however, didn't have the same
constraints. She had the freedom to speak her

mind, and she would. It sounded like Aaron had already turned a corner. She'd give Ashley another week—two tops—to get down off her high horse and realize her mom had made the best possible decisions for all of them under very trying circumstances. If Ash didn't reach that realization on her own, Erin had no problem pointing out the error of her godchild's ways.

She settled back in her chair. She'd always liked this part of the day, when her work was done and it was time to relax and recharge. Tonight, the sun had painted the sky in reds and golds as it dipped below the horizon. From their nests, birds sang their good-night songs. In the deepening twilight, tiny flashes of light came from fireflies flitting above the grasses and bushes. She took a deep breath and caught the faintest scent of roses from the plants on either side of the door.

She sighed contentedly. For the first time in more than two decades, the itch to go, to be somewhere else had faded. It might come back one day, but for now, she was right where she was supposed to be. Right here in Sugar Sand Beach.

Seven

Nina

Nina eyed the tall, dark-haired man who leaned oh-so-casually against the doorjamb. Zeke Henson punched numbers on the calculator app on his phone as if he didn't have a clue that he was the best specimen of the male species in Sugar Sand Beach.

Make that the entire state of Florida, she corrected.

From the roots of the dark brown hair he wore a tad longer than fashionable to a closely cropped goatee that hugged a nicely rounded jaw line, he raised the bar on the boy-next-door look to new heights. The urge to get closer stirred within her. She wanted to see if flecks of green dotted his wide blue eyes. Or if his full lips were as kissably soft as they looked. Her pulse began to race.

Oh, stop. Just stop.

The man might have jaw-dropping good looks, the kind that stopped most women in their tracks, but she wasn't one of them. Besides, she bet he had an ego to match. No one could look as fine as he did and not take advantage of it. She could not afford to lose her head—or pay some inflated price—just for the privilege of being around all that eye candy. Day in and day out. For as long as it took to remodel her kitchen.

Control yourself, woman!

Slowly, she filled her lungs with air and held the breath for three long seconds before she exhaled evenly. She repeated the process until her heart rate dropped to normal. Then and only then did she marshal her thoughts and pose the question she needed Zeke to answer.

"So how much is it going to cost to knock out that wall?" She braced herself for a price that was well out of her ballpark.

His movements languid, Zeke slipped his phone into a back pocket and gave her a disarming smile that threatened to undo the effects of all her breathing exercises. "To take out the whole wall, move the electrical plug, patch the drywall, and lay in new hardwood to fill in the gap where the old wall used to be, I reckon that'll run about a thousand dollars."

Nina blinked. She'd checked out prices online and had a pretty good idea of what the job should cost. Zeke's estimate was well below that and far below the spending limit she and Michelle had agreed upon. She had to ask. "What's the catch?"

"No catch. Chris said you all were good people and I should give you the Friends and Family discount." Zeke tipped his open palms toward the ceiling and shrugged. "Besides, I'm awful tired of my mom's cookin'. 'Bout time we had us a new restaurant in town."

He lived with his mother?

Disappointment formed a hard lump in her stomach. Nina swept an appraising glance over the man's face. This time when her interest flared, she squelched it with a firm hand. Despite an age-defying tan, the laugh lines around Zeke's mouth and the crow's feet at his eyes put him in his late forties or early fifties. He might look like a Greek god, but no one reached that point in life and still lived at home unless they had a serious character flaw...or two...or three.

Which wouldn't keep her from working with the contractor. Chris had recommended him, after all, and she trusted Chris to give her good advice. If she'd asked him about the local dating pool, no doubt the handyman would've sent her in a whole different direction.

Not that she was looking for a date. Between the upcoming craft fair and getting the cafe ready to open, she had far too much on her plate to add any kind of relationships to the activity menu.

"So what do you think?"

At the sound of Zeke's voice, she reined in her wandering thoughts.

Vaguely aware the contractor had been talking while she'd been off in la-la land, she summoned her most apologetic smile for the man who'd crossed the room while she wasn't watching. "Sorry. I didn't quite catch all that. Would you mind repeating that bit about the entrance?"

"That's okay." Zeke's smile slanted to one side as if women lost their heads around him all the time. "It's probably best if I show you anyway."

He beckoned, and Nina followed him through the kitchen, across the hall and into the parlor. Standing in the middle of the room, he pointed to the wall that separated the space from the formal dining room.

"Now here's an idea that'll run you a bit more, but I think it'll be worth it in the long run.

Instead of removing this entirely, we could create an arch between the two rooms. That'd be pleasing to the eye. It would also give you the option of closing off one space for private parties or if, say, you wanted to keep one area closed for breakfast."

Nina nodded. The change made perfect sense.

"Then come back over here." Zeke retraced his steps to the parlor door, where he placed his hand on the jamb. "We'd widen this and the one into the kitchen for ease of access."

Nina's eyes misted. Zeke's proposal was a definite improvement.

"Now step into the hall with me for a sec," came his deep voice. Once they were in the passageway, he slipped behind her. His hands landed on her shoulders. Gently, he turned her toward the front of the house. "What would you think of erecting a wall, say, right there." Moving in front of her, he gestured to a spot between the doors that led to the parlor and dining rooms. "It would divide the hall and keep your guests from inadvertently wandering into the kitchen. They could enter and exit from the front of the house. Wait staff could go in and out of the rear door."

She felt a thrill of excitement that had nothing to do with Zeke's good looks or the faint trace of aftershave that floated in the air. Zeke might live with his mama, but he had rock-solid design skills. Only one question remained. Could they afford to have so much work done?

"What's all this going to cost?" She braced for an answer she didn't want to hear.

One of Zeke's dark eyebrows dipped. "My crew can do all this in one week. If we can start Monday, I can cut you a really good deal."

"Next week?" Nina squeaked. She'd been hoping to delay the remodeling until after the craft fair. "I thought maybe later this summer. That won't work?"

"No. Sorry." Zeke gave his head a sorrowful shake. "After next week, I'm booked solid into December. It's only by pure chance that I have an opening at all. I'm sure Chris told you I had a big job fall through a couple of weeks ago. Me and my boys, we done fished till we filled every freezer in town. Which means we'll be sitting around twiddling our thumbs for the next ten days or so. You'd actually be doing me a favor it you let me put my boys to work on your place, so I'm willing to go this low." Zeke pulled a pencil and a three-by-five card from the pocket of a plaid, short-sleeved shirt. He scribbled briefly on the card before he held it out.

Nina held her breath and glanced down at

the number. The bid was more than double Zeke's original estimate but only slightly higher than her budget.

"This is a bit more than I'm authorized to spend," she told him honestly. "I'll have to run it by my partners." She'd talk with Michelle right away. As for Reggie and Erin, the sisters were on their way to the Keys, but they'd be checking in by phone each day. "You're sure you can complete the work in a week?"

"Everything but the wood flooring. We'll get that down," he assured her, "but we can't stain or seal it till all the other work's done. It'll only take one man to finish the floors. I'll make sure he won't be in your way or make a mess."

She extended her hand. "As long as the others agree, I think you've got a deal, Zeke."

"Great!"

She felt oddly disappointed when Zeke's larger hand enveloped hers in a grip that was solid and warm. She'd been hoping for a jolt of electricity or, at the very least, a tiny buzz. Instead, his touch only provided her with an awareness of his strength, the calluses on the pads of his palms, the slight sandpapery feel of his skin. This time, it was a little easier to remind herself she wasn't looking for romance. Not now. Not with so much to accomplish before the cafe opened.

143

Especially now that she'd need to sandwich the remodel into her schedule. With the workers creating dust and debris, she'd have to shut down the kitchen for a week. Which meant, once Zeke and his crew finished, she'd have to really hustle in order to get ready for the craft fair in time. Until then, she'd concentrate on hiring an assistant who could help her meet the deadline. She'd already received several promising resumes in answer to her ad. She'd get started making calls and interviewing candidates right away.

In the meantime, though, she needed to break it to the others that they were in for a week of meals from Maggie's Diner. Because, no matter how neat and tidy Zeke and his crew were, no one wanted mashed potatoes with a side of sawdust.

Eight

Nina

*I*n the quiet of her room, Nina slipped her arms into her chef's whites and pulled the double-breasted jacket square around her shoulders. She carefully pushed each of the knotted buttons through their holes, then smoothed the hem over her favorite pair of loose-fitting chef's pants. Watching her every move from his favorite spot on her bed, Mr. Pibbs mewed softly.

"Sorry, boy," she cooed. "There won't be any tidbits for you to try today. This"—she ran a hand over the sleek chignon—"is all for show." Although cooking wasn't on her agenda—Zeke and his men had taken over the kitchen and dining areas—she felt it was important to project a professional air while she interviewed candidates for the cafe's sous chef position. Over the past few days, she'd spoken with every applicant by phone and eliminated all but three. Each of the finalists was coming to the house today for a face-to-face meeting. She crossed her fingers and whispered a prayer that the right person had already applied for the job.

As if he understood, Mr. Pibbs unsheathed his claws and stretched.

"Uh, uh, uh," Nina admonished. "Don't you scratch up my comforter. Be a good boy and I'll bring you a treat later."

Mr. Pibbs hissed, but he complied with Nina's request. As his claws retracted, she blew kisses on top of his head. The last couple of days, the kitty had grown restless. Not that she blamed him. She'd been forced to confine the big tabby in her room ever since the remodeling began in earnest on Monday.

She'd discovered that little necessity the first day the crew had been on the job. Normally Mr. Pibbs hid from visitors. This time all the noise had made the cat curious, however, and he'd checked out the construction area. Which was fine until he decided to play in a pile of sawdust. She'd been able to trace his movements through the house by the trail of yellow paw prints he'd left in his wake. But it could have been worse, she'd reminded herself as she cleaned up after the cat. At least Mr. Pibbs hadn't gotten interested in a pan of fresh paint.

"You're such a goofball, you know?" she asked, giving the kitty a final pat. She checked his food and water bowls. Satisfied that, no matter what his thoughts on the subject, he wouldn't actually starve to death over the next several hours, she closed the door firmly behind her and headed downstairs to get ready for the interviews.

On the first floor, masculine voices mingled with the sound of saws and hammers. As tempted as she was to stop and check on the workers' progress—okay, maybe she did want to take a peek at Zeke, too—she aimed her footsteps toward the front parlor. There, the Keurig and a selection of mugs had been moved to one end of a long sideboard until the construction crew finished their work. She had the room to herself—Michelle and the others no doubt opting to enjoy their morning beverages someplace that offered a little more peace and quiet. A few minutes later, she carried her own cup into what used to be Nancy Simmons's office and closed the door, blocking out most of the workers' noise.

The scent of lemon and linseed oil floated in

the air in the room where bookcases lined two walls from floor to ceiling. She crossed to the Queen Anne-style desk, which boasted a beautifully stained top of solid ash supported by ornately curved legs Michelle called cabrioles. Setting her cup on a coaster, Nina took two pens and a pad of lined paper from the supply cabinet. When she'd arranged them "just so" on the desk, she placed the resumes of the three best candidates in a neat stack beside them. Although she'd gone over their qualifications several times already, she flipped through the resumes once more while she sipped her coffee.

On paper, at least, the three cooks were as different from one another as they could possibly be. Mark Dyer had recently moved to Florida from Tulsa, where he'd acquired ten years' experience working as a line cook. Nina was particularly interested in hearing about his work at a farm-to-table, Michelin-rated restaurant that offered a unique tasting menu in lieu of the standard list of entrees and appetizers. Her next candidate, Paul Reasoner, was currently unemployed and living in nearby Fort Walton Beach. Two definite pluses. He didn't list any formal training among his qualifications, though he'd worked with top chefs from around the country. Last but not least, Krystal Evers rounded off the list of choices. The woman had graduated from one of the better culinary schools earlier this spring. She didn't have a lot of experience, but her resume left Nina with the impression of a young cook who was eager to learn.

At 9:55, she downed her last sip of coffee. She straightened the stack of resumes until the edges aligned precisely and took a steadying breath. Her nerves thrummed. She'd never given an interview before, but she'd been on the receiving end often enough to know the questions to ask, the answers she hoped to hear. She rose, smoothed one hand over her chef's whites and, leaving the office, crossed the house to the window overlooking the parking area. There, she waited for her ten o'clock appointment.

And waited…and waited.

When fifteen minutes passed and Mark Dyer failed to show, she checked her phone for messages. Dismay turned her smile upside down when there weren't any. She gave Mark another ten minutes, then crossed his name off her list. Accidents happened, people got sick, they missed turns—she understood all that. But failing to show up for an interview without at least texting sent a message of its own. One she could neither overlook or excuse.

Just before eleven, she resumed her position by the window. An unfamiliar car already sat in the parking lot, and she felt a spark of anticipation flare in her chest. Her hopes dimmed within seconds when a short, stout man barged into the house as if he owned the place. Nina's lips thinned as she took in the shoulder-length hair Paul Reasoner had worn in a greasy ponytail. The stains dotting his shirt told her he hadn't dressed to impress. He'd doused himself with enough body spray that someone else might not have noticed the scent of bourbon that seeped from the man's pores. Nina did, though, and wrinkled her nose.

As far as first impressions went, hers of Paul Reasoner wasn't good. But her grandmother had always preached, "Marry in haste; repent at leisure." And though she definitely wasn't going to marry Paul, she didn't want to rush her decision, either. They'd gone over the basics on the phone; he knew all about her plans to open the cafe in the fall. With the kitchen closed for the remodeling, she ushered him down the hall to a spot where he could take a quick peek at the work in progress.

"As you can see," she said breezily, "we're making some minor renovations. The expanded dining area will more than double our seating capacity. We're also widening doorways and making a few more improvements to create a more efficient workflow."

Paul's eyebrows arrowed down over his nose as he studied the layout through thick plastic sheeting. "Tell me customers won't actually be able to see into kitchen?" he asked archly.

"Yes," Nina assured him. She loved the idea.

"Today's top chefs refuse to have customers looking over their shoulders every minute," Paul insisted. "When I worked with Chef Humbold at Star Shine, he had his entire kitchen redesigned to make it completely separate from the dining area. Chef Gregor at Three Seasons divided the front and the back of the house with a floor-to-ceiling wall."

Though the distinctly nasal quality of Paul's voice made her clench her teeth, Nina only said, "You're fortunate to have worked in such well-known kitchens." She swallowed as doubts crowded her thoughts. The kitchens were some of the top in the food scene, and Paul's implication was clear—if she ever wanted to make a name for herself, she should follow the examples set by Humbold and Gregor. Slowly, she shook her head. Every chef had their own preference. In her dream kitchen, she'd always been able to look out over the dining area and see customers' reactions to her creations. So no. She wasn't going to change things on Paul's say-so. But she did want to know a little more about the man's work history. "Why'd you leave Three Seasons?" she asked.

"I'm trying to better myself. When I've learned all I can from one chef, I move on," Paul answered, managing to sound both pompous and patronizing.

His answer begged the question of how he ended up applying to work at her cafe, but she let that question slide for the moment. As it was, she had enough other issues with the man. They hadn't exactly hit it off. She doubted things would ever improve, but on the off-chance that she'd misjudged Paul, she gave him one more chance.

"Are you available to start work on Monday? We'll have a booth at the Sugar Sand Craft Fair over the weekend of the Fourth. I'll showcase some of the dishes we'll serve in the cafe. I've been told to expect huge crowds. There's a lot to do in order to get ready for the event." The tasting menu she'd developed relied heavily on items she could prepare and freeze ahead of time.

"A craft fair?" Paul asked. Disdain dripped from his voice like wax dripped from a lit candle.

His expression announced to one and all that she'd lost her marbles. "No chef worth his salt would even consider working a booth in a craft fair."

"That's not exactly true," she corrected. "Guy Fieri got his start by running a pretzel stand."

Paul's chest puffed out. "No respectable chef," he corrected.

And Guy wasn't?

Nina scoured Paul with a searing, searching gaze. Though the man's credentials were top-notch, so far he'd challenged her at every turn. Plus, he'd shown up for the interview looking like he'd just rolled out of bed after a weeklong bender. She released a long, slow breath. There was no point in delaying the inevitable.

"I don't believe this is the right fit for someone with your level of experience," she said as she extended a hand. "I apologize for taking up your valuable time."

Paul shook his head as if to clear it. A moment later, he blinked up at her through red-rimmed eyes. "That's it? You don't even want to ask me about my experience, my goals?"

"I don't believe that'll be necessary. I have everything I need." She firmly believed good working relationships were the keys to success in any kitchen. Despite having met him less than fifteen minutes ago, she already knew she and Paul would never in a million years work smoothly together. She managed a half-smile while she guided him to the front door, where she gave him a firm, "I wish you all the luck in your future endeavors."

The man was going to need it.

As Paul's car disappeared down the driveway a few minutes later, she shook off the heavy weight of self-doubt the cook had left in his wake. Aware that she needed to regroup, she headed for the parlor. She spotted Michelle seated on one of the couches and smiled at her friend.

"Two down, one to go," Nina quipped as she positioned a fresh cup on the Keurig and inserted a French Roast pod. She needed the extra caffeine to boost her spirits.

"Oh? Any luck so far?"

"Nope." Nina jabbed the brew button. "The first was a no-show. The second, Paul, was—as they say—a piece of work. I'm pretty sure he tied one on last night and was still feeling the effects. We didn't make it as far as the office before I'd made up my mind. He was definitely not 'my man.'" Her fingers framed the last two words in quotes.

"Let's hope the next applicant is better."

Michelle sipped her coffee. "What time do you expect him?"

"Her. Her name's Krystal. She's not due for another thirty minutes. Why? You need something?" She'd be happy for a distraction while she waited for the next interview.

"I was just thinking about our plans for Sugar Sand Beach's senior citizens."

In a departure from the norm, Nina added a spoonful of sugar to her coffee. She nodded while she stirred. She'd agreed with the others when Michelle first mentioned providing a comfortable space where the town's elderly citizens could meet.

"I know we'd talked about using the spare room off the library, but what do you think about setting things up in here instead?"

Nina sank onto a chair opposite Michelle. "It's definitely more spacious. We already have a coffeepot in here. It's only a few steps from the kitchen in case we need to replenish the cookie tray or check on the sugar and creamer."

"My main concern is that Uncle Jack and his friends might be in the way of our overnight guests."

"I don't see why that should be a problem. At their age, they're not likely to go whooping it up around here."

"Not hardly. Uncle Jack's ninety if he's a day," Michelle agreed with a smile.

Nina sipped her coffee. "Ask Reggie and Erin, but I'm fine with letting our seniors use this area. This house is so big, it has plenty of room for everyone." In addition to several sitting areas off the upstairs bedrooms, the first floor boasted an enormous family room, several parlors, a formal living room and a fully stocked library.

Michelle looked as if she might say something else. Before she did, though, the doorbell chimed. Nina checked her watch. A full twenty minutes stretched before Krystal's appointment. Had the young woman arrived early? Abandoning her coffee, she ran a hand over her chef's whites.

"Good luck," Michelle raised her own mug in a toast.

"Thanks. I don't know what I'll do if she's not any better than the last two candidates." She crossed her fingers and hoped Krystal wouldn't be the third strike of the day.

Nina breathed a sigh of relief at her first glimpse of the neat and trim woman standing on the front porch. Krystal Evers was nothing like the other applicants. First of all, she'd shown up. Not just on time but early. Also to her credit, she'd obviously taken pains with her appearance.

From the dark hair she'd pulled into a neat bun at the back of her neck to the crisp white shirt she'd tucked into navy slacks, everything about her said she wanted to be taken seriously. Nina saw a younger version of herself in the woman and warmed to her immediately.

"Good morning," she greeted the new arrival. "I'm Chef Nina. Welcome to the future home of the Sugar Sand Inn and Cafe. I take it you're Krystal."

At the question, the young woman's head bobbed. "Krystal Evers, Chef." Her eyes dropped to her feet. "I hope you haven't already filled the position."

"No. It's still open. Come on in." As she had with Paul, she walked the young woman as far as the doorway to the kitchen. Zeke's crew had divided the room in two by hanging opaque tarps from floor-to-ceiling. Designed to confine the dust and debris in the construction area, the plastic sheeting did its job better than Nina had expected. She couldn't spot a bit of dust on the countertops or appliances. "The remodeling crew should finish enough of their work this week to let me get back in the kitchen by Monday," she said.

"Oh, this is beautiful," Krystal whispered. "It's so roomy and bright. I love the layout, too.

In cooking school, we just had a two-by-two workspace, so having this much counter to work with would be a dream come true." She pointed past a somewhat murky figure working on a ladder on the other side of the curtain. "The cafe's guests will sit there?"

"There, and in the original dining room beyond it. We're opening the two rooms up to create a bigger seating area," Nina explained.

"Nice."

One word, but it spoke volumes. "Let's go back to the office where we can get to know each other a little better," Nina suggested. She'd make the girl jump through all the hoops, but she wasn't sure it was necessary. Unless Krystal confessed that she'd lied about everything on her admittedly scant resume, she was a shoo-in for the job.

Once the young cook was settled in the guest chair across from the ornate desk, Nina folded her hands and placed them on the desk. "So, Krystal. What made you want to become a chef?"

Krystal's eyes strayed to the left for a second before her focus centered on Nina. "To tell the truth, it's all my grandmother's fault," she said with a tremulous smile. "I spent every Saturday at her house while my mom worked. Granny and I spent most of that time in the kitchen together.

She was always making something wonderful. Pot roast or marinara sauce. Chocolate cake or lemon pie. Working around food became a part of me. When it came time to pick a career, I couldn't think of anything I'd rather do with my life."

Nina could name a half-dozen of the top chefs who'd learned their skills practically at their grandmothers' knees. Her own grandmother had introduced her to not just a love for food but dishes that were beautifully prepared and presented. She leaned forward just a bit. "Your grandmother, is she still alive?"

"Yes." Krystal stared into the distance for several beats. "She's very ill, though. Everyone in the family is concerned."

"I'm sorry to hear that. I'll be thinking of her, hoping she gets better," Nina murmured, thinking of her own grandmother and how the woman had influenced her life and her desire to become a chef. She'd grown up spending summers on her grandparents' farm. With family and workers to feed day in and day out, some kind of food preparation was always underway. Throughout the summers, Nina had worked in the kitchen with her grandmother from the time her feet hit the floor in the mornings until she crawled between the sheets at night. She'd loved every minute of it.

"Where do you see yourself in five years? Or ten?" Nina asked next.

Rather than answering immediately, Krystal took a moment to gather her thoughts. "Of course, I'd love to have my own restaurant some day," she said at last. "But I want to work in several different kitchens before that happens. I have a lot to learn." She crossed and recrossed her ankles.

Poor kid, Nina thought when Krystal couldn't seem to get comfortable. It was only natural for the girl to be jittery, wasn't it? She thought back to her first interview for a job she'd really wanted. She'd been a bundle of nervous energy then, too.

Hoping to put the young cook at ease, she moved on. "Let's talk work schedules for a minute. If I were to offer you the job, would you be able to start first thing on Monday?"

"Yes," came Krystal's quick reply. "But…" The girl bit her lower lip.

"But?" Nina braced herself.

"I can be here as early as you'd like, but I can't work any later than four each day. I have, um, I have another job in the evenings."

"Oh? Where is that?" Krystal hadn't listed a current employer on her job application, so Nina had assumed—incorrectly, it appeared—that the girl was looking for full-time work.

"I'm, uh, waitressing at an oyster bar in Panama City. Great tips and I, uh, need the money to make my rent."

Something about Krystal's answer didn't ring entirely true. Nina couldn't tell whether it was the slight stammer that had crept into the girl's voice or her habit of looking over Nina's shoulder when she spoke, but something warned her that the girl was skating on the thin edge of a lie. Maybe Krystal spent her evenings with her boyfriend. Or had family obligations she needed to take care of in the afternoons. Whatever it was, Nina told herself that what Krystal did in her free time was really none of her business. Slowly, she said, "I can work with those hours. For now." She waited a beat before she added, "After the first of the year, we're hoping to open for the dinner service. If we do, I'll need you here in the evenings. In that case, would you be willing to give up your second job?" She watched Krystal's expression carefully.

The young cook shrugged. "I don't see why not."

Pleased with the response, Nina broached the final topic of the interview. "As I mentioned when we spoke on the phone, the cafe won't open until the fall. In the meantime, we're doing what we can to drum up interest for our little restaurant, as well as the inn." Equally important, she wanted—no, needed—she needed to get people excited about the cafe before Tobias pulled whatever dirty trick he had up his sleeve. Because she had no doubt whatsoever that he had one. She gulped. "Are you familiar with the Sugar Sand Beach craft fair?"

Krystal's eyes narrowed. "No?" she answered, doubtfully.

According to her resume, Krystal had spent most of her life in nearby Panama City. That made her practically a local. Yet she'd never been to the craft fair? Never had her face painted at one of the kiddie booths? Or played with the rabbits in the petting zoo? How could that be?

Nina shrugged aside her questions. Maybe the event wasn't all that well known. Or maybe Krystal's family took their annual vacation over the holiday weekend. When she'd been Krystal's age, she'd been more interested in checking out restaurants and bars than eating kettle corn while shopping for home decor items anyway.

"It's held over the Fourth of July weekend," she explained. "We've rented a booth and plan to offer samples from the cafe's menu. Between now and then, I'll have my hands full getting everything ready. And, of course, it'll be all-hands-on-deck for the weekend itself."

Suddenly, Krystal's eyes brimmed with unshed tears. The young woman clamped one hand over her mouth.

"What is it?" Nina asked.

"Chef, I think you know how much I want this job. I'd love to work with you, to learn from you. I think you can teach me a lot, and getting in on the ground floor of a new restaurant, well, chances like that don't come along every day."

"But?" Nina asked, knowing there had to be one.

"But I have a previous commitment for that weekend." Krystal's words rushed out of her mouth like water spewed from a dam. "I was going to bring it up once you offered me the job. If you offered me the job," she corrected.

"And this obligation, I take it it's not something you can easily get out of?" She didn't need to know whether Krystal was serving as a bridesmaid in a friend's wedding or had planned a weekend getaway. She just needed to know if she could count on the girl.

"No. I'm so sorry. I hope that doesn't mean I'm out of the running." Krystal blinked rapidly. "I promise, I'll work hard for you the rest of the time. I just, I can't work that weekend."

Or after four each afternoon.

Nina tapped her fingers on the desktop.

Could she work with Krystal's restrictions? She nodded. At least for now, she could. True, the circumstances weren't ideal. But considering the alternative—she frowned at the thought of having Paul in her kitchen each day—what choice did she have?

"Let's start with a six-week probationary period," she suggested. By the end of July, she'd know whether the young cook had what it took to be her second-in-command. "If it's not working out for either of us at the end of that time, we'll part ways. No hard feelings. On the other hand, if you're a good fit and like it here, we'll make it permanent, with a slight increase in salary." She'd researched the average wage for sous chefs in the state and knew her offer was a good one.

The grin that broke across Krystal's face sent relief swirling through Nina. Standing, she shook the young cook's hand to seal the deal. She could hardly wait to tell the others.

Nina bent over the packet of forms and house rules she planned to hand Krystal on her first day of work. She'd been lucky enough to have some great mentors in her career. They'd helped her form good work habits from the outset, and she considered it her responsibility to instill those same routines in her young assistant. That included foregoing jeans and T-shirts for chef's pants and aprons, securing her hair beneath a hat or net whenever she was in the kitchen, choosing shoes for comfort and support rather than style.

Movement at the door to the office interrupted her concentration. She looked up from her work to see Zeke's very masculine presence filling the doorway. It took her no longer than a second to decide the man provided a welcome distraction. She gave him a cheery smile. "Hey, Zeke. How's it going?"

"Good. It's all good. You got a minute? I'd like to get your opinion on something in the dining room."

"Oh? I finally get to see what you've been up to this week?" Though she hadn't loved the idea, she'd complied with Zeke's request to keep everyone out of the construction area until the work was complete. Eager for her first real glimpse of the changes he and his crew had made, she sprang to her feet.

"Whoa." Zeke's low whistle sounded an appreciative note. "You're a real chef? Not just a cook?" His gaze traveled slowly over Nina's chef's whites.

"This will be the first kitchen of my very own, but yes." Suddenly self-conscious, she gave the hem of her jacket a nervous tug. It had been a while since a good-looking man had studied her with such interest. She kind of liked the feeling it stirred within her.

"I've met plenty of cooks over the years. Watched plenty of 'em come and go at my mom's place. You're the first chef I've ever met, though."

At another reference to his mom, Nina felt her interest cool a degree or two. Zeke might be ruggedly good-looking, he might run a successful construction company, but the fact remained that he lived with his mother. While that alone might not be a deal-breaker, it certainly waved a red flag.

"Your mom hires and fires cooks?" she asked, confused and not afraid to let it show.

"Not on a daily basis. But you know how it is. The only restaurant in a small town. People come. People go."

"Wait. Are we talking about Maggie's Diner?" Nina's eyes narrowed. Her heart thudded. "Maggie is your mother?"

How was that even possible? The tiny woman who owned the only restaurant in Sugar Sand Beach looked nothing like the tall, handsome figure of a man whose mere presence soaked up all the air in the room.

"Yeah. You didn't know?" Surprise glinted in Zeke's blue eyes.

"Chris didn't mention it. No one else did, either." She and her friends had eaten at the Diner every night since Zeke and his crew had begun working on the cafe. Almost every night, Maggie herself had stopped by their table and asked how things were going with the remodeling project. Yet not once had the restaurant owner—or anyone else for that matter—mentioned her connection to their contractor.

Zeke gave his shoulders an oddly disarming shrug. "Small towns. They say there's six degrees of separation between any two people in the world. You can cut that down to three degrees in Sugar Sand Beach. We're so used to it around here, I guess we don't think about it all that much."

Chris and Reggie had had a similar experience. The story of his wife's death was so well-known among residents of the small town that the handyman had assumed his new friend knew all about it. Nina smiled. "Now that I know you two are family, I'll be sure not to complain to Maggie about the work you've been doing here. At least, not while we're still eating in her diner every night."

Zeke's own smile slanted. "I aim to do such good work you won't have anything to complain about. Ready to take a look?" He moved aside to let her pass.

Nina caught the faintest trace of spicy cologne mingled with the unique scent that was Zeke's own as she fell in beside the contractor. Though she was practically bursting with questions about the remodel—and the remodeler—they covered the short distance from the office to the kitchen in silence.

"I think you'll be pleased with what we've done. The men were glad for the work, and it shows." Zeke pulled the plastic tarp to one side and gestured her into the area.

Watching the changes taking place on the other side of the thick, murky plastic had been like watching the progress through a lens smeared with jelly. She'd had the vaguest impression of wider doorways and more space, but standing at the entrance to the larger dining area, she gasped with surprise. Beyond the curtain, Zeke and his men had done everything she'd asked for...and more. Not only had they created the perfect arch between the dining room and the former parlor, they'd repeated the same curve above the doors that led from the hall, as well as the one that led into the kitchen. In the dining area, an eight-inch swath of unfinished wood flooring was the only sign that remained to remind anyone that the space had once been two separate rooms.

"I don't want to seal the new wood till some of this dust settles," Zeke hurried to explain. "Otherwise, the finish will look cloudy."

Nina nodded. The man obviously knew what he was doing. She trusted him to polish off the details.

"We only have a few minor touch-ups to take care of tomorrow." He pointed out a barely visible rough edge here, a tiny bit of loose tape there. "We're ahead of schedule and have time to paint both rooms if you know what color you want."

Nina ran her fingers lightly over the chair rail Zeke had added. She eyed the stained glass window at the far end of the room. "What do you think of using the same dark green in those leaves for the lower half and that pale peach above the chair rail?" she asked, pointing at the cattails arrayed against a setting sun.

Zeke's head bobbed up and down. "Those colors will go great in here. It'll make that pretty glass a real focal point." A secretive smile graced his face. "C'mon, there's one more thing I want to show you."

Together, they headed back toward the kitchen. Just on the other side of the exit that was now wide enough for two, Nina's skin warmed beneath Zeke's hand when he grasped her upper arm. "Here now," his deep voice murmured in her ear. "This is what I wanted you to see."

Letting him turn her, Nina pivoted slowly toward the wall Zeke had promised to erect in the hallway. Her mouth dropped open. Instead of erecting a permanent barrier, Zeke had hung a new door between the front half of the house and the rear.

Stepping in front of her, he grasped the handle and swung the door wide. "If you like, you can leave the door open whenever the cafe is closed." When Nina didn't respond immediately, he shuffled his feet as if he wasn't sure he'd done the right thing. "'Course, if you hate the idea, I can have the guys drywall it in."

"No!" Nina spun toward the towering hunk of a man, who suddenly looked adorably unsure of himself. "I love it," she said, summoning her brightest, most reassuring smile. "I'm just mad that I didn't think of it myself. This will make life sooo much easier." The new door would save everyone countless steps and probably more than a little aggravation.

"I was hoping you'd say that."

Nina turned pensive. "I'm just a little worried about our budget. Did this put us over?" She'd already had to ask Michelle and the others to expand the original budget. She hated the thought of asking for even more money.

"That's the best part." The skin around Zeke's eyes crinkled as his expression shifted into a wide grin. "Hanging a door isn't much more work than dry-walling the whole thing in. We re-used the door from the dining room so we didn't run up your bill any."

"Whew! That's a relief." Pretending to wipe away sweat, Nina brushed her forehead with the back of her hand. Suddenly thirsty, she announced, "I could use some iced tea. You want a glass?"

"I wouldn't turn one down."

While Nina pulled glasses from the cabinet and took the pitcher from the fridge, she watched Zeke out of the corner of her eye. The big man ambled over to the counter, where he leaned against it.

"Seemed like you had lots of company here today," he observed as she added ice and poured their drinks.

"I was interviewing candidates for an assistant. A sous chef. Someone who can follow my recipes, oversee the other cooks—if and when we hire them—and make sure each order that goes out of the kitchen is right. Consistency, that's the key to success." Handing him one of the glasses, she hopped up on the counter and let her legs dangle over the side.

"Did you have any luck?" Zeke turned to face her.

Nina shrugged. "I hope so. Didn't think I would there for a minute. My first choice was a no-show. He was the best qualified of the finalists, so that was disappointing. The second guy was pretty full of himself." She gestured toward the work Zeke and his crew had done. "He didn't like the concept of an open kitchen. Or, if I'm honest about it, much else about the cafe. I got the impression he'd be difficult. I simply don't have time to deal with a prima donna. Not when I'm trying to get a brand new restaurant off the ground."

Zeke took a long pull from his glass and smacked his lips. "Good tea," he pronounced. "They say the third time's the charm. Was it?"

Nina couldn't help smiling. "Krystal was definitely the best of the lot. She reminds me a lot of myself when I was that age—eager to learn, anxious to please, thankful for the opportunity." She hesitated. She hadn't had a chance to put her misgivings about the girl into words. Slowly, as if trying them on for size, she voiced her concerns. "I really like her, but there's something about her that's just a little bit 'off.'"

"Oh, yeah? Something set your antenna wiggling?"

"Hmmmm. I'm not sure. Her resume is a little thin, but I'd expect that. She's a recent graduate from a well-respected culinary school. Not one of the top places, but it's produced some pretty good cooks. There was just something about her, though, that made me a little bit cautious. I'm trying to chalk it up to her age—she's young. Hopefully, that also means she's teachable."

"When it comes to hiring, I always say 'trust your gut.'" Zeke's lips thinned. "People can look real good on paper yet not be worth the ink it took to fill out an application."

She grinned. "How very insightful. Based on experience?"

"You might say that." Zeke downed half his tea in one long swallow. "I've hired my share of workers who didn't, you know, work. Mostly, though, I was referring to my ex," he said, as if that were explanation enough.

It wasn't.

"Oh?" she prompted, hoping to learn more about the man. Not that she was at all surprised to hear that he'd been married. With his good looks and easy manners, she'd have been shocked if Zeke had remained single his entire life. Especially in a town as small as Sugar Sand Beach.

"Donna and me, we dated off and on all through high school. It was kind of expected, you know. She was a cheerleader. I was into sports. Football, mostly, though I played a little basketball, too. We had the classic high school romance. Except it looked a lot better than it was." He scuffed one foot against the floor. His chest rose as he took a deep breath. "Anyways, we'd date. Then, for one reason or another, she'd break up with me. Every time it happened, I'd tell myself it was never gonna work out. Not to be a fool and take her back. But, of course, I did." He sighed. "The rest is the same, sad familiar story you'd hear in any bar every night of the week. We got married, had two of the sweetest little girls you ever did see. But Donna, she was just going through the motions. Soon enough, she found someone else. Up and left me when Lily was five and Megan was seven. Took the girls and moved to Fort Walton Beach."

"I'm so sorry, Zeke." Nina rotated her glass between her fingers. Her mouth had gone the kind of dry no amount of iced tea would ever dampen.

"Aw, don't be. I knew going in it was a big mistake, but I went ahead and did it. I'm glad I did. Otherwise, I wouldn't have Lily and Megan. Megan's twelve now. Great at sports and always on the go. Lily's ten and just starting to come into her own. Loves helping out in the kitchen and helping out at the nursery at church on Sundays. They still have me wrapped around their little fingers."

"Do you see them much?" Knowing she'd hate it if Zeke turned out to be an absentee dad, she crossed her fingers.

"All the time," he said, his chest puffing out a little. "Fort Walton's just an hour away. I make sure I'm in the bleachers for every softball game. I go to every recital. I tried for full custody, too, but for all her faults, Donna's a good mom. I ended up getting the girls on alternate weekends and holidays, plus one month out of every summer. That was easier to do when they were little and didn't have so much going on. Lily's still young enough that she loves coming to Dad's and Grandma's house. But now that Megan's almost in her teens, juggling her schedules and visits isn't so easy. Teenagers," he said with a long-suffering sigh.

"They're always up to something. Usually with their posse." It felt like only yesterday that she and Michelle and Erin had gone everywhere together.

"Anyways, that's why I recommend listening to your gut whenever you take on someone new."

"I am. I did," Nina assured him. "I'm looking for someone permanent, but I offered Krystal a temporary position. I want to be sure she's right for the job before I commit."

"Sounds good." Zeke nodded. "Sorry if I bent your ear more than you wanted. Bet you didn't expect to hear my whole life's story." He downed the rest of his tea and pushed off the counter.

"Actually, I'm glad we had the chance to talk. Now that I'm going to be here permanently, it's good to get to know the neighbors." Especially ones as tall and handsome as Zeke.

Nine

Reggie

"Hey, Jimbo!" Reggie slid from her high perch on the driver's seat of the freshly washed and waxed van. As soon as she'd gotten back from the Keys with Erin, she'd spent two whole days sprucing up the vehicle's exterior and tinkering under its hood. After she'd replaced assorted hoses and refilled the required liquids, the engine purred like Mr. Pibbs getting a belly rub. But was the van one worn timing belt away from a breakdown? She'd turned to an expert to find out for certain.

"Back at ya, Ms. Reggie." The thin man in the grease-stained work uniform unfolded his long frame from a plastic folding chair that had been strategically placed in the shade of the two-bay garage. He peered over her shoulder. "What brings you in this morning? That van need work?"

"Some. Don't know how much." Jimbo had painted the garage's cement exterior white, which gave the building a clean, fresh look. It also reflected the bright morning sun with a vengeance. Reggie cupped one hand over her eyes as a visor. "I got it started, but I need you to give it a good going-over, including the wheelchair lift. I think it needs new tires, too, after sitting in one place for so long. I want to make sure everything's in tip-top shape."

From beneath his baseball cap, Jimbo studied the van. "You fixin' t'sell it? I don't mind getting your business, but you don't need to bother with repairs an' such. I know someone in Destin who'll give you a fair price for it as is."

How sweet of Jimbo to try and save her some money. The mechanic was definitely what the folks in Sugar Sand Beach called "good people." She smiled up at him. "Thanks, but the four of us have thought it over, and we'd like to donate it. You've heard about the house the town is building for Robert Phelps?"

"Who hasn't?" Jimbo swatted at a mosquito and missed. "Most everybody from miles around's been pitchin' in to make it the best it can be. I've hammered a few nails there myself on my days off."

"Next time there's a work party, let me know." She stepped into the shade where she could see better. "I can't hammer a straight nail to save my life, but I'd be happy to help out with the landscaping. I'll let Michelle, Nina and Erin, know too. I'm sure they'll pitch in."

"That's awfully neighborly of you gals," Jimbo said.

"We want to do our part to show our appreciation to someone who's given so much for our country." Which brought her back to the reason for her visit. "From what we've heard, Robert's going to need a wheelchair-accessible van when he finally gets released from the VA. This one's just been sitting in the garage taking up space. We thought, if it's in good enough shape, we'd let him have it."

Jimbo swept a baseball cap from his head and mopped his forehead with a red bandanna he plucked from a back pocket. "Now that's a mighty big offer. I remember when Ms. Nancy bought that van. Ordered it from a place that tricked it out special for her. It's got a few years on it, but it has to be worth a pretty penny. You sure ya'll want to just give it away?"

"Only if it's in good running condition. I think it is, but I'm no mechanic. Which is why I'm bringing it to you." She listed a few of the things the vehicle had going for it. "I checked the mileage—the van has less than ten thou on it. It's been garage-kept all this time, so the paint's like brand new. But we want to be sure there's no surprises. That everything's in good working order."

"Well now." Jimbo slipped one hand into the deep pocket of his pants. "Tell you what. I'll look it over myself this afternoon and give you a call. You want to give me your number?"

Reggie did as she was asked. "You'll let me know how much any repairs might cost?"

"It'll just run you the parts and the cost of the tires." Jimbo nodded. "I'll donate my time and labor. I can't let you newcomers out-neighborly me, can I?

Jimbo's laugh let her know he was only half-serious. Impulsively, Reggie leaned forward and gave the taller man a friendly hug. "Thanks so much, Jimbo!"

The mechanic stepped back, his face glowing red. "Glad to do my part, Ms. Reggie." His brows arrowed down along with his lips. "Say, you aren't walking back to your place, are you? You need a lift?"

"Nah, I'm good," she assured the man as she dangled the keys to the van from her fingers. "Chris ought to be here in a minute or two.

We're picking up paint for a couple of the upstairs rooms."

"You say 'hi' to Chris for me. Tell him we need to go fishing one of these days." He plucked the keys from Reggie's outstretched hand. "I'll be in touch later today."

Apparently eager to get to work, Jimbo had the van moved into the empty bay and the hood up almost before she knew what was happening. She waved goodbye just as Chris's pickup truck slowed to a stop at the curb. Butterflies fluttered in her tummy when she spotted him behind the wheel. Reggie shook her head. She'd missed Chris more than she thought she would while she was down south with Erin.

Seconds later, she sprang from the running board onto the passenger seat with a friendly but definitely not too friendly, "Hey, stranger. I sure appreciate the ride."

"Hey yourself. It's been a while."

"It has," she nodded. The interior of the cab smelled of window and leather cleaner, a sure sign Chris had spiffed up a bit after he'd agreed to pick her up. He'd taken pains with his own appearance, too. Gone were his usual well-worn jeans and T-shirt. In their stead, he'd donned khaki shorts and a short-sleeved shirt. With a collar, no less. The urge to embrace him stirred

181

within her. She resisted it with a stern reminder that she might be officially separated, but it'd be months before her divorce was final. Until it was, Chris was definitely off-limits.

Hoping for a distraction, she glanced into the back seat. Her plans to play peep-eye with Chris's little daughter faded when she spied the empty car seat.

"Where's Hope?" she asked. "Did that new tooth pop through yet?" Before she left for the Keys, the baby had been teething and miserable.

"Mom's got her. And yep, she's back to her happy self." Chris put the truck in gear. "Are we still picking up paint?"

"Uh-huh," Reggie replied, glad to talk about something as mundane as the job ahead of them. "Michelle ordered it yesterday. Ronnie promised to have it ready for us."

Chris waited for a lone car to pass before he pulled away from the curb and headed for the hardware store at the opposite end of the block. "How was your trip?"

"Too long and too short at the same time." She laced her fingers together and stretched. "Eight hundred miles—that's a lot of driving for one day. And those bridges—I thought they'd never end. I'm not sure I would have agreed to go if I'd known we'd spend so much time over open water." She shuddered. Bridges were definitely not her thing. "At least Erin and I kept each other company on the way down. On the way back, she drove her Jeep and I drove the truck. Making it across the Overseas Highway on my own wasn't much fun." Forty-two bridges dotted the road that ran from the mainland through the Keys—she'd counted every one of them. Erin understood her fear, though, and had kept her on the phone the whole time. And she'd managed. Still, she hadn't drawn an easy breath from the time they'd left Key West until they'd stopped for gas outside of Homestead. Just thinking of making the trip again sent a shiver down her spine.

"Did not know you had a thing about bridges." Chris lifted one eyebrow. "You probably didn't like coming across the Bay, either, did you?"

"Not especially." She avoided the three-and-a-half-mile bridge across the Choctawhatchee Bay as much as possible.

"I'll keep that in mind. If we ever decide to go to someplace like Crestview for dinner, we can take the long way around." Chris's words faltered. "Not that we'd ever go to Crestview. Or go out to dinner together. But if we did…" Color crept up his neck while his voice trailed off.

Reggie turned to look out the window so Chris wouldn't see her smile at the thought that—someday—they might actually go on a date. Although neither of them was ready to take that step yet, her midsection warmed with the hope that they might be before too long.

After a couple of long seconds, Chris cleared his throat. "Did you get to see the sights while you were down in the Keys?" he asked. "Or were you too busy?"

The awkwardness of the last few moments faded fast. She nodded. "I took one of Erin's bikes and rode down Duvall Street and out to Mallory Square while she was talking to the people at the rental office about leasing the cottage out year-round. I only had a couple of hours, so that's about all I saw."

"Did it live up to all the hype?"

"You've been, haven't you?" She couldn't imagine anyone spending their entire life in Florida, like Chris had, without visiting the chain of islands at least once.

"Oh, yeah. But I imagine it's changed a good bit since I was there." Chris pulled into one of the angled parking spots in front of the sand-colored hardware store. "I spent a week in the Keys the summer after high school. We were just kids, so it was nonstop fun. Partying on the beach every night. Fishing and surfing all day. Not sure I could handle that kind of life forever, though." He put the truck in park and turned off the engine.

"Me, either." She slipped out before Chris and met him on the sidewalk. "It is pretty down there. I definitely loved the colorful houses and the scenery. The crowds were a bit much, though, and this is supposed to be the slow season. I'd hate to see what it's like in the middle of winter. It made me doubly glad the town council decided to keep Sugar Sand Beach just the way it is." Though it'd only been a few weeks, she'd come to think of the small town filled with friendly, helpful neighbors as her home.

"Sounds like you're planning to stick around for a while," Chris said, sounding a wee bit tentative.

"Sure am," Reggie quipped with a grin. "Also thanks to the town council, we have an inn and a cafe to run. Speaking of which, let's go get that paint."

"Yeah, let's." This time, Chris reached the door before her and held it open.

The interior of the hardware store provided a welcome respite from the blinding sunlight. On the downside, it was, well, dark. Reggie propped her sunglasses atop her head as ancient floorboards creaked beneath her feet. She'd learned on previous visits to let her eyes adjust to the dim light or risk knocking over a display of, say, heavy weather gear. As she lingered near the door, she noted that the store looked even more crowded than it had on earlier supply runs. Generators blocked some of the narrow aisles that were already barely wide enough for one person. Rows upon rows of low shelving units had recently been restocked with everything from garden hoses to gas cans to more blue plastic tarps than she'd ever seen in one place. Above those shelves, pegboard walls stretched toward the ceiling. She spied one that offered socket wrenches of every imaginable size on one side, while small power tools hung from the other. At the end of an aisle, umbrellas stood in a white, five-gallon bucket. Another held rolls of plastic sheeting. Various lengths of rebar poked out of another. Meanwhile, overhead fans circulated currents of air that smelled of paint and nails and freshly cut wood.

"You think anyone's here?" Reggie asked when no one stood behind the counter where an ancient cash register sat. Somewhere in the distance, an electric saw buzzed in short bursts.

"Ronnie's probably checking her orders

against today's delivery." When Reggie shot him a questioning look, Chris explained. "The delivery truck comes on Tuesdays. Ring the bell beside the register. She'll be right out. I'll be over there." Chris aimed a thumb toward a wall where built-in drawers held what looked like half the world's supply of nails.

Reggie edged around a campfire display that had been erected by the front door. Behind it, cast-iron pots and pans filled the shelves of an open bookcase. Thinking it was some kind of miracle that she reached the counter without knocking something to the floor in the crowded store, she searched for a silver bell among the discarded nuts, bolts and rolls of tape on the countertop. She didn't find one of those, but there was a buzzer. She pressed it, and sure enough, a plumpish woman dressed in blue overalls emerged from the rear of the store only a few seconds later.

"Good to see you, hon." Ronnie brushed frizzy red curls out of her eyes. Sweat trickled down the sides of her cheeks. "Whew! It's hotter than blazes in back. Must be a scorcher outside."

"It's nothing like down around Orlando, but it's warming up." Erin had been right when she said stepping out of the car in the middle of the state would be like stepping into a steam bath.

"I swear, it gets hotter and hotter every year. And you know what all that heat brings?" Ronnie looked at her expectantly.

Reggie drew a blank. "Bugs?" she ventured.

"Hurricanes," Ronnie said with authority. "You ever been through one of them?"

When Ronnie pinned her with a demanding look, Reggie swallowed. "Nooo," she said slowly.

"Didn't think you had. You being from Virginia and all. Well, let me tell you, we've got everything you need right to get you clear through November when the season ends."

Reggie shuffled her feet. She distinctly remembered a case of stubby white candles on the top shelf of the pantry. What more could they need?

Evidently, Ronnie knew exactly what the situation might require. The store owner launched into a lengthy explanation. "Now, I'm sure Nancy kept plenty of emergency supplies on hand, but you never know what's gonna happen when the wind blows. Being right on the beach like you are, you have to watch out for the storm surge. It could flood the house. You'll need sandbags to keep that from happening. They're over there against the wall. You'll need a generator in case you lose power. Or at least, a camp stove and fuel. Some of them cast-iron pans wouldn't hurt, either." Ronnie pointed to the display Reggie had nearly knocked over. "Lots of debris gets tossed around. A big ol' branch could punch a hole in your roof. When that happens, you're gonna want'a put a tarp over it pronto-like to minimize the damage. We got plenty of 'em. Fact is, you might wanna pick some up now and so they'll be handy when you need them. What do you say?"

Reggie swallowed. Holes in the roof were more than a little outside her comfort level. To say nothing of surviving a storm so powerful it might wash away the entire house. She shivered as she recalled scenes from one disaster movie after another. An urge to buy out the entire store surged through her. "I'll take—"

"Ronnie. Ronnie. Ronnie," Chris chided as he rounded one of the rows carrying a small paper bag. He wagged a finger at the store owner. "Shame on you. Trying to scare a newcomer like that."

Chuckling, Ronnie put up both hands like she was under arrest. "Hey, you can't blame a gal for trying. Look at this place." She gestured toward the full shelves. "I got a lot of inventory to move."

"Yeah, but you don't have to sell it all to Reggie," Chris admonished. He turned to her.

"Don't you get caught up in all Ronnie's hurricane nonsense. That house of yours has been standing for over a century. There's no reason to think it won't last another hundred years."

Reggie's jittery nerves had just begun to settle when Ronnie shook her head. "I'm just repeating what the weatherman said. He says it's gonna be a banner year for storms. The time to get prepared is now. You saw what that Michael did to Mexico Beach a few years ago."

Reggie's stomach plummeted. Three years ago, a strong Category 5 hurricane had all but leveled the tiny coastal town less than a hundred miles from Sugar Sand Beach. Damage had been widespread and so devastating, the national news had covered the story for weeks. Churches in northern Virginia had banded together to send an entire flatbed loaded with bottled water and other supplies into the area. When her own pastor had asked the congregation for contributions for the relief efforts, Reggie had dipped into her grocery money to help out. She swallowed. Doubtfully, she looked up at Chris. "Could that happen here?"

Chris made a dismissive gesture. "Michael was a once-in-a-lifetime hurricane. I'm not saying it can't happen again, but in this case, the odds *are* ever in our favor." He grinned at the reference to a recent blockbuster movie. "Besides, those big storms don't spring up overnight. The weatherman will start tracking 'em a week or more before they come anywhere close to the United States. On the off chance that one does take aim at this particular section of the Gulf, it'll be all over the news. We'll all have more than enough warning to hang the shutters and get out of Dodge."

Turning back to Ronnie, he eyed the store owner with sympathy. "Same goes for you, Ronnie. There's no need to fret so much this early in the season. You know good and well nothing's gonna happen before August or September." Though hurricane season ran from June through November, only one major storm had ever struck Florida early in the summer.

"You're right, Chris. You're right. I'm sorry." Ronnie's cheeks flushed, but Reggie couldn't tell whether heat or embarrassment made the owner redden. "I was just unloading the new shipment that came in today. It's all hurricane supplies, and I guess it got me all worked up. But Chris is right, hon," she admitted. "We've never had a hurricane make landfall here. There's no reason to believe one will."

"Well, that's a relief," Reggie said. The reassurance both Chris and Ronnie had offered helped settle her nerves for good this time. "Just in case, though, I'll take two of those blue tarps you were talking about." Hopefully, they'd never need the thick blue sheets for their intended purpose, but they could always use another drop cloth or two. "Meanwhile, I'm here to pick up the paint Michelle ordered. Is it ready?" Before all the talk about hurricanes had distracted her, she'd been planning to get started on the cut work this afternoon.

"It sure is." Ronnie hefted four gallons of paint from somewhere near her feet and set them on the counter.

Reggie eyed the dabs of Sea Salt Green and Pale Ocean Breeze the owner had placed on the lids after blending the paint. The colors were so close she could hardly tell them apart, but she was sure Michelle would know the difference. She made a note to ask which one went with which room before she and Chris got started.

"Anything else? Rollers? Brushes? Edging tools?" Ronnie asked with a hopeful gleam in her eyes.

"We have everything we need for now." Before she left this morning, Reggie had laid out the necessary supplies in one of the rooms. At Ronnie's disappointed look, she added, "We're having the whole exterior painted in a few weeks, so get ready for a big order." Before she'd signed the contract, Michelle had insisted the contractor purchase his paint from the only hardware store in Sugar Sand Beach.

"And I'll take these nails." Metal sifted with a soft, chinking sound as Chris placed his small paper bag on the counter. "You can ring them up separate from Reggie's order." He reached for his wallet.

Reggie sliced one hand through the air. "Ignore him," she instructed, "and add them to our bill." She smiled up at Chris. "It's the least we can do after you picked me up from Jimbo's this morning."

In the middle of ringing up their purchases, Ronnie stopped to snap her fingers. "That reminds me. I hear you're giving Nancy's van to our wounded warrior project."

Reggie felt her eyes widen. "How do you know that?" Outside of their small group, Jimbo was the only person in Sugar Sand Beach who knew they intended to donate the vehicle. And he'd only learned of the plan minutes earlier.

"Oh, a little birdie told me," Ronnie answered without giving so much as a hint. "I just want you to know the whole town thinks it's wonderful. Frank and I talked it over. We want to help out, too. We'll throw in a bucket full of car care stuff—cleaning products, wax, tire shine, some of those high-tech dry cloths. Just let me know when you need it and I'll have it ready."

"Wow! That's mighty nice of you." When she and her friends had talked about donating the vehicle, they'd hoped some of the other businesses in town would add their own contributions. None of them had imagined it would happen in the blink of an eye, though.

As she and Chris loaded the paint and their few purchases into the back of his pickup a few minutes later, she turned to him. "How on earth did Ronnie and Frank find out about the van?"

"Word travels along the grapevine in Sugar Sand Beach faster than greased lightning," Chris said with a grin. "Jimbo probably mentioned it to Gus when he walked across the street to get his morning coffee. Either Gus shared the news with his next customer or someone overheard their conversation. From there, the news spread."

Reggie shook her head in awe. In Virginia, the foreman on her landscaping crew had relied on a phone tree to let everyone know whenever a job got postponed due to inclement weather or some other problem. It hadn't been the most reliable method of communication. More than once, Reggie had battled slippery road conditions only to have her cell phone ring just as she was pulling up to the job site. If they'd had access to the Sugar Sand Beach grapevine, that would never have happened.

On the flip side, everyone now knew they planned to donate the van. Which meant at least four faces would turn mighty red if Jimbo discovered the vehicle needed costly engine repairs. She crossed her fingers and said a silent prayer that, whatever problems Jimbo uncovered, nothing would make them scrap the project.

She checked her phone. Jimbo hadn't called while they were in the hardware store. Not sure whether that was a good sign or a bad one, she promised to keep her cell phone handy for the rest of the day.

While Chris unloaded their supplies at the house a short time later, she sought Michelle's input on the paint colors. "Quick question," she said, popping her head into the library, where Michelle was hard at work on the brochures and displays they'd need for their booth at the craft fair. "Which colors go in which rooms?"

Michelle punched a key on her laptop before she looked up. "Use the Sea Salt Green in the rooms with the cherry trim. I think it'll bring out the warmth in the wood."

Reggie nodded agreeably. Ask her which flowers would look best in which room, and she'd have a ready answer. But paint? Not so much. "That leaves the Pale Ocean Breeze for the suite across the hall, the one with the white fireplace mantle."

"Right," Michelle said, rising. "And now, I need to get moving or I'll be late for my appointment with Dave." She checked the slim watch she wore on her left wrist.

"Oh? Another meeting with Da-ave?" Reggie asked in a sing-song voice.

"Yes. But don't you get any ideas. This is business. We're going over the partnership agreement."

Uh-huh. She'd seen the looks Michelle and Dave gave each other when they thought no one was looking. Something was brewing beneath that thin veneer of friendship. She'd bet on it. Tossing a "Think of poor me and Chris slaving away while you're gone" over one shoulder, she waved cheerily and headed for the stairs.

By the time she'd stopped in her room to swap out her shorts for paint-splattered jeans, Chris was waiting for her. "Michelle wants us to use the Pale Ocean Breeze in the suite with the white woodwork," she told him.

As Chris hefted two cans of paint and carried them to the right suite, she quickly swallowed a disappointed sigh. As much as she'd enjoyed seeing him in the shorts he'd been wearing earlier, she had to admit the loose white overalls he wore now were more suited to the work they'd be doing. Before her thoughts had time to drift any further in a direction she'd prefer they not wander, he was back, waving his phone at her.

"My battery's nearly dead. Do you have a charger?"

She made a show of patting her pockets. "Not on me," she said with a sheepish grin. "But there's a charging station on the sideboard in the family room. You can plug in there."

"Got it. I'll be right back."

Smiling, she listened to the sound of his footsteps on the stairs while she opened one of the cans of pale blue paint, gave it a quick stir and poured some into two waiting trays. The drop cloths she'd spread over the hardwood floors rustled as she took one tray to a corner, where she began cutting in around the molding. Chris soon joined her and, with the radio tuned to a country music station, they made quick work of edging the ceiling, corners and baseboards.

"You want me to start on the other room while you finish up here?" she asked an hour later. While Chris used the paint roller on the prepped walls, she could get a head start on the adjoining sitting room.

"That works. Have you heard anything from Jimbo yet?"

Reggie carefully wiped her fingers on the damp rag she used to take care of any dribbles. She hadn't heard her cell phone ring, but it wouldn't hurt to check. Gingerly, she pulled the device from the pocket of her overalls. It chimed before she even had a chance to look at it.

"Hey, are you psychic? That's probably him now." She thumbed the green Accept Call button and held the phone to her ear. "Reggie here," she quipped.

"Regina Frank?" an unfamiliar voice asked.

Something in the formal tone coming through the speaker straightened Reggie's spine. "Yes. This is Regina."

"Ms. Frank, this is Deputy Snider with the Walton County Sheriff's Department. There's been an accident, and I'm trying to reach Chris Johnson. I've been told you might know where he is?"

Reggie's entire body went so numb, she nearly dropped the phone. She managed to hang on to it and, without bothering to answer the deputy, held the device out to Chris. "It's the Sheriff's office," she whispered. Her heart thudded in her ears. "Something's happened. Something bad."

Ten

Michelle

*M*ichelle pushed away from the desk and stretched her arms over her head. It had been a long morning, but the day was already shaping up to be a very productive one. After working the kinks out of her shoulders, she studied the image on her laptop. The new brochure they'd hand out at the craft fair was coming along nicely, even if she did say so herself. She powered down the computer and closed the lid.

That wasn't all she'd accomplished. She'd also had a chance to talk with Zeke. She'd been impressed by the work he'd done in the kitchen and dining areas. So much so that she wouldn't consider using anyone else to remodel the turret. Fortunately, the hunky contractor had been quite enthusiastic about her idea of turning the storage area into a private getaway for newlyweds and other special guests. The only downside was that Zeke and his crew couldn't fit her into their schedule for six months. Which meant he wouldn't be able to start the job until the Christmas holidays. She could work with that, though. After all, it'd probably take her that long to decide on all the design details. Plus, she needed Erin, Nina and Reggie's approval for the project.

For now, though, it was time to get ready for her meeting with Dave Rollins. She and the lawyer had been slowly sketching out the scope of the partnership agreement and had a few more details to work out. Details the tall attorney preferred to discuss in his office. Not that she minded the drive into Destin. Or spending time with the man she'd come to think of as more than just her lawyer. In the few months they'd been working together, Dave had become a friend. A good friend.

Would their relationship deepen into something more? She hesitated. *Did she want it to?* She wasn't entirely certain. Now that the truly heart-wrenching pain of losing Allen had finally faded, fond memories of their years together had flooded back. She missed her late husband. She probably always would. But she also knew Allen wouldn't want her to spend the rest of her life in mourning, any more than she did.

Was Dave the answer?

Only time would tell. She did know that, whether she and Dave were handling details of the estate she'd inherited or simply chatting about their children over coffee, she enjoyed his company. Thinking of him made her days brighter, her footsteps lighter. She sensed he felt the same way about her, but neither of them had made a move toward taking things any further than a lunch or two at Maggie's Diner.

For now.

On her way to her room, she caught the smell of fresh paint and the sound of music drifting down the stairs. The smell transported her back to the day she'd come home from a meeting of the neighborhood watch to find that the twins had banded together and painted their rooms jet-black. She'd been so shocked she hadn't known whether to rush them into therapy or ground them for life. And those paint commercials guaranteeing one-coat coverage? They didn't apply to black, no matter what the stores claimed. She'd spent weeks re-doing the walls before she'd finally achieved a pale gray both she and the twins could live with…until the next time they redecorated.

She sighed. Thinking of the twins reminded her of the breach between them. Would it ever heal?

She thought Aaron might be ready to patch things up. He'd called several times lately. Mostly, they'd talked about the website he was building for the inn. It was a start, though, and for that she was grateful.

But Ashley? Three whole weeks had gone by since the last time her daughter had deigned to speak to her, and then Ashley had only called to ask for an advance on her allowance so she could buy an outfit she just *had* to have. Michelle had been happy enough to finally hear her daughter's voice that she'd agreed before she thought about it. Later, she'd kicked herself for giving in too quickly. She firmly believed that teaching her children to stand on their own two feet was part of her job as a parent. Not giving in to their every whim was part of the process.

In her temporary quarters at the top of the stairs, Michelle changed into one of her favorite shirtwaists, freshened her makeup and ran a comb through her hair. She was lucky, she admitted, rubbing one of the silky strands through her fingers. Despite humidity so high the air practically wept, her hair remained straight as a board.

But wait! Was that a—

Her heart rate doubled when her gaze zeroed in on a silver thread among the otherwise dark strands. She winced as she plucked the offender from her head. Holding it between her fingers, she stared down at her first gray hair.

Was it time to see a colorist? She shook her head. That wasn't even a question. Some of her friends wore middle age well. She wouldn't be one of them. She had no choice. She had to make an appointment with a hairdresser. The sooner, the better. She was overdue for a cut, anyway.

Moments later, the tires of her white Escalade hummed as she followed the four-lane road that skirted the coastline from Sugar Sand Beach to Destin. She'd just passed the Maple Street Biscuit Company, famed for breakfast and lunch sandwiches served on fluffy biscuits, when her cell phone chimed. She accepted the call with the push of a button mounted on the steering wheel.

"Hello," she said, her attention focused on a pool service truck passing her on the left. The long pole of a net used for sweeping leaves and trash from the water bounced as the truck hit a pothole.

"Mummy! Oh, good! I finally caught you!"

Michelle's foot lifted off the gas pedal as Ashley's voice blared from the car speakers. The pool truck sped off. She swallowed, lowered the speaker volume and took a breath. "Ashley, honey. How are you?"

A horn tooted a friendly warning to keep moving. Apologizing to the driver behind her with a wave of her hand, Michelle pressed on the gas pedal. The big SUV surged forward, and she once more matched her speed to the flow of traffic.

"Are you in the car? You're not driving and talking on the phone, are you?"

Preferring to interpret the odd note in her daughter's voice as concern instead of criticism, Michelle reassured the girl. "Not to worry, Ash. My phone's in my purse." She'd developed the habit of hands-free calling when she lived in Virginia, where hefty fines were imposed on anyone caught behind the wheel with a phone in their hand. Although Florida's laws were more lenient, she thought the practice made sense and had stuck with it.

"Mummy, guess what?" Her words coming at Ashley's typical lightning speed, her daughter rushed on without giving Michelle a chance to answer. "Aaron and I talked it over. We both have the third week in August free. We're going to fly down and see you. Isn't that great?"

It was exactly that, if only a little confusing. Ashley seemed to have forgotten all about storming out of the house on the anniversary of her father's death. Or how difficult things had been between them ever since. Michelle shrugged. If it meant reconciling with her children, she'd let bygones be bygones. "That's great, honey," she said. "Let me know which flights you want, and I'll book them."

Sure, it'd be easier if the twins made their own reservations and paid for them with the emergency credit card they shared. But their father had given them clearly defined examples of what constituted an emergency. A flat tire or engine trouble on the road? Yes. Want to gas up for a weekend at the beach? No. Caught the flu and have to pay for an unexpected prescription? Yes. Mouthwash or groceries? No. A trip two months in the future didn't make the approved list.

"We'll get right on that," Ashley promised.

"So how have things been?" Michelle ached to hear what had been going on in her daughter's life.

"Good. Better than that. The director approved my proposal for our leadership retreat next year. Mummy, I'm so excited. I can't wait for our first gathering in the fall. This could really make a difference in these girls' lives, you know?"

Michelle did know. When they were in college, she, Erin and Nina had all participated in their sorority's efforts to help at-risk teens. None of them had taken charge of the large project like Ashley had, though. "I'm so proud of you," she said with heartfelt maternal pride.

"Did I tell you about…"

A smile played across Michelle's lips as her daughter chattered on about her summer classes, her friends' breakups and hookups and a boy who'd recently caught her eye. She'd passed the iconic city limit sign proclaiming Destin to be the "luckiest fishing village in the world" when her daughter finally paused to take a breath.

"Aunt Erin says hello," Michelle said as she took advantage of the lull. "She'd love to take you kayaking while you're here. Nina is sure to fix all of your favorite dishes. Are you on any particular diet these days?"

"Oh, I'm positively dying for some of Nina's spaghetti Bolognese. Nobody makes it as good as she does."

"I'll tell her," Michelle said, smiling at her daughter's flair for the dramatic. "I'm sure she'll have a huge pot simmering on the back of the stove when you get here."

"What about you, Mummy? Have you had any fascinating guests at the inn?"

Surprised that Ashley would bring up the topic that had caused so much tension between them, Michelle nonetheless smothered a sigh. Her daughter was a hopeless romantic who thought all one had to do was snap her fingers and—voila—a hundred-year-old house became an inn overnight. That only happened in Hallmark movies. "We're still working very hard to get the place ready to open in the fall. There's so much to do—painting, landscaping and some remodeling. By the time you come down in August, though, we'll have all the big stuff taken care of. You and Aaron will be our first guests."

"Oooh," Ashley cooed. "Like the soft opening of a restaurant."

She hadn't thought of it quite that way, but she supposed it was. Hopefully, her kids would love the inn so much, they'd make this the first of many trips.

Traffic was light in Destin, and it was still early for her appointment when she pulled into a parking space in front of Dave's office. As long as she had some time and Ashley was in a good mood, there was one more thing she wanted to tell her daughter. She took a deep breath. "You know, your aunt Reggie did the sweetest thing for me."

"Oh, yeah?"

Michelle described how Reggie had secreted away two of Allen's prized rose bushes and presented them just before the open house last month. "I was so touched," she finished. "I finally felt at home here."

"Do you miss Daddy?" Ashley asked.

Michelle's heart broke at the sudden vulnerability in her daughter's voice. "I do," she reassured Ashley. "I think of him all the time."

"Me, too," Ashley whispered. After the briefest of pauses, her rapid-fire delivery began again. "Oh, I wish you could see this. Laura McClintock just walked past my room. You know how snooty she is. She's headed for a mixer over at the Union. And get this, she's wearing socks *and* sandals!" Ashley laughed as if the other girl had committed a fashion faux pas of the highest order. "Listen, I gotta run, but I'll get that flight information to you tonight. Love you, Mummy."

"Love you, too, honey," Michelle said despite the almost certain knowledge that her daughter had already ended the call. Ashley was, after all, Ashley. She shook her head. Some things never changed. She pressed one hand to her heart. Was it possible that the bond she shared with her daughter was one of those things that never changed?

Oh, they'd have their ups and downs, like in any normal relationship between parent and child. But the idea that she'd once more made it onto her daughter's A-list wouldn't be denied. Of all the things she could ask for in the world, she wanted to be more than just a footnote in her children's lives. She wanted to sit in the front pew the day Ashley walked down the aisle. To share the mother-and-groom dance with Aaron at his wedding. To be her children's friend and confidante. To play an important part in her grandchildren's lives when, and if, that time ever came. For the first time in several months, all those things seemed like real possibilities. The hope filled her with a schoolgirl's giddiness as she walked across the herringbone sidewalk into Dave's office building. His receptionist, Josh, buzzed him and showed her right in.

"Someone's in a good mood," Dave said, meeting her at the door, where he greeted her with a handshake that lasted a few seconds longer than absolutely necessary. "What's up?"

"Excellent news. Ashley called while I was on my way here," she gushed. "She and Aaron are finally coming for a visit. In August."

"That's *great* news! No wonder you're glowing." Dave beamed down at her.

"I know I shouldn't get my hopes up, but it sounds like they might actually have forgiven me for leaving Virginia." She didn't casually discuss her problems with Aaron and Ashley with just anyone. But Dave wasn't just anyone. Having endured his own daughter's growing pains and lived to tell the tale, he'd been willing to listen when she needed someone to talk to.

As he ushered her into his office and closed the door to protect her privacy, he said, "Wait till they see what an amazing job you and the others have done with the inn. I'm sure they'll be impressed."

Despite his enthusiasm, Michelle detected a note of concern in Dave's voice. She glanced up at him. The tiny lines around his mouth had deepened. "Is something bothering you? Something about the twins?"

"Let me slip on my attorney hat," he said, adopting a slightly more formal air. "Now that you and Aaron and Ashley have patched things up, I do have to ask how that might impact your decision to move forward with the partnership agreement."

"I haven't changed my mind." Michelle gave her head an emphatic shake. Erin, Nina and

Reggie had invested time, money and countless hours in transforming Nancy Simmons's beach house into what would be a first-class inn. They deserved a share in its future. "I fully intend to honor my promise to make us equal partners in this venture. Nothing that happens between Aaron and Ashley and me will change that."

"I suppose, then, we'd better get to it."

As she usually did, Michelle headed for the guest chair opposite Dave's desk. The light touch of his fingertips at her elbow pointed her, instead, toward a smaller table in a corner of the office. Framed photos of the attorney with various dignitaries hung on the walls in the cozy seating area. Michelle's brief glance took in no less than three pictures of him with the current and previous Florida governors.

"I thought we'd work here today, if that's all right with you," he said, pulling out a chair for her.

Glad not to have the wide expanse of Dave's desk separating them, Michelle took the offered seat. For the greater part of an hour, they discussed the finer points of the partnership— how decisions would be made, the roles and responsibilities of each person, which of them had the authority to enter into binding agreements. The breadth and scope of the details were a bit overwhelming, and Michelle was happy to follow Dave's suggestions for most of it. When they came to the division of assets and liabilities in the unlikely event that a rift occurred between the partners, however, she balked.

"I can't imagine that happening," she protested.

"I'm not saying it will," Dave soothed. "But part of my job is to make sure there's a plan in place to deal with all possibilities, rather than to wait and have something happen that no one ever considered."

Michelle crossed her ankles and folded her hands on the table in front of her. "The four of us have been friends forever. There's hardly been a harsh word between us in all the years we've known each other." It felt like borrowing trouble to include the language Dave had suggested adding to the contract.

"I don't have to tell you how quickly life can spin out of control. Love, marriage, birth"—he paused—"death. All of you are single right now. Some day, that might change for one, two, maybe all of you. From what you've told me, you don't trust Nina's ex. But say they get back together. Who knows what trouble that could cause."

"I suppose that's possible," she conceded. She

was all but certain Nina was too smart to make such a dumb move, but she'd seen others follow their hearts into places where their brains told them not to go.

In the end, they decided that all assets and liabilities would be divided equally among them if, or when, the partnership dissolved. Which, Michelle insisted, could only happen by unanimous decision. The business of the day completed, she began to gather her things.

Dave leaned back in his chair. His expression turned pensive. "Before you go, there is one more thing I'd like to discuss."

Michelle relaxed. As difficult as it was to hammer out the details of an agreement that could last a lifetime, or longer, she didn't mind spending a bit more time with Dave. Not at all. "What's on your mind?"

"I'm afraid I can't continue as your attorney once this partnership is finalized," he said without preamble.

Michelle felt her brows knit. Dave had worked for her birth mother and served as executor of her estate. He'd even gone so far as to hire a private investigator to track Michelle down and prove she was Nancy Simmons's rightful heir. He'd played a pivotal role in helping her and her friends earn the respect and friendship of the people of Sugar Sand Beach. All that aside, she'd thought *they* were friends. Now he was abandoning her?

"Why? Did I do something wrong?" she asked. Her lower lip trembled.

"Not at all. But the ethics of attorney-client relationships are very clear," Dave answered.

"I don't understand," she admitted. She hadn't asked him to do anything unethical, had she?

"Please don't be upset." Dave reached for her hand and cradled it in his. "It's not you. It's me. You see"—he cupped her hand between both of his—"I've enjoyed our time together so much. Maybe too much. It creates an ethical dilemma, since dating a client is more than frowned on. The only way to resolve it is to ask one of the other partners in the firm to handle your account. That is, if you're interested in seeing me socially. If not..."

"Oh!" she whispered, finally understanding where the conversation was headed. The idea that he might be ending their relationship had brought tears to her eyes. She blinked them away. Slipping her fingers free of his grasp, she squeezed his hand. "I am," she answered, taking a chance.

The faint worry lines that had formed in

Dave's brow smoothed. His smile widened. "In that case, I'll make arrangements for Mark Dansen to take over your case once the partnership is in place. You'll like Mark. He's one of the best."

"The partnership," she murmured, recalling the real reason for her visit today. "And when will that be?" She'd like to have everything signed and official before they held the inn's grand opening.

"I'll make sure everything gets wrapped up by September 17th," Dave said without checking his calendar.

"That's a very specific date," she noted. "Why then?"

"Because I have two tickets to see *Harvey* at the Destin Community Theater on the eighteenth, and I'd like you to go with me. Do you think you might be free?"

She pressed a hand over her heart. For good measure, she batted her eyes. "Why, Dave Rollins, are you asking me out on a date?" she asked in her best imitation of a Southern belle.

Dave's eyes sparkled. "Why, yes, Ms. Robinson, I believe that's exactly what I'm doing."

"In that case…" She took a big breath. It was time for her to take the next step in the new life she was building for herself in Sugar Sand Beach.

"I accept." Their date wasn't for several months yet, which gave her plenty of time to get used to the idea. She appreciated that Dave was taking things slow and not rushing her. Slow was good. Especially when, not too long ago, she'd been sure the romantic side of her life had died with her husband. But, thanks to Dave, she had a second chance at life and now love.

She had no idea how much longer they would have lingered there, her hands in Dave's, but a series of soft chimes coming from her purse forced her to break the connection. She slipped her phone from the bag. Reggie's name on the screen elicited a frown. The younger woman knew she was in an important meeting. She held up one finger, the universal signal that she'd keep the call short.

"Hey, Reggie. Dave and I were just wrapping things up here. Can I call you back in a few minutes?" she asked.

"Good. You're still in Destin. We've got a bit of an emergency."

Road noise coming through the speaker told her Reggie was headed somewhere in a hurry.

Michelle stilled. "What is it?"

"It's Chris's mom. She fell. She was taking Hope for a walk, and she fell." Panic edged Reggie's words.

Michelle froze as the day Allen collapsed rushed back at her. He'd been on the phone when she'd just happened to walk past the den he'd been using as his office. His voice had cut off mid-sentence. There'd been a crash, and she'd spun on one heel. She'd rushed into the room to find her husband of twenty-five years sprawled on the floor behind his desk.

Her mouth dry, she whispered, "Is it—is it her heart?"

"We don't know yet. It was serious enough that a neighbor called an ambulance. Someone must have told the paramedics that Chris worked for us, 'cause a deputy called looking for him. He's on his way to the emergency room at the hospital there in Destin. I wanted to go with him, but I have to pick up Hope from the neighbor's."

"You're going to babysit? Are you up to that? Where are Nina and Erin? Can they…?" Outside their immediate circle, no one knew how infertility had played such a factor in Reggie's life that, until recently, she'd shied away from young children and, especially, infants like Hope.

"Nope. It's just me. Erin went kayaking earlier. I tried to reach her, but she's out of cell phone range. Nina went on a supply run. Besides, I'm fine. Hope is, well, she's special."

No one could deny the adorableness of the cherubic six-month-old, but Michelle thought it might have taken more than a drooly, sweet grin or the smell of baby lotion to break through Reggie's aversion to youngsters. She'd seen the way Chris and Reggie worked together. How much they enjoyed one another's company. Was their deepening friendship responsible for Reggie's change of heart? Michelle filed the question away to ask another place, another time.

"Say no more," she told Reggie. "I'm on my way to the hospital now. When you talk to Chris, tell him I'll look for him there." She clicked off. A single glance from Dave told her he'd heard enough of the conversation to understand the urgency of the situation.

"I'll drive." He was already reaching into his pocket for his keys.

"You don't have to come—"

He cut her off with a look filled with sympathy. "What kind of friend would I be—for you or Chris—if I let you go alone? At times like these, we all need as much support as possible." He buzzed Josh on the intercom. "Clear my calendar for the rest of the afternoon. Family emergency."

Michelle grabbed her purse, and within minutes, they were headed across the parking lot. As they hurried to Dave's car, she had to admit, she was glad for the steadying grip of his hand around hers far more than she'd expected.

Eleven

Reggie

Following the prompts from the map app on her phone, Reggie steered down the road in an unfamiliar part of Sugar Sand Beach. Homes on the acre lots varied from squat older houses constructed of sturdy concrete to two- and even three-story modern residences wrapped in pastel siding. She passed one lawn where thick St. Augustine grass looked like it had been manicured by someone holding a tiny pair of scissors. The next yard featured sparse clumps of grass that sprouted in a yard mostly made up of gray sand. Not for the first time, she wondered what kind of place Chris called home. Was he like the cobbler who spent all day making shoes for other people while his own children went barefoot?

She'd barely considered the question when the computer-generated voice on her phone announced, "You have arrived at your destination." Pleasantly surprised, Reggie pulled to the curb in front of a tidy clapboard house with a yard full of thick, freshly mowed grass. She checked the slip of paper with the name and address of Chris's neighbor, not that she needed it. Hope's stroller sat outside the house next door. One leg of a pink teddy bear stuck out of the shopping basket beneath the seat.

"Binky." Reggie whispered the name of Hope's current favorite stuffed animal. The child carried the toy with her everywhere. Shutting the engine off, Reggie unbuckled her seat belt and stepped from the truck.

The forlorn screams of a very unhappy baby shattered the peace of the quiet neighborhood. Reggie's stomach clenched. Ignoring the narrow, cracked sidewalk, she bolted straight across the yard, pausing only long enough to grab the stuffed animal from the stroller. An instant later, she rapped firmly on the neighbor's front door. Her heart hammered while she waited for it to open.

When no one answered, she knocked again. "Mrs. Bees," she called loud enough to make herself heard over the crying child. "Mrs. Bees, it's Reggie. Chris's friend. He asked me to come and help you with Hope."

She was just about to try the knob when a very thin woman with sparse white hair swung the door open. Reggie breathed a sigh of relief mingled with concern at the sight of the sobbing child perched on the woman's bony hip. Mrs. Bees peered out owlishly. "What's that you said?" She patted the baby's back. "There, there, sweet thing. Hush now so I can talk to our company."

Glad to finally put a name to a face, Reggie studied the frazzled version of a woman she'd seen at the open house and again at the town council meeting. On both of those occasions, Mrs. Bees had been well-dressed, with her thinning hair pulled back in a bun. Today, half her hair had escaped, her glasses were missing, and she was still wearing her robe and slippers.

Reggie cleared her throat. "Mrs. Bees, where are your glasses?"

"Can't see a thing without 'em," Chris's neighbor replied in a wavery voice. "Sweet thing here kept pulling 'em off. I finally left 'em on the counter where they wouldn't get broke. Are you here for Hope?" Her tone carried a desperate, pleading note. "She won't stop crying."

"Why don't you let me hold her for a minute

while you get your glasses," Reggie suggested. If she thought she'd have some convincing to do, she couldn't have been more wrong. Mrs. Bees instantly leaned forward. Reggie didn't hesitate. She plucked the squalling child from a pair of frail arms.

"I'll be right back," Mrs. Bees promised.

"Take your time." Reggie kissed Hope's damp curls. "Hey, sweetie. Look who I have. It's Binky." She wiggled the pink teddy bear in front of the baby.

Hope took one look and cried harder.

"Okay," Reggie murmured. "Time to break out the big guns." She tucked the bear under her arm. With her hand free, she covered her eyes with her fingers. "Peep-eye," she cooed.

As if a switch had been thrown, Hope's mournful shrieks cut off abruptly. She stared at Reggie, tears dampening her cheeks, her lower lip trembling.

Reggie dropped her hand for a quick peek, then just as quickly hid her eyes again. "Peep-eye," she called and repeated the process.

On the third repetition, the baby clamped her chubby little hands over her own eyes.

"Oh!" Reggie exclaimed. This was new. When they'd played before, Hope had been content to let someone else do all the work. She whispered a soft, "Peep-eye." Sure enough, Hope dropped her little hands for a bare moment before she covered her face again.

"Well, I guess we know what you like." Reggie laughed. She gave the baby's round belly a teasing poke and was rewarded with a tentative giggle. "What say we take you home when Mrs. Bees comes back?"

"Bah-bah," Hope babbled.

"You want your bottle? We can do that." Chris had said there were extras in the refrigerator. Reggie leaned in through the open doorway. "Mrs. Bees, did you find your glasses?"

"Oh, yes, dearie. I'll be right there."

Reggie heard a toilet flush somewhere in the house. The muffled sound of a dog's excited barks followed. A minute later, a noticeably less flustered Mrs. Bees joined them on the porch. Reggie took in the freshly combed hair and the glasses that sat a little crookedly on the older woman's nose and smiled. The poor thing had probably been dying for a moment of privacy.

"Chris and I were painting at the house when he got the call about his mom. He sent me to help out with Hope. If that's all right with you. We can stay here, if you'd like." If she were in Mrs. Bees's position, she didn't think she'd readily turn the baby over to a relative stranger.

"You're one of the girls who moved into Nancy Simmons's old house, aren't you?"

"Yes, ma'am." Reggie smiled while watery blue eyes treated her to a questioning glance. "My name's Reggie," she reminded the woman.

"You have a way with young 'uns." Mrs. Bees nodded to the baby. All her crying must have tired Hope, because she rested her head against Reggie's shoulder. "You wouldn't have known where to find his daughter unless Chris sent you." Fatigue etched the woman's face. "I love that little girl like I love my own grandchildren, but she plumb wore me out," she apologized. "Have you heard anything about Doris? I hope she wasn't hurt real bad." Mrs. Bee wrung her hands.

"I haven't heard, but Chris promised to call as soon as he knows anything. I'll be sure to let you know." After the deputy's call, Chris had told her his neighbor saw his mom fall and called for help. Had Doris tripped over one of the cracks in the sidewalk? "Do you know what happened?" she asked. "Chris didn't have any of the details."

"Oh, it's my fault, I'm afraid." Mrs. Bees's hands churned faster. "I was taking Buster for a walk—he's a beagle and usually so well-behaved. But he got excited when he saw the stroller and took off like a rocket. I keep him on one of those retractable leashes. You know the kind?"

Reggie nodded.

"The next thing I knew, he'd run all around the stroller and Doris. It was awful, I tell you. One minute Doris was standing there, and the next she was on the ground. And Buster, he was so upset, he was barking to beat the band. I ran— well, I'm too old to run, but I went as quick as I could—and called the ambulance. Then that nice Deputy Snider asked me to take Hope." Mrs. Bees's focus seemed to drift. "He's such a nice boy. His parents live in Palatka, and he has a sister somewhere nearby. What's her name? Oh, yes. Cathy, that's it. She does my hair. I have an appointment with her tomorrow. Doris is supposed to drive me." She snapped back to the present. "Oh, I do hope she's okay."

Relief swirled in Reggie's chest and brought tears to her eyes. The whole way here she'd worried that Chris's mom had suffered a stroke or heart attack. Apparently, though, she'd been tripped up by a dog's leash. She might still be seriously injured—she could have broken a hip or suffered a concussion in the fall—but those things could be fixed. Mrs. Bees, on the other hand, had wandered off there for a bit. Should she do something about that?

Reggie drew in a steadying breath. For now, her primary goal was to take care of Hope. That didn't mean she'd ignore the situation, though. She eyed the heavy Cadillac sitting in the carport that jutted out from the house. Did the woman still drive? Judging from the thick layer of dust coating the vehicle, she thought not. Still, it was better not to take the chance.

She resettled Hope on her hip. Offering to take Mrs. Bees to her appointment was the neighborly thing to do. "I'll be happy to take you to get your hair done tomorrow. What time would you like me to pick you up?"

"Oh, dearie. That's so sweet, but you don't have to do that."

Reggie overrode Mrs. Bees's protests and insisted on taking the woman to the salon. Once that was arranged, she patted the baby's bottom. "I think this little one wants her bottle. Is it all right if I take her to Chris's?" she asked.

"By all means. And do let me know how Doris is doing as soon as you hear anything."

After offering assurances that she would pass the word along, Reggie slipped Hope into her carriage and wheeled the baby home. At the door to the house, sudden doubts niggled. Had Doris locked up when she left? Would Chris be upset that she'd taken Hope to his house? She'd find out the answers to both questions soon enough, she supposed. Lifting the baby from her carriage, she snuggled Hope close. The knob turned easily in Reggie's grasp a few seconds later. With one less thing to worry about, she carried the baby over the threshold.

Home once again, Hope perked up. Her blue eyes open wide, she asked, "Bah bah?"

"Yes, we're going to get you your bottle," Reggie assured the little one. She stepped into a smallish living room where most of the furniture had been pushed together to form a pen of sorts, with an oversize ottoman serving as the gate. She pushed the footrest aside for the moment. In the play area, a colorful, cushiony pad covered the hardwood floor. A neatly folded quilt provided extra padding at one end. Building blocks and large plastic rings in bright colors and a set of stacking cups were scattered about. Reggie plunked the baby in the middle of her toys, handed her the beloved teddy bear and, after sliding the ottoman back in place, went in search of the kitchen.

It wasn't hard to find. The house was cozy with a narrow, galley kitchen and dining area off the living room on one side and a hallway that presumably led to the bedrooms on the other. Satisfied that Hope was content for the moment,

Reggie hurried to the refrigerator. Sure enough, three prepared bottles sat on the top shelf. She took one and shut the door.

Hope must have recognized the sound, because the baby let out a yelp and began to fuss.

"Coming, sweetheart," Reggie reassured the child as she wrenched off the protective cover over the nipple.

She hurriedly retraced her steps toward the baby, bottle in hand. She'd only covered a few feet when she stopped dead in her tracks. Did she need to warm the bottle? She scanned the counters. No bottle warmer sat among the baby supplies on the otherwise spotless Formica. Should she call someone? Chris? Or Michelle?

Sitting on the quilt-covered floor, Hope bellowed in earnest. Deciding it might be best to let the baby take the lead, Reggie covered the rest of the distance between them. Hope's little legs flailed as Reggie scooped her off the blanket. In her arms, the baby lunged for the bottle. Reggie watched carefully when Hope popped the nipple in her mouth and sucked. Would the cold milk confuse the baby? Would she be frustrated?

Hope only grunted happily and continued to suck. Reggie's breath shuddered through her chest. She sank onto the couch, the child in her arms, thankful she'd made the right choice. Hope stared up at her, her eyes wide.

"You've had a very big day, haven't you?" Reggie whispered. She tapped one finger on the baby's nose.

Hope flung herself sideways as if to say, "Leave me alone. I'm drinking."

Reggie barely won the battle against laughing out loud. She eased back into the comfy couch and, while the baby worked on her bottle, she took a better look around. From the glossy hardwood floors to the bit of lace edging on the sheer curtains at the windows, the house had been decorated in a classic American style that suited Chris's personality and gave off a welcoming vibe. She wondered if the feminine touches she spotted here and there—a throw pillow in a floral print tucked into a corner of a chair, a crocheted afghan over the back of the sofa—had been his wife's idea or if his mom had added them. Regardless, someone had done an admirable job of child-proofing. Knickknacks that might prove tempting to a baby had been moved to high shelves. The TV swung out from an arm mounted on the wall, the remotes placed in a sturdy basket out of the child's reach. The electrical outlets featured child-proof locks.

She ran a hand over the nubby fabric of the

three-piece sectional done in neutral grays. The furniture was both sturdy and functional, with no sharp edges to harm an active toddler. "You have a very good dad," she whispered to the child.

A glance at the baby told her Hope had drained every last drop of her bottle. "My goodness, that was fast. You were hungry, weren't you?"

In reply, the baby tooted. Or Reggie thought she'd tooted until a smell she recalled from her babysitting days wafted up. "Oh, Hope!" Grinning, Reggie waved a hand. "I think the next thing on the agenda is to get you changed."

Only three doors branched off the short hallway on the other side of the living room. Reggie chose the one on the right and stepped into Hope's nursery.

"Oooh, pretty," she cooed to the baby. Although the space wasn't large, white walls made the room appear larger. A cascade of flowers painted over the baby's crib created the impression of movement. Girly-girl elements like pink curtains at the window, a plush pink throw rug and an upholstered rocking chair in pale pink were tempered by a bluish-gray crib and chest of drawers. Reggie zeroed in on the changing table, where diapers had been stacked neatly beside a basket containing all the necessary supplies.

Once she'd taken care of business, she and Hope returned to the living room, where they sat on the floor and played peep-eye until the child's interest waned. Hoping to avoid another crying jag, Reggie made a tower out of building blocks and pretended to be horrified when Hope promptly knocked it down. Her reaction elicited a series of giggles, and for the next twenty minutes or more, they made a game of building and demolishing the stack. The next time the baby's interest faded, though, Hope faded right along with it. A few moments later, she crawled into Reggie's lap and snuggled against her.

"Is it sleepy time?" Reggie whispered. She settled them both on the couch. Hope stirred until she found a comfortable position with her thumb in her mouth. The baby had just conked out and was sleeping soundly pressed against Reggie's shoulder when her cell phone trilled.

She froze. But when the baby didn't stir, she slipped the phone from her pocket. "Hello," she said, just above a whisper.

"How's Hope?" Chris asked.

"She's fine," Reggie assured him. "She had a bottle, a diaper change. We played, like, a thousand games of peep-eye. She drifted off a few minutes ago. I'm sitting on the couch holding her." She gave Chris a minute to absorb the news before she asked, "How's your mom?"

"She'll be all right. No broken bones, thank God, but her ankle is pretty badly sprained. They're going to discharge her. She'll have to follow up with her own doctor in a day or two."

"That's very good news." Realizing she'd braced herself for much worse, Reggie let out a long breath.

"Yeah," Chris said, echoing her relief. "Mom's coming home with me. We should be there in time for me to feed Hope and put her to bed. How are you holding up?"

"Surprisingly well." Reggie brushed her fingertips over the baby's soft curls. Hope didn't stir. "I think she's warming to me."

"Listen, I really appreciate you taking care of her." Chris waited a beat before adding, "This couldn't have been easy for you. Are you sure you're doing okay?"

"I'm fine," she assured him. It was sweet of him to ask. There'd been a time not so long ago that the mere thought of being around a baby, knowing she'd never have one of her own, had been too much to bear. Chris and his sweet daughter had shown her how wrong she'd been.

Twelve

Nina

My grandmother taught me how to make short-crust. I still use her recipe. It produces a light, flaky pastry that lends itself to many uses." Images of the days when she and Granny had worked side by side flashed through Nina's head. Her grandmother had filled her hand pies with fruit, dusted them with sugar and served them as dessert. The crust worked just as well for savory fillings. Which was why Nina had chosen to use it in one of the sample dishes she'd serve at the craft fair.

She lifted the strainer containing a thick tomato-y sauce from the catch bowl. "Ordinarily I wouldn't dream of draining my Bolognese," she told Krystal and Lily. "But since we're using it in hand pies, we have to. Otherwise, they'll get soggy. No one likes a soggy pie."

Nina feigned a look of horror, and Zeke's daughter giggled. Standing beside the young girl, Krystal didn't so much as crack a smile. The assistant chef never even looked up from the cell phone she'd slipped from the pocket of her apron the moment Nina had begun the demonstration.

Was she taking notes? Or checking on her grandmother…again?

From the concerned frown her assistant wore, Nina thought it was probably the latter. She stifled an exasperated groan. She really shouldn't blame Krystal for worrying about her grandmother. After all, it was only natural to check in on a sick relative. Besides, this lesson should be old hat to anyone who'd graduated from culinary school. The impromptu class was really for Lily's benefit, and the little girl was paying enough attention for everyone. Still, Nina couldn't help wishing Krystal would spend less time on her phone and more time cooking.

Satisfied that she'd removed enough liquid from the thick sauce, Nina added the final item to the mise en place she'd assembled on the kitchen counter. From left to right, a hundred rounds of short-crust pastry sat under a dampened tea towel. Next came the large bowl of meaty sauce. Spoons and crimping tools came next, followed by a bowl of egg wash and brushes. Stacks of parchment-lined baking sheets rested at the end. She glanced up at her helpers.

Lily stood at the edge of the counter with her thick, blond curls tucked into a neat hair net, a too-big apron wound around her thin frame, her lips slightly parted. She stared in rapt attention, looking as excited as a kid in a candy shop. Nina crossed her fingers and hoped Lily's older sister was likewise enjoying her time with Erin. The two of them had taken the kayaks out shortly after Zeke dropped the girls off this morning.

Beside Lily, Krystal continued to type furiously on the phone she'd kept within reach since reporting for work last week. Between the frequent checks on her grandmother and the notes she took whenever Nina shared a recipe or a cooking technique, the thing was hardly ever out of her hands. The trouble was, Krystal seemed so intent on her phone that she often overlooked the finer points of whatever Nina was trying to help the girl learn. And no matter what culinary school she'd graduated from, there was always more to learn in a working kitchen.

Nina tried telling herself she should be flattered to have an assistant who took such pains, but honestly, all that note taking was getting on her nerves. Several times today, she'd been tempted to tell her helper to put the phone down and simply pay better attention. Not that she'd dream of giving such an order in front of the impressionable Lily. The child was all wide-eyed innocence, a trait her father would prefer she hold on to for as long as possible. So, for now at least, Nina swallowed her irritation and continued showing her helpers how to make a perfect hand pie.

"First you take one of the pastry rounds, like this." She lifted one from the stack, being careful to tuck the towel back in place so the others wouldn't dry out. She lay the circle on the lightly floured counter and smoothed it. "Next place about two tablespoons of the Bolognese on one half and complete the fold." Gently, she worked her fingers under the dough before folding it over the sauce. She checked the edges, which matched perfectly. "Then run the crimping tool all the way around to seal the sauce inside. I usually use one like this." She held up a wheel on a wooden handle. "But there are other methods. Lily, you might prefer to use this." She plopped the pie into a device that resembled a pair of dentures and gently closed the lid. "Don't press too hard or you'll end up cutting off the edges altogether. Brush a little egg wash over the top and—voilà—all done." She settled the finished product on the baking sheet.

"Yes, Chef," Lily whispered breathlessly.

Wiping her hands on one of the green-and-white kitchen towels she'd purchased for the cafe, Nina stepped away from the counter. "Okay, now it's your turn. Let's see how well you can make a hand pie."

Lily stepped forward eagerly. One corner of her bottom lip tucked between her teeth, she followed Nina's example step by step. Meanwhile, Krystal slipped her phone into an apron pocket before she moved closer to the counter.

"Krystal." Nina canted her head toward the hand-washing sink Zeke had installed. This had to be—what?—the fourth time today she'd had to remind her assistant to wash her hands after handling the device. She fought an urge to roll her eyes.

What were they teaching young chefs in culinary school these days? Not proper food-handling techniques, apparently. Why, when she'd been a student at the Culinary Institute, hand washing had been so deeply ingrained that she'd grown accustomed to having chapped, dry fingers. Krystal, not so much. Her perfectly manicured hands remained soft and smooth.

"Yes, Chef." Krystal's cheeks reddened, but at Nina's reminder, she walked to the sink, where she washed and dried her hands before she proceeded to assemble a hand pie that wasn't quite as neat as Lily's.

"Excellent job, Lily," Nina coached. "A little less pressure on the crimping wheel, Krystal." She clapped her hands lightly. "Let's get busy now. I'd like to have two hundred of these ready for the freezer by the end of the day." Another batch of pastry and sauce sat cooling in the fridge.

For the next half-hour, Nina divided her time between lavishing praise on Lily, encouraging Krystal to do her best work and transferring the finished pies to the oven and from there to the cooling racks. She'd just taken the third sheet pan from the Aga when Krystal placed another haphazardly crimped pie on the parchment and began removing her apron.

"Krystal?" Nina frowned.

"It's time, Chef." Krystal nodded to the big clock Zeke had mounted on the kitchen wall.

"Right," Nina said on a long, slow breath. She studied the ingredients spread out on the counter. They'd barely put a dent in the work she'd hoped to accomplish today. The unbaked dough wouldn't stay moist until morning, not even tightly wrapped and stored in the fridge. To finish the job, she'd have to work far into the wee hours. Her own fault, she supposed, for agreeing to Krystal's shortened schedule. She gritted her teeth and nodded.

"I can stay," Lily piped up. The girl slipped another perfect hand pie onto the baking sheet. "This is fun."

Fireflies and stars twinkled by the time Nina sank onto one of the chairs on the front porch with an icy glass of the inn's signature drink in her hand. She propped her aching feet on the footrest and crossed her ankles. "Thanks, guys. I would never have gotten all those pies baked and in the freezer without your help."

"Thank you!" Reggie raised her glass in a mock toast. "Gold Coast Sunset on a week night? Yum." She swirled the ice in her glass and sipped.

"You deserve it. We all do." Nina took a long swallow.

After Krystal's departure, Lily—bless her heart—had done her best, but the child was only ten. It hadn't been long before her workspace looked like a war zone, with red Bolognese sauce splattered everywhere. Nina, meanwhile, had tried to do everything at once. Filling and shaping pies. Timing the sheets in the oven. Sliding the baked pastries onto the cooling racks.

Reggie had been the first to notice the chaos when she'd trooped downstairs with a load of brushes and rollers to wash. She'd wisely headed out the door without saying a word. At the time, Nina thought her friend was merely escaping her frenzied efforts to assemble, bake and store over two hundred hand pies. But no. Reggie had merely dumped her supplies in the tool shed's deep sink, leaving them to soak overnight while she circled back upstairs. After showering and dressing in record time, she'd returned to the kitchen, where she stole the pot holders right off Nina's hands and set to work.

Michelle, Erin and Lily's older sister Megan had joined them a bit later. Soon laughter and chatter had replaced the chaos, and almost before Nina knew what was happening, the last batch of hand pies was cooling on the kitchen counter.

The best moment, though, came when Zeke bit into the tasty treats his daughters had set aside for him. He'd sauntered into the kitchen smelling of sawdust and *man* and not entirely sure what kind of greeting he'd receive. Would the girls still be angry at him for foisting them off on Nina and her friends after their regular babysitter took an unexpected day off? When he'd called to ask if Nina's offer to have the girls over still stood, he'd warned her they could be sullen and difficult to handle. Especially Megan. The delight in the man's eyes when both of his daughters chattered about their day like a pair of happy magpies had been priceless.

She turned to Erin. "I hope Megan didn't give you any trouble today. It was nice of you to take her out on such short notice."

Erin interlaced her fingers and stretched her arms over her head. "She was great. Honest. We had a good time, and I learned some things."

"Oh?" This from Michelle, who sat in one of the side chairs.

"Yeah. Like teenagers don't want to see the sights as much as they want to race." Erin chuckled. "Keeping up with her gave me quite the workout."

The rattan webbing in her chair squeaked as Michelle leaned forward to grab a carrot stick from the tray of cut veggies centered on the coffee table. "Teenagers are a handful," she acknowledged. "But it was nice to have youngsters around here today. I wouldn't mind if Zeke pawned his daughters off on us from time to time."

"Shhh!" Nina whispered. "Don't say that too loud, or the next thing you know, we'll be running a summer camp." Not that she'd mind spending more time with Lily. Or Megan either. Both girls were sweet in their own way. It didn't hurt that they were quite handy in the kitchen.

"We'll all benefit from a successful showing at the craft fair, so I didn't mind pitching in this afternoon." Michelle broke her carrot in two. "But what happened to your assistant? Where was she?"

"Krystal was, um…" Nina lowered her feet and sat upright. Slowly, she began taking the pins out of her hair. "She has another job in the evenings. She leaves here at four. On the dot. Maybe even a little earlier." She ran her fingers through her hair, freeing the long tresses from their tight bun.

"Yeah? And how is that working for you?" Erin wanted to know.

"I thought as long as I could only offer her part-time work, it would be okay. She assured me she'll let the other job go once we open for dinner service and can give her forty hours a week. But as you saw this afternoon, it's not working out as well as I'd hoped. I thought she'd have realized we were in a bind and stayed later—it's what I would have done when I was starting out and trying to prove myself."

Michelle chewed thoughtfully on a bite of carrot and swallowed. "Not everyone has your drive and dedication," she pointed out.

"I am driven," Nina admitted. She'd had to be. Lazy chefs had very short careers. Was Krystal cut from that kind of cloth? "I don't expect her to have my passion for the job, but…" She sighed. The girl was a puzzle. Trying to solve it, she voiced her concerns. "There's a lot about her I can't figure out. When she said she got her love of cooking from her grandmother, I thought, 'Oh good, she's just like me.' The truth is, she's not. During her interview, she gave every indication that she was eager to learn, hardworking and dedicated. When we're working together, though, it's a whole other story. I mean, she does whatever I tell her, but she needs constant direction, supervision. Whenever there's a break, she goes off on her own. Then there's the phone thing. I think that's what's driving me batty most of all. She's on it constantly."

"She does what, now?" Reggie, who'd been in the process of taking a drink, lowered her glass.

"Her phone. She's always on it. She says she's taking notes, but it drives me to distraction. I remember when I was just starting out and the chef would demonstrate some new technique or recipe, I couldn't wait to get my hands on whatever he was fixing. Try it myself, you know?"

"Yeah. Watch and learn. That's how I learned how to graft stock, from watching one of the master gardeners at the plant nursery." Reggie nodded.

"Krystal's not like that. She's got her head bent over her cell phone so much that I'm afraid she's not paying attention to the subtleties." The girl's misshapen hand pies were a prime example.

"That does seem odd," Erin allowed.

"Doesn't it though?" Nina shrugged. She was developing serious qualms about her new assistant. "Unless things improve, I'm not sure she'll last."

Michelle, their usual voice of reason, spoke up. "Maybe she's intimidated and afraid to make a mistake, so she's being extra cautious. Give her some time to settle in and get used to your routine before you decide."

The idea had merit. After all, Krystal had only been with her for a week. The younger cook might still be learning her way in an unfamiliar kitchen. Nina hoped that's all it was, but she couldn't shake the feeling that she was missing something. Some clue as to what made the younger woman tick.

She brushed aside her concerns like she'd brushed flour from her hands earlier this afternoon. She'd given Krystal a six-week probationary period. During that time, she'd take advantage of every opportunity to get to know her helper. And who knew? Maybe the girl would surprise her and show more interest in the work.

Whether she did or not, though, one thing had to change. Krystal's cell phone had to go.

Thirteen

Erin

"Thanks for stopping by. Take one of our cards in case you want to book a tour in the future." At the entrance to their booth at the craft fair, Erin handed the business card for the Sugar Sand Inn and Cafe to the young couple who'd admired the kayak on display. She'd taken two steps toward the table where Dave and Michelle sat when a woman she didn't recognize broke out of her place in line for the sample plates and came straight at her.

"I just can't thank you enough!" the woman exclaimed. "C'mere and let me give you a hug!"

The words were barely out of the woman's mouth before a pair of fleshy arms wrapped around Erin and enveloped her in a cloud of Jean Nate.

"*Umph!*" Erin's breath rushed out. The woman squeezed tighter than the green anaconda she'd encountered on a trip through the Brazilian rain forest some years back. Was she going to walk around with bruised ribs this time, too?

"What you and your friends have done for my Bobby, why, it's just the sweetest thing in the world. Me and Robert Senior will be grateful to you for the rest of our lives."

Black spots appeared in Erin's vision as the woman continued to squeeze. The van, she thought. The donation had been on the lips of nearly every person who'd passed through the tent this morning. Realizing the hugger had to be none other than the mother of the wounded soldier, Erin searched for a name, if only to ask ever so politely if the woman could give her some air. "Mrs. Phelps," she finally gasped. "We were glad to help out."

As if it suddenly dawned on her that she was strangling the object of all her gratefulness, Mrs. Phelps relaxed her hold.

Erin drew in a gulp of cologne-scented air and coughed. "It wasn't just me," she wheezed. "The whole town pitched in."

Once word had spread that their new neighbors from the Sugar Sand Inn planned to donate a van—an entire van!—to go along with the house the town was building for a very deserving soldier, individuals and businesses alike had pitched in to fill the vehicle with all manner of gifts. By the time the van rolled down Main Street in yesterday's parade, towels and linens, pots and pans and a year's supply of cleaning products spilled out the open cargo door. A basket on the passenger's seat held coupons good for car washes, oil changes and groceries plus gift certificates from restaurants as far away as Panama City and Destin. Small wonder that Bobby's mother had been overwhelmed. Erin and her friends had all shed a tear or two when they saw the generous outpouring.

"Any idea when Bobby will get to come home?" she asked.

"I spoke with him just yesterday. His therapists are all so proud of how hard he's working. They think he might be released in time for Thanksgiving. Christmas at the latest. Won't that be wonderful?" Mrs. Phelps smoothed the voluminous shirt she wore over baggy shorts.

"Next time you talk to him, tell him we're all pulling for him." Erin indicated her friends and neighbors with a sweep of one hand.

After another hug, a gentler one this time, Bobby's mother rejoined the line of people who slowly moved toward the sample table. Erin, meanwhile, retreated to the back of the tent, where she took a moment to regroup.

"Our booth is drawing men like flies to honey," she murmured under her breath as she sipped water from an eco-friendly bottle.

One after another, Zeke and Chris and Dave had put in appearances this morning. The first two left earlier, but Dave was still hanging around.

Of course, she wouldn't dare complain. Not after all the help Zeke and Chris had given them. Dave, too, although, his assistance had been more brain than brawn. They all recognized and were ever so thankful for the lawyer's involvement in their lives. Without him, Michelle and Nina would still be struggling to keep body and soul together in Virginia's competitive job market. And Reggie? As much as Erin didn't like to think about the possibility, without Dave's help, her sister might still be married to that oaf of a husband of hers. As for herself, she'd probably be halfway across the world...and wishing for something more. So, yeah, Dave was truly a godsend.

And then there were Zeke and Chris. They'd already been waiting when, shortly after sunrise, she and Michelle, Reggie and Nina had slowly driven their heavily loaded vehicles over the lumpy field to their designated spot for the craft fair. It had taken all six of them to erect the large canopy tent that would serve as their base for the next two days. From that moment on, until shoppers thronged the aisles, the contractor and the handyman had worked up quite a sweat. She'd lost count of the number of trips they'd made back and forth—hauling tables and chairs from the bed of the pickup truck, coolers and a gas grill from the back of the Jeep. To say nothing of the mountain of paper products and plasticware Nina had insisted they'd need for the weekend event. That alone had filled Michelle's SUV.

Though she'd been busy, too, Erin hadn't overlooked the frequent glances Chris and Reggie had shared. Or the soft smile that had shaped Zeke's lips whenever Nina singled him out for a task. Any more than she could overlook the sparkle in Michelle's eyes as she looked up at Dave right now. The tall, distinguished lawyer lingered at the table where Michelle was handing out flyers and brochures for the Sugar Sand Inn. From the way he leaned down to talk with her, Erin could tell the man was interested. But she'd bet money it wasn't the inn that had stirred his interest.

Were her friends falling in love in Sugar Sand Beach?

They might be.

Could she blame them if they did?

No, not at all. If anything, happiness made her chest expand every time she considered that Michelle, Reggie and Nina might find their very own Mr. Right.

Where did that leave her, though? As some nearly forgotten third—no, make that seventh— wheel? The old maid who tagged along on group outings. The one the others uttered worried whispers about.

Will she ever find love? Will she grow old alone? And her personal favorite, *Maybe we should find someone for her,* followed by a parade of blind dates.

No, just no.

She didn't need anyone to set her up or to fret about her love life or lack thereof. If she had to, she'd sign up for every dating app in existence in order to avoid that fate. She was perfectly capable of handling her own search for the right man. If and when she wanted one. *Thank you very much.*

But not today. Not while hundreds of potential customers browsed through tents featuring everything from bottle-cap artwork to hand-carved tiki poles. Or when the line of people willing to pay a dollar a plate for a sample of Nina's cooking snaked out the door and two booths down.

She spared a quick glance at the four-woman kitchen crew. Wearing the kid-size green aprons Nina had purchased especially for them, Megan and Lily greeted each customer with a smile. While the teen handled the money, the younger girl relayed orders to Reggie and Nina. In what had been possibly the smartest move she could make, the chef had decided on only two offerings. The first was an appetizer plate featuring a couple of Nina's special cheese crackers, several tiny bison balls and a hand pie, plus a nice piece of freshly grilled grouper topped with a to-die-for mango chutney. The alternative was a dessert plate crowded with cookies, mini éclairs and lemon bars. Nina had instituted an iron-clad no substitution rule, which simplified things. And at a dollar a plate, she hadn't heard a single complaint.

Behind the girls, Erin's friends moved at warp speed. Reggie took preassembled dessert plates from coolers while Nina warmed the appetizers on the grill and arranged things just so on small paper plates. Try as she might, Erin couldn't see how to help out without disrupting their flow. She was about to pitch in anyway when the wavery voice of an older woman stopped her.

"We couldn't have asked for better weather for the craft fair, could we?"

"No, ma'am, Miss Polly," Erin said as she turned to face the tiny owner of the flower shop. Puffy white clouds filled the skies, keeping the temperature down to a balmy eighty-three, which, compared with the ninety-degree heat wave they'd endured the previous week, was practically a cold front. "It's absolutely perfect."

"Looks like the cafe is doing a booming business." Polly aimed her chin at the line. "I've heard nothing but good things about the food."

"Have you tried it? I'd be happy to get you a plate," Erin offered.

"Oh, pshaw. We wouldn't dream of jumping the line. Would we, Wally?" Polly glanced up at the man who stood beside her. "Oh, I'm sorry. I forgot you two hadn't met. Erin, this is my son Wally. Wally, Erin—I'm sorry, honey. I forget your last name."

"Bradshaw. I'm Erin Bradshaw," she said, extending a hand to the tall, slender man. Beneath a mop of curly dark hair, his blue eyes took on a watery look behind thick lenses set in square tortoiseshell glasses. The man with the unfortunate name had rolled up the sleeves of the chambray shirt he wore over unfashionably long shorts. He had the whole geeky look going for him.

"Walt," he corrected, taking her hand in a grip that was firmer than she'd expected. "Welcome to Sugar Sand Beach. My mother says you and your friends took over the old Simmons place?" His thin lips curved into a killer smile that lent a movie-star quality to his nerdy boy-next-door looks.

Momentarily distracted by that smile, Erin swallowed, hard. "Uh, yes," she managed. "We're turning it into an inn. And a cafe. We, uh, we open in the fall. Would you like a brochure?" Good grief, she was as tongue-tied as a teenager.

"Thanks," Walt said. He gave her hand a pump before he let it go and tapped his shirt pocket. "I have one."

She was definitely out of practice and needed to brush up on a few skills before she signed up for one of those dating apps, Erin told herself. She took in the glossy tri-fold sticking out of Wally-Walt's pocket as she caught Reggie's eye. Off to one side, she held up two fingers and waited until her sister nodded that she understood before Erin turned to their guests. "So do you live in town, Walt?" she asked to be sociable.

"Panama City. I'm here a couple of times a month to see Mom. I keep telling her she should move in with me. I have plenty of room, and the Gulf is only a few steps from my back door. I know she'd love taking her morning walks along the beach." Walt gave one shoulder an indulgent shrug. "But she says she's not ready to quit the flower business."

"Now, Wally." Polly's lips pursed. "You know I'm gonna keep Posies open till the day I die. How else will I know what's happening around town?"

Erin grinned. As one of the members of the town council, Polly liked keeping her thumb on the pulse of Sugar Sand Beach. She turned to Walt. "And what do you do in Panama City?"

"As little as possible," he said with a disarming shrug. "I own a part interest in a couple of businesses there."

"I bet that keeps you busy." She should know. It had taken her and her friends months to get the inn and cafe ready to open. But it was happening. By fall, their dream would be a reality.

"Not really. I'm just the money man. Other people handle the day-to-day stuff. I spend most of my time fiddling around on my computer. Or reading. Right now, I'm concentrating on biographies of all the presidents."

He had a house on the beach but spent all his time indoors?

Count me out.

"Wally sold an apt to one of those giant computer companies," Polly said with a fair amount of maternal pride.

"An app, Mom," he corrected. "I'm working on another one."

Which explained the slightly geeky vibe, Erin supposed. She spotted Reggie on her way over with double orders of both the appetizer and dessert plates. "Can I interest you in some samples from our cafe?"

"Now Erin, honey, I told you not to go to any trouble on our account." Despite her protest, Polly snatched a plate right out of Reggie's hands.

"Nonsense," Erin replied while Reggie handed the rest to Walt. "Not after all you've done for us." She whispered her thanks to her sister and made the necessary introductions. To Walt, who now stood carefully balancing the other three plates, she said, "There are picnic tables in the shade just around the corner."

"Thanks," he said with a nod to the food. "This looks great. Ready, Mom?"

"Oh, yes, dear. We shouldn't take up any more of these girls' time." A wide grin on her face, Polly was already double-timing it into the crowd that thronged toward the food aisle.

"You come back any time you want, Miss Polly," Erin said to Walt's back as he trailed behind his mother.

"He's kinda cute," Reggie whispered once Polly and her son had disappeared.

"He's okay. Not my type, though. More's the pity. I think he's loaded."

"Oh yeah?" Reggie took one step forward. "Maybe I should make a play for him."

Erin punched her sister lightly on the arm. "I think Chris might have a thing or two to say about that."

"Really?" Reggie paired the comment with a look that was pure wide-eyed innocence.

"Yeah, really," Erin said dryly. Her sister knew full well that Chris was more than a little interested in her.

"Reggie, I need you." Nina's call interrupted their teasing.

"Yes, Chef," Reggie answered, already moving to grab another dessert plate from the ice chest.

Erin lingered, staring at the empty spot where Walt and Miss Polly had stood. It really was too bad that Walt wasn't her type. She could use someone in her life. Not that she wanted to settle down or anything. But now that Reggie was spending more and more time with Chris, while Michelle and Nina nurtured budding relationships with Dave and Zeke, it'd be nice to have someone to catch an occasional movie with or meet for drinks on a Saturday night.

Of course, that begged the question of what her type actually was. For perhaps the first time in her life, she didn't know the answer. Ever since her marriage to Ron had crashed and burned on the rocks of broken promises, she hadn't stayed in one place long enough to develop a long-lasting relationship. Oh, she'd had the occasional fling, mostly with the rough-and-tumble crowd who lived like she did, moving from one place to another, always on the go. Once in a great while she'd meet someone special on her travels, someone who, under different circumstances, she wanted to get to know better. But none of them had ever been worth staying put for. She'd never once considered changing the flight reservations that would take her from Borneo to Alaska for the summer tourist season or from the Ukraine to the Keys in the winter. Now that she was planning to stay in one place for a good long while, she supposed she ought to put some effort into figuring out what the perfect man for her might look like.

Yeah, she'd get right on that. Right after she spoke with the young couple who were flipping through pictures of the canoe trips she'd taken through the Topsail Preserve. Did they want to book her guide services? Or could she drum up some business from the photographer who was admiring the kayak she'd propped against one of the tent walls?

Fourteen

Nina

Nina flagged Erin to take over the grill. In need of a break, she stepped outside the rear of the tent, bottle of water in hand. Nothing in all her years of working in some of the most hectic kitchens in Northern Virginia had prepared her for the onslaught of customers at the craft fair. She'd been working the grill nonstop since the gates opened this morning. Before that, actually.

Though the handout hadn't mentioned blue ribbons, she'd half-expected the judges who roamed through all the booths, clipboards in hands. What was a fair without judges, after all? These had definitely surprised her, though, by arriving in their tent a half hour before the gates opened. Luckily, she'd been taking a test batch of grouper off the grill at that exact moment. She hadn't even had a chance to give the fish a taste test before the judges had scooped up every bite and, murmuring their compliments, moved on.

She'd been tempted to kiss Zeke full on the lips just about then. Not because she was falling for the guy, although she thought she might be. No, she just couldn't think of a better way to thank him for all the help he and Chris had given them in setting up the tent and getting ready for the crowds. And yeah, she supposed she owed Chris a kiss, too, though his would be the garden-variety peck on the cheek.

Um, mmm, mmm, Zeke. The man's name was fast becoming a part of her vocabulary. At least a half-dozen times a day she caught herself saying, "Zeke did this" or "Zeke said that." Best of all, she was pretty sure he felt the same way about her. Otherwise, he wouldn't hang around so much, would he?

Now that he and his crew had finished the work in the dining area, he constantly found one excuse after another to swing by the house. He'd insisted on staining the new flooring strips himself, a task that had required multiple treks through her kitchen. One day, he'd stopped by to check the plumbing under the hand-washing sink. On another, he'd dropped off a set of restaurant-grade floor mats that had just happened to land in his lap. Seeing his tall, muscular frame in the doorway never failed to stir an urge to get to know the man better. A lot better. As much as she'd wanted to explore those feelings, though, she told herself she had too many irons in the fire to let their relationship grow beyond a casual friendship. But once the craft fair was over, she fully intended to see if there was anything to that spark of attraction she felt for the man.

In the meantime, this was Zeke's month to have the girls, and thanks to his busy work schedule, Lily and Megan had become regular fixtures around the inn. Which wasn't at all a bad thing. She enjoyed having the girls around far more than she'd expected. Megan had proven herself very handy in the kitchen whenever she wasn't kayaking or fishing with Erin. The older girl had a deft hand with pastry tools and had taken to decorating pies with flair. And little Lily? Nina smiled. The youngster was turning into quite the cook, too. Just last week she'd made her very first crème brûlée...with only the teensiest bit of help.

Krystal, though, wasn't nearly so happy to have the girls underfoot, as she called it. Nina twisted the cap on her water bottle and sighed.

She'd tried every trick in her arsenal to get through to her new assistant. So far, nothing had worked. No matter how much encouragement she offered, Krystal remained disinterested and aloof. Things had gotten so bad that she'd finally called the woman into her office last week and spelled it out for her. Speaking plainly, she'd told Krystal that her attitude had to change or she wouldn't last past her probationary period. Unfortunately, instead of improving, the woman had only grown more distant. On several days, she'd turned downright sullen. Admitting she'd made a mistake was hard for her to do, but Krystal was giving her no choice. She'd have to let the woman go, and the sooner, the better.

But that was next week's problem. Today, she needed to focus on the craft fair. Lowering herself onto an empty ice chest, she downed half the bottle of chilled water in long gulps. Her mind raced as she reviewed where things stood.

Megan and Lily were working out beautifully as their counter help. The two girls relayed orders and kept track of sales better than the front house staff in the last restaurant where she'd worked. They definitely deserved a bonus, and she made a mental note to think of some special way to thank them for all their hard work.

Reggie and Erin had been godsends. There'd been a time or two when Reggie had been moving so quickly to pull dessert plates out of the coolers that her hands actually blurred. Erin, too. She'd filled in whenever and wherever needed—giving Megan and Lily frequent breaks or, like she was doing right now, taking over the grill.

But not everything had gone smoothly. Even with Polly's warning, Nina admitted that she'd underestimated the crowds. At the rate they were serving people, she guessed they'd run out of prepared dessert plates before lunch tomorrow. The appetizers would last a little longer, but by early afternoon, they'd exhaust that supply, too.

Should she spend the night creating more? She shook her head. She'd spent the last six weeks prepping for the craft fair. It wasn't possible to recreate all those dishes in a single night. Not even if she drafted everyone in the house to help her. Then there was the massive amount of supplies they'd need. Would the stores even be open after the gates closed this evening? She let out a long, slow breath. By the time they sold the last plate tomorrow, they'd have served well over a thousand people. For a first showing, it was more than enough. Next year, though, she'd double…everything.

She swigged the rest of the water, removed the chef's toque from her head and mopped her brow with a napkin. Stretching her feet out in front of her in the thick grass, she watched a fat bumblebee hover over a white trefoil. A battery of soft pop-pop-pops came from a nearby stand where congenial workers prepared a fresh batch of kettle corn. The sizzle of onions, chilies and various meats came from the fajita truck two booths down. The smells drifted in the thin breeze. They mingled with the scent of fresh-grilled grouper that rose from her own tent. The combination was not at all unpleasant, and the germ of a new recipe began to take shape. For a few minutes she played with the idea of finely grinding popped corn, adding spice and using it as a breading for fish. As she considered how different peppers and seasonings might blend together, the noise of footsteps, conversations and the muted shouts of vendors barking their wares faded into the background. That was, it did until she picked one voice out of the hubbub.

"Appetizers or desserts? Those are my only two choices?" The man laughed as if someone had told a not-so-funny joke. "Make mine the appetizer plate, then."

Nina jerked upright. Silky smooth and polished, that voice could only belong to one person.

Tobias.

What was he doing here? And why now? It was well after two. Any chef worth his salt would be in his kitchen, prepping for the all-important dinner service on a busy holiday weekend. Then again, Tobias always had followed his own rules. Rules that included foisting as much of the work—and the responsibility—off on his underlings as possible.

She shook her head. Whatever. She and Tobias no longer worked together. How he chose to run his kitchen shouldn't matter to her. His being here, though, that could only spell trouble. Filing the unfinished recipe away for another day, another time, she slipped on her chef's hat. She stood just as Erin pushed aside the tent flap.

"Um, Houston, we have a problem," she whispered.

"I'm on my way," Nina said, squaring her shoulders. She paused to listen.

"Grilled fish and mango?" Tobias asked in a stage whisper. "For a tired, old-fashioned recipe, it's surprisingly good," he said. "And what's this—a cheese cracker? Not bad."

LEIGH DUNCAN

The nerve of the man! This was war!

Nina clenched her fists while she fought down an urge to march into the tent and throttle her former lover. So much for keeping the negativity at bay. Tobias was the one who'd proposed a truce, yet he'd broken it at his very first opportunity. Why was she not surprised? She hadn't honestly expected him to honor their agreement, had she? He might sound like he was paying her dishes a compliment, but his ruse didn't fool anyone. It certainly didn't fool her. Damning her cooking with faint praise was exactly the kind of mean, nasty trick she'd expected him to pull. She supposed she should be grateful he hadn't done something worse.

But she was an old hand when it came to dealing with Tobias and his tricks. Two could play this game, and determined to come out of this one on top, she plastered a smile over her anger like she'd slap a Band-Aid over a cut. Smoothing her apron, she walked into the tent.

"Tobias, what a surprise!" she exclaimed, deliberately not calling his visit a pleasant one. "I didn't expect to see you here today. I thought, what with your own restaurant to run, you'd be far too busy to spend the afternoon at our little craft fair." As for her, she'd have to be on her deathbed before she'd abandon her kitchen staff to go on a jaunt mere hours before the dinner service.

"Chef Nina," Tobias said with a smile that was so fake, Nina could practically smell the artificial flavoring. "I had no idea you and your, um, helpers"—he shot a disparaging glance at Megan and Lily—"had a booth this year. When I saw your sign out front, I absolutely knew I couldn't miss it. Even it meant standing in that hideously long line."

Nina gritted her teeth at the implication that service was slow. With attendance at the fair breaking every record in the books, lines snaked out in front of all the food tents and trucks. "I'm so sorry you wasted your precious time in line along with everyone else." Did the man really think he deserved special treatment?

Zing! Color rose in Tobias's cheeks as her barb hit its mark. He recovered quickly.

"Tsk tsk," he remarked. He flicked the meatball on his plate with one finger. "My food is cold, and I believe this fish is undercooked."

It most certainly is not! A muscle in Nina's cheek twitched. She ought to kick the man's butt to the curb.

"My fault, Chef," Erin interrupted. "I took the fish off the grill while you were on break."

Nina knew good and well there was nothing

wrong with Tobias's food, but she refused to argue. The customer was always right, she reminded herself, even when he wasn't. And especially when he stood at the front of a long line of hungry customers who had nothing better to do than listen to the man rant.

"Oh, no! I'm so sorry," she said using her most concerned tone. "Here, let me get you a fresh one." She watched carefully as Erin plated the next serving. Taking the dish from her friend's outstretched hand, she fussed over it a bit, adding a tiny extra dollop of chutney and two extra crackers. "Here you go," she said, at last serving his food to Tobias.

"Much better, thanks," he answered with a condescending sneer. "That's very nice of you. To return the favor, I'd love to treat you and all your friends"—his wide gesture included all the people who'd waited while he held up the line— "to a complimentary appetizer the next time you visit my new restaurant, the Happy Dolphin, in Panama City. Be sure to mention seeing me, Chef Tobias, at the craft fair."

Glancing away from the onlookers, Nina rolled her eyes so hard she was almost afraid they'd get stuck at the top of her head. She was on to Toby's tricks. The freebie would draw people in to his restaurant, where anyone who took him up on his offer was bound to order a meal to go with it.

"Thanks so much," she said tightly. "Now, if you wouldn't mind moving along, I think you've kept these good people waiting long enough." She aimed a friendly smile to those who'd had no choice but to listen in on every word.

She stood, her arms folded across her chest until Tobias blended into the crowd and disappeared.

"You okay, Chef?" Reggie asked at her elbow.

"Of course," she answered, her chin up, an unwavering smile for the crowd on her face.

"That man is trouble," Reggie whispered. "He never even touched that food. Just threw his plate in the garbage on his way out."

Nina took a breath. "At least it's over. He's out of our hair now."

But was he, really? Nina stared at the spot where she'd last seen Tobias. It wouldn't surprise her at all to learn the man had another trick or two up his sleeve. There was nothing she could do about what might or might not happen in the future, though, and customers were waiting. "Frankly, I'm just thankful he didn't do something worse." She clapped her hands lightly. "Let's get back to work, everyone, shall we?"

And, to a chorus of "Yes, Chef," that's exactly what they did.

Fifteen

Michelle

"We have that grouper sandwich you liked so much on special," Sally suggested.

Seated in their usual booth at Maggie's Diner, Michelle and Dave exchanged knowing smiles.

"No thanks, Sally," Michelle said. She picked up her menu. "I've had enough fish to last a lifetime."

Nina had been testing grouper recipes for weeks leading up to the craft fair. As her guinea pig, she, along with Reggie and Erin, had dutifully critiqued each dish until the chef had honed in on the exact blend of spices and toppings. Then there'd been the craft fair itself. They'd kept the grill up and running nonstop for two days in order to serve the hungry crowds. By the end of the second day, Michelle's hair, her clothes—even her skin—had reeked of fish and smoke. She'd had to shampoo and condition twice to get rid of the smell.

She handed her menu to the waitress. "I'll have a small house salad, blue cheese on the side, and a cup of vegetable soup."

"Soup and salad, right?" Sally asked. She tilted her head toward the booth behind them, where another customer was talking on her cell phone loud enough for anyone on the opposite side of the diner to hear.

"Give me a turkey sandwich. Hold the mayo. Hold the chips." Dave pitched his voice above the noise and smiled up at their favorite waitress. "Did you make it to the craft fair last weekend?"

"Wouldn't'a missed it." Sally wrote down their order in quick, bold strokes. "Maggie, she closed the diner a half day on Sunday so's we could all go. Y'all were all sold out by the time I got to your booth, Michelle, but I've heard folks talking. They say the food was so good, they can't wait till the cafe opens for real."

Michelle gave the waitress a look filled with sympathy. "I'm sorry you missed us, but Nina will be glad to hear that people are looking forward to the cafe. I'll be sure and tell her."

Sally pocketed her order pad while she

scanned the table. Both Michelle and Dave had opted for iced tea, and their glasses were still nearly full. The plastic basket next to the wall held packets of sugar and artificial sweeteners, salt and pepper shakers, as well as freshly filled bottles of Tabasco sauce and ketchup. A soup cup held a selection of creamers. "I'll have your food out shortly. Y'all wave or something if you need refills."

Michelle raised her eyebrows at her lunch date after their waitress had hurried toward the kitchen. "Hold the mayo? And the chips?"

"I'm eating extra healthy this week. No sugar. No fats. I have lab work at the end of the month." Dave drank his tea, which he'd ordered unsweetened.

Michelle's brow furrowed. "You aren't having any problems, are you?" She was developing strong feelings for Dave. She'd absolutely hate it if anything happened to him.

"Nope. Not at all," he answered sincerely. "Nothing's changed since my last visit. I think I told you then that my doctor said my numbers were up a bit. I'm just doing my best to ward off problems before they happen. Cutting back on the bad stuff. Getting more exercise."

"Smart." She sipped the tea she'd likewise ordered unsweetened. If Allen had given his health the same amount of attention, would he still be alive? She gave her head a shake so subtle she doubted even the man seated across from her noticed. Traveling down the "What If" road wouldn't do any good. The past was the past. She couldn't change it. The future, though…

She felt a smile tug on her lips as she glanced up at Dave. "I can't thank you enough for all your help last weekend."

Wearing faded jeans and a polo shirt, the lawyer had shown up at their booth minutes before the bell in the clock tower of the First Baptist Church had rung five times. The sound marked the craft fair's official close. The last few shoppers hurried off while, from one end of the field to the other, vendors closed up shop for another year. Along with Zeke and Chris, Dave had loaded their equipment into the vehicles and helped break down the tent. At the house, he'd fetched and toted until every last item had been returned to its rightful place.

Leaning forward, Dave placed both hands over his hips and rubbed his lower back. "I'm getting too old for this kind of thing," he complained.

Michelle caught the glimmer of humor in his eyes and knew he wasn't serious. "Maybe I should get you some liniment for your aging, aching muscles," she teased.

"Only if you'll rub it on for me," he returned.

Her face heated when he called her bluff. Without bothering to hide the movement, she fanned her cheeks. There was no sense in denying that the idea of a shirtless Dave intrigued her. She wouldn't even try.

She caught his eye and beamed a winning smile in his direction just as movement near the door caught her attention. Momentarily distracted, she watched as a woman she vaguely recognized bustled down the aisle between the booths and tables. The new arrival sported over-teased hair with flipped-out ends, and Michelle quickly averted her gaze so she wouldn't get caught gawking at the hopelessly out-of-date style. Her bench jiggled as the woman slid into the booth behind her.

"It's so good to see you, darlin'," the new arrival practically shouted. "I'm sorry I'm late, but Kathy was super busy this morning. I almost felt bad for making her try something new with my hair. What do you think?"

"I love it!" squealed the woman who'd been talking on the phone only seconds earlier. "My appointment's next week. Maybe I'll ask her to do mine the same way. Would you mind?"

"Gosh no. You'd look super…"

Michelle lost interest in the conversation

quicker than ice melted on a hot Florida sidewalk. She shot Dave an apologetic look, but he only lifted his eyebrows as if he, too, thought their neighbors' conversation was a little light on substance.

"Here you go, hon." Sally slid their orders onto the table and held up one finger to the women in the next booth. Giving everything another quick survey in case her customers had given in to a temptation to down a bottle of ketchup, she said, "Y'all let me know if you need anything."

Michelle barely had time to nod before the busy waitress dashed off. While Dave piled lettuce and sliced tomato on top of a generous serving of turkey, she added a tiny dollop of blue cheese dressing to her salad.

"Have you heard from Sara lately?" she asked. She tasted her soup while she waited for Dave's answer. It was hot, tomato-based and brimming with green beans, corn and bits of celery. Exactly like she liked it.

Dave swallowed a bite of his sandwich. "Court's in session, so she's busier than usual." He beamed with pride for the daughter who clerked for a judge in Tallahassee. "We only talked for a few minutes on Saturday, but she's planning to be here the week your kids are in town."

"That's wonderful. I'd love for Ashley and Aaron to meet her. They fly in that Friday. Maybe we can have a cookout at the house Saturday afternoon and they can all get to know each other." She grinned. "You can come, too."

"Why, thank you, ma'am. I'll check my calendar." Dave paused for half a sec. "Yep. I'm free." He reached for his glass.

His eyes met hers over the rim, and what Michelle saw in them made her heart beat just a little faster. She broke the connection before anyone else could notice and cleared her throat. Sugar Sand Beach might look like a sleepy little town, but people here loved their gossip. The last thing she or Dave needed was for word to spread that they were a couple before they so much as went out on their first date. A date she was looking forward to more and more.

By unspoken agreement, they stuck to safe topics while they ate. Dave asked about her children, and she filled him in on her latest conversations with the twins. He shared an amusing story about the receptionist in his office. She was in the middle of asking his opinion about a giveaway she'd planned for the inn's grand opening when one of the women in the booth behind her mentioned a restaurant in Panama City. She paused to listen.

"...The Happy something. I can't remember the name."

"The Happy Dolphin? I haven't been there. You have?"

Michelle stilled. The women were discussing Tobias's new place. Whatever she'd intended to say to Dave died on her lips. She pressed one finger over them, signaling him to listen. Which, considering how well the women's voices carried, he'd have no difficulty doing. Michelle was pretty sure Maggie could hear them in her office.

"Charlie and I went two weeks ago. Adorable little place. Nice artwork on the walls. I think you'd like it." Michelle recognized the voice of the woman who'd been talking on the phone.

"I don't know," Eunice whined. "You know how picky I can be. How was the food?"

"Excellent."

The other woman's voice struck a false note that caused Michelle to sit up straighter. She canted her head and listened harder.

"But?" Eunice left the word hanging. "What aren't you saying, Candice?"

The woman named Candice sighed audibly. "You went to the craft fair, right?"

"Huh. You know I did. We kept running into each other there all day. I'd come out of one booth and there you'd be, going into the one next door. Too funny." Eunice laughed.

"Yeah, but did you check out the booth for the inn that's supposed to open this fall?"

"Of course! I wouldn't miss it. You were at your sister's when they had the open house. They've done wonders with that old place. It got me to thinking, Frank's Uncle Pete is coming down to spend his usual two weeks with us this winter. I'm trying to get Frank to put him up at the inn. It would make my life so much easier."

"You don't want him to stay with you?" Candice sounded shocked.

"Have you met Uncle Pete?" From Eunice's tone, everyone within hearing range knew that Pete and Candice were well acquainted. "He can be such a grouch sometimes, don't ya know. Why? Do you think it'd be wrong to have him stay there?"

"I don't know," Candice hedged. "I can't imagine making any member of my family go to a hotel. People might talk. Might say I didn't love them enough. But then, I'm lucky I don't have an Uncle Pete to deal with."

"You don't think that way about me, do you?"

Michelle relaxed a bit as an obviously worried Eunice sought reassurance from her friend. She made a special note to watch for a reservation for someone named Pete in the coming weeks.

"Of course not," Candice declared. "I know you. You're one of the sweetest, most generous people in Sugar Sand Beach. Others might not know you as well as I do. That's all."

"They should mind their own beeswax. Pete is staying at the inn as long as I can talk Frank into it. But I think we got sidetracked. You were telling me about your dinner. I want to hear more about it. Maybe I can get Frank to take me there for our anniversary next month. We're always looking for a new place to try."

The leather cushions of the other booth squeaked, and Michelle pictured the two women leaning closer to each other to share a secret. An odd tension crawled up her back.

"Well, it was the strangest thing," Candice said without bothering to lower her voice. "Our waiter brought out a bread basket to get us started. I hate it when they do that. It always means it's gonna be a long time before I get my real food. Anyway, there were these little crackers in it, and I swear, they tasted exactly the same as the ones I got at the craft fair."

"The spicy ones that came with the fish?"

"Uh-huh."

"That's nothing," Eunice declared. By the way she spoke, she was obviously not impressed by Candice's big reveal. "A lot of restaurants buy things from that big box store in Destin. The cafe and the Dolphin probably just got the same brand or something."

"Maybe," Candice said, but doubt edged her words. "It was strange, though. To get the exact same cracker in two different places. And that's not all."

"What else?"

Michelle thought Eunice was merely humoring her friend. However, she sensed there was more to Candice's story and that she wouldn't like it. She braced herself.

"You know how Charlie always orders the prime rib. He said this one was pretty good. Definitely not the best he's ever had. But good. Me, I chose the special. I'd had a hankering for seafood, and our waiter swore theirs was the best. But you know what?" This time Candice answered her own question without waiting for Eunice's response. "The fish we got at the craft fair was *exactly* the same. Had the same topping on it and everything."

"The mango? Gosh, that was good! I could've eaten a gallon of that all by itself."

"It was incredible," Candice admitted.

"That's why I remember it so well. I'm telling you, the fish I had at the Happy Dolphin tasted exactly the same."

"Are you sure?" Doubt colored Eunice's tone. "I've met that cook at the inn. Nina something. She's a nice lady. All those women are. Why, look at that van they donated and tell me that's not the most generous thing. I can't see any one of them copying another restaurant's recipe. That'd be like stealing."

Michelle's heart sank. She pressed her hand over her lips and slid lower in her seat.

"Well!" Candice said in a huff. "You remember the stink there was two years ago at the bake sale when Mildred Connors tried to pass Betty Gramble's carrot cake recipe off as her own, don't you?"

"Oh, my word! They're still talking about it at the Garden Club. Nobody dares to bring a carrot cake to the meetings anymore. They're all afraid someone will ask if it's Betty's." A sad, wistful note crept into Eunice's voice. "I so love me a good carrot cake."

"Right," Candice said, sounding somewhat mollified. "I mean, how many times have you ever walked into a diner and had a Monte Cristo as good as Maggie's?"

"Well, never," Eunice admitted.

"That's my point. It's not possible for two different cooks to come up with identical dishes. Not unless one of them is cheating."

"I don't know," Eunice said without a whole lot of conviction. "You don't think Nina or one of the others is the one who cheated, do you?"

"Well, it stands to reason, doesn't it? The cafe isn't even open yet. The Happy Dolphin's been around a little while now. It's…" Candice paused. "It's fishy." She brayed a laugh at her own joke.

Menus rustled in the other booth. Having exhausted the topic, the two women turned to a different one. "What are you going to have for lunch?" Candice asked. "I'm gonna have the chicken salad. I love the way they make it here."

"Not me. You've got me wanting a Monte Cristo. Do you think I should have the fries?" Eunice asked.

Michelle's stomach turned over. She pushed the salad she'd barely touched aside while the women behind her began discussing an upcoming club meeting. She looked at Dave. His expression mirrored the same sick feeling she felt in the pit of her stomach.

"I've lost my appetite. Do you mind if we leave?" She'd deliberately kept her voice barely above a whisper to avoid being overheard.

"Good idea." He blotted his lips with his napkin. "Let's talk outside."

Tears formed in Michelle's eyes. She took a deep breath and blinked rapidly. That kept the tears at bay for now, but it wouldn't be long before they overcame her defenses. She hurried out the door before that could happen.

Standing in the shade of the big oak tree in the parking lot a few minutes later, she blotted her eyes with a tissue. When her vision finally cleared, she searched Dave's face for any sign that she might have misunderstood the conversation they'd both overheard. Her hopes faded when worry knotted the lawyer's brows, too.

"I don't understand how this could happen," she moaned. "How could Tobias and Nina have the same recipes?"

"I have no idea." When Dave shook his head, a lock of silver hair fell onto his forehead. He brushed it back. "They're not, um, close, are they?"

She swallowed. "Not at all. You should know, Nina and Tobias have history. A very nasty history. It was a long time ago, but when they broke up, it devastated her. I'm not just talking about your standard issue heartbreak. He destroyed her professionally. That man..." She drew in a breath. "He's a devil, that one. Nina's been afraid he'd pull something ever since he showed up."

"You know you're going to have to tell her what you heard," Dave cautioned. "You don't want her to be blindsided if word gets out."

"Hmph." Michelle ran trembling fingers through her hair. There wasn't a doubt in her mind that Tobias was up to his old, horrible tricks. She needed to make sure Dave understood that, in this case, there was only one side— Nina's.

"Those are Nina's recipes," she insisted. "It took lots of trial and error for her to get them exactly right. Especially the topping for the grouper. I know, because we had fish for dinner every night for weeks while she fine-tuned the recipe. And those crackers? She's been serving those as our afternoon snack since we got here."

Dave held up one hand. "You're preaching to the choir. I've enjoyed enough of Nina's cooking to know she's an excellent chef. She doesn't need to steal someone else's recipes. Furthermore, I don't believe she'd even consider it." Dave's brows smoothed. "There could be something else going on here, though."

"What?" She was ready to grasp at any straw, no matter how slender.

"Maybe it's all a big misunderstanding. Candice could be wrong. The dishes could be similar but not exactly the same."

For two seconds, maybe a tad longer, she held on to that hope before reality came crashing down. "It doesn't matter. You're right—I have to tell Nina, and I have to tell her right away. As loud as those two were talking, it'll be all over town before nightfall."

"I'm afraid that's true." Dave slipped his hands in his pants pockets. "Gossip spreads like wildfire here. And those women? Candice and Eunice? They just tossed a lighted match onto a patch of dry grass."

Michelle buried her head in her hands. She didn't know how Tobias had orchestrated such a devilish trick or what they could do to put an end to his shenanigans. She did know, however, that once she, Reggie, Erin and Nina put their heads together, they'd figure out a way to turn the tables on Nina's personal nemesis. First, though, she had to break the news to Nina.

How was she going to tell one of her best friends that what she feared the most had come to pass?

Sixteen

Nina

"Thanks, Reggie."

Holding the heavy tray, Nina sidestepped through the door and onto the front porch as another glorious Florida sunset faded in the western sky. "Remind me to AirDrop those pictures I took at the craft fair to you. There's some cute ones of Hope and Chris and you."

After they'd served the last of the appetizer plates on Sunday, Reggie and Chris had taken the baby to get her face painted and to see the rabbits in the petting zoo. Someone had given Hope the cutest whiskers and a kitty nose.

"I bet his mom would like to see them," Nina suggested. "How's she doing, by the way?"

"Much better. Her doctor says she can try

going without the cast next week. But she won't be ready to start chasing after Hope for a while yet."

Chris's mom had been hobbling around on a walking cast ever since she'd sprained her ankle. While she recuperated, the handyman had been bringing his daughter to work with him. Along with Zeke's girls, they'd all taken turns watching the baby so Chris could continue to prep the exterior of the inn for the painters.

"That's fine. We've all quite fallen in love with little Hope." Nina nudged Reggie. "I think you have, too."

She chalked Reggie's lack of response up to a sign that her friend wasn't yet ready to discuss her relationship with the baby's father. She turned to Michelle and Erin, who'd already taken their usual places on the porch.

"Nothing fancy tonight, folks," she announced. "Just crackers and iced tea." She lowered the tray onto the coffee table. "But there's a beautiful chicken roasting in the oven for supper. The veggies for tonight's cucumber-and-onion salad came straight out of our own garden. Tea anyone?" She held up a glass.

When no one reached for it, curiosity stirred in her chest. She glanced up. The faces of her three best friends in the world stared back at her.

Erin's eyes were shuttered. A muscle in her jaw ticked. Deep-set lines crisscrossed Reggie's forehead, which aged the younger girl at least ten years. Michelle stared steadfastly at a spot over Nina's shoulder. She gulped.

"What's wrong?" she asked tentatively. She tried to think of something she'd done to put those concerned expressions on her friends' faces and drew a blank. Whatever it was, it had nothing to do with her.

Or the craft fair, either. That had been a huge success. Visitors to their tent had been so interested in the inn that Michelle already had several bookings for the fall, while Erin had fielded so many questions about kayaking that she was thinking of offering eco-tours to both guests and non-guests. But the real draw had been the tidbits from the cafe's menu. Lines for those had formed early and lasted until the supplies ran out. By charging a dollar a plate, they'd recouped all their expenses and then some. Better still, if she didn't count Tobias—and who would?—not one customer had complained about the food or the service.

Michelle expelled a long, forceful breath. "There's something I—we—have to tell you. You'd better sit down."

"O-kay." She held on to the glass of iced tea

while she gave her friends a quick study. "Somebody want to give me a hint? What's this all about?"

"It's Tobias," Erin said.

"I might have known," she whispered. Slowly, she sank onto the cushions of her favorite chair. Mr. Pibbs, who'd been lounging on Reggie's lap, immediately leapfrogged onto hers. As if he sensed she needed comforting, the big tabby propelled himself up until his head rested on her shoulder. Nina stroked the cat from head to tail. She took a fortifying slug of tea and looked up. "What's he done now?"

"I met Dave for lunch at Maggie's earlier today," Michelle began. "He said to tell all of you hello."

Nina gave the dark-haired woman a tentative smile. Michelle deserved to have someone special in her life, and Dave seemed like a nice guy, but where was this going? "What's that have to do with Tobias?"

"I'm getting to it. It's just…well, this isn't the easiest thing to say."

To Nina's horror, Michelle teared up. Her own stomach clenched. She ran through several awful scenarios. "Are the kids okay? Dave and you didn't have a fight or anything, did you?"

"Let her finish," Erin interrupted. "She's getting to it."

"It's all right. No. Nothing like that." Michelle blotted her eyes on the napkin Erin handed her.

Nina gave Mr. Pibbs another thorough rubdown. Whatever was bothering her friends, it couldn't be too bad as long as nothing had happened to the twins. Dave, on the other hand, would have to answer to her—to all of them, really—if he did anything to upset Michelle.

"The problem is, there's an ugly rumor going around town. About you. And Tobias," Michelle began.

"That's ridiculous," Nina scoffed. "There is no me-and-Tobias."

"Not that kind of rumor," Reggie said. The lines across her forehead tightened.

"I'm making a mess of this." Michelle tucked her hair behind her ears. "Let me just put it out there before I make things worse." She took a breath. "There were a couple of women sitting behind us at the diner. I wasn't trying to listen in on their conversation, but it was kind of hard not to—they weren't exactly whispering. One of them, some woman named Candice, had eaten at the Happy Dolphin recently and was convinced that some of the dishes she had there were identical to the ones you served this weekend."

"That's preposterous!" Nina bolted upright so fast, Mr. Pibbs sank his claws into her shoulder in order to hang on. "Yeow!" she exclaimed. Gently, she removed the cat's paws and settled him in her lap. "She had to be wrong."

"That's what I thought. So I had Reggie get takeout from the Dolphin this afternoon. There's no doubt about it. Tobias is using your recipe for these cheese crackers"—Michelle pointed to the small bowl of chips on the tray—"and the grouper. And who knows what else."

"There is something a little bit different about the fish," Reggie put in. "But it's so subtle, I can't put my finger on it. I saved a serving in the fridge in case you wanted to taste it."

"You bet your sweet bippy I do." Nina placed her hands on the arms of her chair and started to rise.

"I'll get it." Reggie jumped up from her seat and disappeared into the house. She returned a few minutes later bearing a takeout container and brandishing a bottle of vodka. After handing the Styrofoam box to Nina, she poured a generous slug over ice before filling the rest of her glass with tea. "You guys might not need this, but I do. Anyone else?" she asked, holding out the bottle.

They passed the vodka around, each one adding a shot to their drinks. When they'd finished, Nina nuzzled Mr. Pibbs. "Sorry, boy. You'll need to get down for a minute while Mommy looks at something." She lowered the kitty to the floor.

Her eyes narrowed as she eyed the package with suspicion. The clasp slid open with the standard squeak. Without looking inside, she wiggled the lid back and forth. "Styrofoam. Please," she hissed. "Do you know how bad this is for the environment?" Nearly all the plastic ended up in landfills, where it might take up to five hundred years to break down. She'd opted for recyclable containers for the cafe.

"Go ahead. Take a look," nudged Michelle.

"Yeah. Okay." No sense in putting off the inevitable. The dish was either hers or it wasn't. Sitting here with a half-opened box on her lap wasn't going to tell her what she needed to know. She let the lid fall open.

Tiny bits of cubed mango and pineapple, a fine dice of red and green pepper, bits of jalapeno and shallots covered a generous serving of grilled, white fish that did, indeed, look like something she'd prepare. She sniffed, her nose easily separating the identifiable smells of lime and garlic. Taking the fork Reggie handed her, she broke off a tiny piece of fish. Done to perfection, it flaked facedown on a buttery sauce. She speared it and tasted celery and paprika up front with back notes of cinnamon and ginger. Before it went on the grill, the fish had been dusted with a combination of spices identical to her house-made mix. She chewed thoughtfully on a piece of mango.

"Crap," she whispered when she'd swallowed.

"The same as yours?" Erin asked.

"Not exactly. But it's close enough. Too close to be a coincidence." She scooped up a forkful of the salsa and let all the flavors roll across her tongue. "This actually isn't the topping I used for the craft fair, but I'm pretty sure it's an earlier version of mine. How on earth…"

She stopped, unable to finish the question. It was impossible for anyone, much less Tobias, to get their grubby little hands on her recipes. Especially the one for the fish. She hadn't decided on the final ingredients for the topping until the week before the craft fair. Not only that, but she didn't keep copies of her recipes anywhere. Not on her computer, where something as simple as a coffee spill could erase a decade's worth of work. Not jotted down on a notepad in the kitchen where a passerby might see it. No, the only written copy was in a journal she kept under lock and key in her room.

"You don't suspect Lily or Megan, do you?" Reggie asked. Zeke's daughters had spent a considerable amount of time working in the kitchen with Nina over the last few weeks.

"I don't see the connection." She dismissed the idea with a wave of her hand. "How would they even know Tobias?"

"Maybe Zeke did some work at the Happy Dolphin?" Erin suggested. "I heard another restaurant had that space last year. I'm sure Tobias had the place remodeled."

"I suppose it's possible that Zeke did some work there. I'll ask him." Nina tugged her phone from her pocket while she gave the idea another minute's thought. Slowly, she shook her head and set her phone aside. "No. Even if Zeke did work there, it still doesn't track. Megan and Lily are eager to learn, but neither of them have the skills to pull this off. It would take someone with years of experience to watch me in the kitchen and figure out the proportions and ingredients I use in a particular dish."

A round of relieved sighs rose from the group. They'd all become quite fond of Zeke's daughters. No one wanted to blame them.

With the girls ruled out, Erin probed deeper. "What about one of men who worked on our own renovations then? I know it's a stretch, but could one of them have picked up an old recipe or something while they were hanging the tarps or building the arches?"

Again she shook her head. "We closed down completely that week. We either ate at Maggie's or had takeout. Besides, at that point, I hadn't finalized the list of dishes for the craft fair. Much less the recipes."

"Who else has been here?" Reggie asked.

She considered the question for a long minute. "The health inspector," she said after a bit. "He stopped by twice." Lance Parker had had nothing but praise for the remodeled kitchen and dining areas. "The county sent the building inspector out." Zeke had pulled the necessary permits and arranged for the required inspections. "That's about it." She'd exhausted her list of possibilities.

"Except for Krystal," Erin said slowly.

Nina's heart sank. "Until I put a stop to it, she was always taking notes on her cell phone," she allowed. "I suppose she could have left it lying around where someone else could see it. But it would take some weird set of coincidences for it to wind up in Tobias's hands."

She chewed her upper lip while she considered this new possibility. For someone who had claimed she wanted to learn from an experienced chef, Krystal had been a disappointment from Day One. Despite tons of encouragement, the young cook had remained distant and, quite frankly, bored with her work. Things had gotten so bad, Nina had decided to let the woman go at the end of her probationary period. But was Krystal a thief? She didn't want to believe it.

"There's only one way to find out." Reggie poured herself a second helping of boozy iced tea and grabbed a handful of crackers. "You'll have to ask her." She popped one of the spicy chips in her mouth.

"I would, except she quit this morning. She didn't bother coming in. Just called and said she wouldn't be back." At the time, Nina thought the girl had seen the writing on the wall and saved them both from a difficult conversation. Now she wasn't so sure.

"That ends that." Michelle leaned forward until her elbows rested on her knees. "You can't very well call a former employee and accuse them of being careless...or worse." Her brow smoothed. "Look, we may never find out how Tobias got hold of your recipes, but that's not the real problem. The problem is, he has them. I'm worried that people, like Candice and Eunice, might believe they were his to begin with."

"It's happened before, but I'll die before I let

it happen again." Nina jumped to her feet. "I'll just go to the Happy Dolphin—what kind of a name is that, anyway? I'll go there and confront him." She put a hand out to steady herself.

"Whoa there, Nelly. Hold your horses." Erin grabbed her by the arm. "You're not going anywhere. None of us are. Not after having a drink or two. Let's just sit back down, and we'll all work on a plan that doesn't involve someone getting arrested."

Nina remained upright but swayed. Drinking vodka on an empty stomach probably hadn't been her best idea. Her thoughts felt muddled, confused. Slowly, carefully, she sat down. The moment she did, though, a fresh worry hit her.

"You said those women..." She looked to Michelle.

"Candice and Eunice?"

"Yeah, them. They think I'm the one who stole Tobias's recipes?"

Michelle's fine features puckered. "Candice did. Eunice wasn't convinced."

Nina formed a steeple with her hands. She pressed it to her face, her thumbs under her chin. Michelle was right. It didn't matter how her recipes had ended up in Tobias's possession; once he'd served her dishes in his restaurant, the damage was done. She'd have to leave.

"I have to go," she whispered. "It might take me a few days, but I'll start packing tomorrow."

"What?" three voices chorused at the same time.

"What are you talking about?" Erin asked. "You're not going anywhere."

She shook her head. "It's best for everybody if I do. Tobias has pulled the same dirty trick before. This time won't be any different. He'll take full advantage of the situation. Once the rumors and the whispers start, and they will start—people like Candice and Tobias will see to it—once they start, they'll paint me with a brush so black, I'll never get clean. But it's not me I'm worried about. I can't take the chance I'll pull you and the inn down with me. That's why I have to go."

"Well, that's about the dumbest thing I've ever heard. You're going to walk away without a fight?" Erin asked.

"Yeah, don't you want to clear your name?" Reggie demanded.

"What I want and what I can have are two different things," she insisted.

"Stop." Michelle grabbed her by the wrist and held on tight. "Just stop all this foolishness. You. Are. Not. Leaving. We've got your back. Whatever happens, we are all in this together."

"All for one and one for all," Reggie chimed.

"You don't understand," Nina insisted. She had to make them see how badly this could hurt them. "If people side with Tobias, you could lose everything. This house. The land. All the money you've invested. No one will book a room at an inn where a dark cloud hangs over the kitchen. No one will trust a guide who befriends a cheater. The people in Sugar Sand Beach will turn their backs on all of us."

Michelle's grip tightened. "None of this—not the house, not the inn, none of it will be worth having if you're not a part of it," she said simply.

The words sliced straight into Nina's heart like a sharp knife cut through a tomato. Tears ran in rivulets down her cheeks. Reggie clasped her other hand and wept silently while a damp-eyed Erin slung an arm around her sister's shoulders.

"Okay. I guess you've left me no choice," Nina said, her voice shaky with emotion. "I'll stay."

For a long time, they sat where they were. One by one, they straightened at last, grabbed glasses of tea and a chip or two and sat back in their chairs. By the time they'd stopped sniffling and had used up all the napkins drying their eyes, stars twinkled in the dark sky. Along the sidewalk that led to the parking area, a faint

301

glow came from the solar lights Reggie had installed. The distant sound of waves lapping the Gulf shore filled the air when Erin broke the silence.

"Now that that's decided," she said, "what are we going to do about Tobias?"

Seventeen

Nina

At first glance, the Happy Dolphin looked like the kind of place that should attract a crowd. The dining area was certainly lovely. Ferns and philodendron with glossy green leaves spilled from wooden boxes mounted in simple room dividers that lent a sense of privacy to each table while maintaining the restaurant's open, airy feel. Soothing instrumental music poured from hidden speakers. Arranged in tasteful groupings, photographs of some of Florida's most scenic spots dotted the pale, yellow walls. But on what should have been a busy Friday evening, maybe half the tables were filled. Discreet "reserved" placards leaned against bud vases on only a few of the empty ones.

To Nina's practiced eye, the problem lay in spotty service. The wait staff moved in fits and starts about the room as they refilled beverages and memorized the items their guests chose from menus written on small chalkboards. Occasional runners ferried plates from the kitchen at the back of the house. At a nearby table, two men grumbled impatiently over their cooling meals while they waited for the dishes their wives had ordered. Nina surveyed the clutter of uncleared dishes and half-empty glasses that had slowly filled their own corner table over the last two hours.

Spotty service caused by a slow kitchen, she clarified.

Following their usual custom, she, Michelle, Reggie and Erin had ordered one of every appetizer, which they'd divvied up between them. Although no one had much of an appetite, they'd also sampled several entrees.

Nina pushed her plate away. "I've had enough," she declared. The bright prick of tears stung her eyes. She blinked to hold them at bay. She was too angry to cry. That could come later, after she'd said her piece.

Erin aligned her knife and fork at the center of her plate, the stacked bracelets on her wrist jingling softly. "This is worse than I'd feared."

"I know, right?" Reggie asked. Her sequined top reflected tiny shards of light as she gave her head a sad shake.

The very image of poise and sophistication in a little black dress, Michelle pursed her lips. "Think we could boil Tobias in a vat of cooking oil?"

The question had rolled so unexpectedly off Michelle's tongue that Nina laughed in spite of herself. She caught her breath and pitched her voice low. "How about we hang him from a meat hook?"

"And leave him there until he changes his wicked, wicked ways," Reggie added.

"We could cook up a big pot of Tobias Fricassee or Chili," Erin suggested.

"Now that's the stuff of Southern legends." Nina's eyes sparkled again, but this time laughter, not anger, triggered her tears. "I have the best friends," she sighed, wiping her eyes. "I'd be lost without all of you."

"Now don't go getting all sentimental on us," Erin advised. "We still have a job to do."

Nina sobered. "So I'm not wrong?" She needed reassurance.

"You're not wrong." Seated on her right, Erin patted her hand. At least six of Nina's recipes were represented on the table.

It was time.

Nina blotted her lips with a napkin and signaled their waiter. A momentary pang of sympathy for the guy struck her. Tobias was apt to rake him over the coals later this evening. She hoped the tip she'd leave would make up for the unassuming role he'd play in tonight's events.

"Would you see if the chef has a moment?" she asked when, bending at the waist, the man leaned down. "We'd like to speak with him if we could." She indicated her friends with a flick of her wrist.

Like any good waiter would, the man scanned the table. Seeing only the smiling faces of customers who'd ordered extensively from the menu while they sipped on an expensive bottle of wine, he nodded. "I'll see if he's free."

All he needed was a blare of trumpets, Nina thought, watching Tobias make his grand entrance only minutes later. The chef strutted into the dining area wearing a towering toque blanche that threatened to fall off his head with every step. As he must have expected, a murmur of awareness swept the room. Like a banty rooster's, his chest puffed out beneath his chef's whites. He waved and grinned at several diners while he stopped to have a quiet word with the waiter, who tactfully steered his boss toward Nina's table.

The instant Tobias's gaze landed on her, she swore guilt flickered in the man's eyes. His jovial smile definitely dimmed there for a second. But now that he'd barged into the room, Tobias was committed. He couldn't very well hightail it back to the kitchen without arousing suspicion or, at the very least, curious looks and whispers. Nina watched him regroup, watched the plastic smile reassemble on his face. His arms wide, he crossed the short distance to their table like a gracious party host.

"Nina!" he exclaimed as if he'd happened upon an old friend. "I had no idea you were dining with us tonight. Your name wasn't in the book."

"I'm here with my friends," she said by way of explanation. She'd seen chefs scour the reservations for VIPs, big spenders or troublemakers. Not wanting to tip her hand only to be told that the Dolphin was booked solid for the next three months, she'd asked Zeke to make the reservations.

"I trust you enjoyed your meal. Everything to your liking?" Tobias's grin widened until Nina thought his face might crack.

"It was more or less what I'd expected." Mostly less, she added silently. At the prices Tobias was charging, the tiny servings had come as an unpleasant surprise. So had the unannounced substitutions, like the garden-variety parsley the chef had used in his pesto instead of the oregano promised on the menu.

"You must have one of our fine desserts. Compliments of the house, of course."

"Let me guess—lemon bars or mini éclairs?" Nina arched a brow. She'd served both at the craft fair.

Tobias's smile withered. His voice lost its effusive quality. "Listen, Nina. I have no idea what you think you're…"

She cut him off with a wave of her hand. "Since, apparently, you don't understand, I'll spell it out as plainly as I can." Maintaining a neutral tone was difficult, but she battled down the urge to yell at the man. "Your dishes are rather *familiar*, aren't they?"

She gestured to the meals the four of them had barely touched. She had to give Tobias credit for sneakiness. Other than the grouper and the chips—which she could tie directly to her recipes—he'd deconstructed every item she'd served at the craft fair and incorporated the various parts into his own dishes. The meatballs she'd skewered and served as an appetizer had been artfully arranged atop a bed of salad greens. He'd used her grandmother's recipe for short-crust to make seafood hand pies and reserved her Bolognese sauce for pasta. Her voice turned to steel. "I can't help but ask how you came up with the exact same recipes as mine...this time."

As if someone had thrown a switch, Tobias's demeanor changed. His jaw hardened. His eyes darkened. They narrowed to glittering slits. The hands he'd folded below his waist fisted and landed on his hips. Gone was the fake, obsequious chef. In its place stood an angry bull of a man.

"How dare you! You insult me in my own restaurant?" Tobias's voice bounced off the walls of the corner table and reverberated through the open spaces. Several patrons looked up in alarm. At the table of impatient diners, one woman aimed her cell phone in their direction. "I'll have you know I personally created every item on this menu."

"Oh?" Though she wanted to yell right back at Tobias, Nina forced herself to remain calm and reasonable. "Where'd you come up with the idea to use bison in the meatballs? Or to add chicken livers to the Bolognese? I chose bison, not because it's leaner—which it is—but because it's rich in Omega-3's. And the chicken livers? They add a layer of depth to the sauce."

Tobias's voice turned guttural. "I don't have

to answer to you. You're just desperate to keep your little cafe from going under. You think you can hurt me? Me?" He struck his chest with one fist. "You're nothing but a washed-up has-been. A crab scrambling to escape the pail by pulling down all his brothers who've made it to the top. Get out! Get out of my—"

"Chef Tobias!"

The harsh, commanding voice interrupted Tobias in mid-rant. The chef froze solid as a hand landed on his shoulder with a clap that resounded from one end of the restaurant to the other. The noise made several customers, including Erin, gasp.

"Chef Tobias, I believe you're needed in the kitchen," the newcomer said in a tone that made it clear the subject was not up for discussion.

Nina's gaze shifted between Tobias, whose mouth worked soundlessly, and the new arrival. Despite the rumpled, souvenir T-shirt the man wore over a pair of well-worn Dockers, he clearly exerted some level of authority in the restaurant. An investor? A manager? Whoever he was, she was thankful he'd shown up when he did.

"Now," the other man said firmly when Tobias remained rooted to the spot. He propelled the chef forward with a pat on the back.

Muttering under his breath, Tobias went.

Growing more certain that the newcomer owned the restaurant, Nina watched while he turned to face the other diners. His voice carried well in the room that had gone eerily quiet. "My apologies for interrupting your dinner. Our chef can be a bit hot-tempered, as creative people are known to be." His shoulders rose and fell in a shrug that produced a titter of nervous laughter from several of the tables. "I'm deeply sorry for his outburst. I hope you'll let me make it up to you. Michael?"

At the coffee station, one of the tuxedoed waiters nodded.

"Please serve a complimentary dessert to each of our guests."

"Yes, sir," Michael nodded.

Addressing the room again, the man said, "I'll also see that each of you receives a gift certificate you can use the next time you visit us here at the Dolphin."

At the announcement, the concerned and curious expressions at many of the tables changed into forgiving smiles. A smattering of applause rose and quickly fell. The woman who'd filmed the entire episode tucked her cell phone into her purse. A soft cough from Michael propelled the staff into motion.

While waiters and waitresses hustled through

the restaurant replenishing drinks and taking dessert orders, the stranger turned to Nina's table. He scanned the foursome, his gaze turning quizzical when it reached Erin. His head canted. "Erin?" he asked.

"Walt," Erin answered. "Um, what's going on?"

"I was about to ask you all the same question. What'd you do to my chef?"

"Your chef?" Erin frowned.

"I own the Happy Dolphin." Walt stopped himself. "Well, not the entire restaurant. But I do hold a majority share."

"I had no idea," Erin whispered. "When you said you owned businesses in Panama City, I guess I assumed…" Her voice faded as she appeared to realize they weren't alone. She cleared her throat. "Michelle, Reggie, Nina, this is Walter Denton, Polly's son."

Michelle's head whipped around so fast, her hair flew to one side. "Our Polly?"

Erin grinned. "The one and only. Walt and Polly stopped by our booth at the craft fair."

"I thought you looked vaguely familiar," Reggie exclaimed. She wagged a finger back and forth between her sister and the restaurant owner. "So that's where you two…Small world."

"Quite," Walt agreed. He stuck his hands in his pockets and rocked back on his heels. "Now, would one of you like to tell me why my chef came completely unglued?"

"I believe I'm responsible." Afraid her hands might tremble if she tried to shake the man's hand, Nina only nodded. "I'm Nina Gray. Head chef at the Sugar Sand Inn and Cafe."

"You prepared the food Mom and I had at the craft fair," Walt said, putting two and two together. He gave a polite bow. "My compliments. I thoroughly enjoyed every morsel." He peered closer. "Now what was this fuss all about?"

Recognizing that this was her one and only chance to make her case, Nina took a breath while she framed her answer in a short sentence. She looked the man square in the eye and said, "The menu at the Happy Dolphin relies heavily on recipes Tobias stole from me."

As if by reflex, Walt's arms folded across his chest. "That's a serious accusation."

"I'm aware," she assured him. "This isn't something I take lightly." Leaving the ball in Walt's court, she looked away just in time to catch a sidelong glance from the woman at the next closest table. A woman who obviously was listening in on their entire conversation. She tilted her head in the diner's direction. "It might be best if we moved this discussion someplace a little more, um, private," she suggested.

Walt must have caught her drift, because he asked her to join him in his office.

For Walt's sake, Nina agreed. So far, the man had done an excellent job of mollifying his customers and soothing any ruffled feathers, but another heated discussion would undoubtedly lead to several bad reviews on social media. Get too many of those, and a new restaurant was doomed. She had no interest in destroying Walt's livelihood. Especially now that she knew how he was related to Polly.

She turned to Erin. "Come with me?"

Ordinarily, she'd want Michelle's cool head by her side, but Erin and Walt had a connection, no matter how tenuous. Which might come in handy. If she had any hope of clearing her name and getting any kind of justice at all, she'd need all the help she could get.

Eighteen

Nina

"I t's the third door on the left," Walt said. After waiting for a runner to pass carrying a heavily loaded tray, he pointed down a narrow hallway that led off from the main corridor. "I'll join you in a minute."

Nina wasn't at all surprised when Walt continued on toward the kitchen at the back of the restaurant. Regardless of whether the man believed her or not, she had no doubt a discussion of the decorum he expected of his chef lay in Tobias's immediate future. Without a word, she followed the owner's directions to his office.

"Tiny, isn't it?" Erin asked as they stepped inside.

"It's actually quite spacious compared to

some," she replied. In restaurants where every possible square foot was devoted to paying customers, owners and managers often shared cramped quarters. In this one, a small desk and several file cabinets took up most of the floor space. Piles of receipts and the soft hum of a computer told them the owner had been working on the books when he'd either overheard the fracas in the dining area or been summoned there by concerned staff.

True to his word, Walt joined them a scant minute later. He propped himself on one corner of the desk and got straight to the point. "You say Chef Tobias stole your recipes. It's quite obvious he disagrees. Why should I believe you over him?"

Nina's respect for Polly's son rose a notch. He could have blindly taken Tobias's side. Instead, he was giving her a chance to prove she was in the right.

"Because I'm telling the truth," she answered. She pulled herself erect while she did an admirable job of not squirming under Walt's searing gaze. "The recipe for the short-crust he uses in his seafood hand pies was handed down to me by my grandmother. She and I used that exact same recipe for fruit tarts, which we made every summer on her farm."

"Tell him about the crackers," Erin urged.

"Okay," she nodded. "The original recipe came from an author who served them at the launch party for her latest book. I asked her for the recipe, and she gave it to me. I've tinkered with it a bit—added more spice, punched up the flavor until I was happy with it. But Erin will tell you, I've been making those crackers for years."

"She's telling the truth." Erin held up two fingers. "Scout's honor. We brought a big bag of them with us on the way down here from Virginia."

Walt gave his chin a thoughtful rub. "You certainly sound sincere, but you must realize I have an obligation to Tobias. I stopped by the kitchen on my way here and asked him to join us." The sound of heavy footsteps echoed from the hallway. "That's probably him now."

Sure enough, sans his impressive hat, the chef barged into the room two seconds later. "Listen, Walt. I shouldn't'a lost my temper out there." He hooked one thumb over his shoulder toward the dining room. "But I won't stand…"

The instant Tobias realized he and Walt weren't alone, Nina swore the temperature in the office plummeted twenty degrees. At the same time, the stench of garlic and sweat wafted over her. She coughed. "Geez, Toby. Shower much?" she asked dryly. She took his growl as a no.

"What're they doing here?" the angry chef demanded. "You're not letting them fill your head with their lies, are you, Walt?"

"We're just talking, Chef." Walt held up both hands. "Trying to resolve this beef between you two before both our restaurants suffer."

"Tell her to get out and stay out, and that'll be the end of it." Tobias folded his thick arms across his chest.

"All in good time, Chef," Walt said. "All in good time." He took a breath, seemed to consider what he wanted to say next, then focused all his attention on the man who ran his kitchen. "Chef Nina was just telling me the origin stories of a couple of her recipes. I'm sure yours are just as valid and interesting. I'd like to hear how you came up with the idea for using bison in those little meatballs. Aren't they usually made with beef?"

"You want to know why I switched? I don't see why I should have to defend myself," Tobias retorted while pinning Nina with a look that made her skin crawl. "But I'll tell you why. 'Cause bison's loaded with Omega-3's. Less fat, too. It's healthier for you than beef."

"Son of a—" Nina swore under her breath. Not twenty minutes earlier she'd hand-fed those lines to Tobias. That was one mistake she'd never make again. Crossing her fingers behind her back, she prayed the owner wouldn't ask Tobias about the Bolognese sauce. If he did, she might as well kiss her career goodbye now. She breathed a tiny bit easier when Walt's next question concerned a new addition to the Happy Dolphin's offerings.

"You added grouper to our menu about two weeks ago. Why was that?"

Tobias shrugged. He adopted a patronizing tone. "We change things up all the time. That's why we opted for those little chalkboards instead of printed menus—so it's easy to take advantage of fruits and vegetables when they're in season."

"A reasonable answer," Walt declared. "Thank you, Chef. I take it you deny there's any truth to Chef Nina's accusations? You didn't, shall we say, *borrow* her recipes?"

"Humph." Tobias's upper lip curled. "I couldn't have. I've never even stepped foot in her kitchen."

Nina let her eyes narrow. Tobias had avoided giving Walt a direct answer. Instead, he'd insisted that he hadn't been in her kitchen. Which was true, as far as it went. But it didn't eliminate the possibility that someone else had done the job for him.

She shook her head. She was searching for a

lifeline, and she knew it. No one—not even her best friends—knew about her journal or where she hid it. The odds of some stranger getting into the house without anyone noticing and stumbling upon her hiding place were so small, she couldn't even calculate them.

Walt idly scratched the back of his hand while he thought for a moment. "Well, it seems we've reached an impasse," he announced finally. "Chef Nina, isn't it possible that you and Chef Tobias developed similar recipes independent of one another?"

Her head snapped up. Walt was giving her an out. Asking her to withdraw her complaint and go on her merry way, no harm, no foul. From her perspective, though, his solution had one major flaw. Trust. She didn't trust Tobias to play fair any further than she could throw him. And yeah, yoga kept her strong and flexible, but that didn't mean she could pick up a man who had fifty pounds on her and toss him into the compost heap. No matter how much she might want to.

"I'm afraid I don't buy it," she said, her voice heavy. "I don't believe Tobias just happened to decide to serve grouper at the Happy Dolphin. Or that he came up with the exact blend of spices, fruits and vegetables it took me weeks to create. Any more than I believe he crawled out of bed one morning with a sudden urge to add chicken livers to his Bolognese. Or that he magically came up with the same mix of flour, salt, butter and ice water my grandmother used in her pastry. And I certainly don't believe he duplicated my recipe for lemon bars on his own. He's allergic to lemons." She'd learned that little fact over ten years ago when she'd been experimenting with limoncello recipes. Tobias had picked up a piece of peel and broken out in hives.

"Ha!" Tobias exclaimed. "That proves it! I didn't create the lemon bars. My sous chef did," he taunted.

"Amber?" Walt asked.

"Yeah." Tobias swiped his hairline, where a fresh batch of sweat beaded. "She was happy to have one of her own creations added to the menu."

The minute the moisture trickled down her former lover's temples, Nina knew without a doubt the man was lying through his teeth. But about what? That whoever this Amber was, she'd created the dessert? Or that she'd happily turned the recipe over to Tobias?

"I'd like to hear how she came up with the dish," Nina said, her eyes on Walt. "Could she join us? Just to, you know, back up Toby's story."

"Absolutely not," Tobias argued. The realization that bringing Amber's name into the discussion had been a mistake dawned on his face for everyone to see. "While I'm wasting my time in here, she's running the kitchen."

The owner breathed so deeply, his nostrils flared. He picked a handful of the receipts up from his desk and put them down again. He had clearly grown tired of the issue and was anxious to return to crunching numbers and balancing budgets.

"Please, Walt," Erin intervened. "Get her in here and we can settle this once and for all."

But Tobias refused to go along with the plan, no matter how sensible it sounded to anyone else. "No." He stomped his foot. "I won't allow it."

The look Walt gave Tobias made Nina very thankful she wasn't on the receiving end of it. The owner's voice slowed, and his drawl became more pronounced.

"After this is over, you and I will have a serious discussion of where your authority ends and mine begins in this restaurant," he warned Tobias. "For now, though…"

Walt whipped his phone out of his pocket and hit a button. Within seconds, he spoke into the mouthpiece. "Amber, come to my office, please. Right away."

Nina's stomach churned. This was it. The moment of truth. Her career and reputation were on the line. Even with Erin's backing, she hadn't been able to convince Walt she was telling the truth. If she couldn't clear her name, right here and right now, a dark cloud would follow her wherever she went. She held her breath and waited for Tobias's assistant, knowing her fate hung on the woman's answer. Would Amber confirm his story? Or deny it?

Beside her, Erin whispered, "Relax. It'll all be okay."

She wished she shared her friend's confidence. The fact was, she didn't. At this particular point in time, there were only two things she knew for sure. First, that Toby was lying. And second, that the chef did not want his assistant to join them. Which, to tell the truth, was the only thing that gave her the slightest sliver of hope.

At a soft tapping, panic rose in Tobias's eyes. While Nina and the others watched in incredulous silence, the chef braced one hand against the door and kept whoever was on the other side from opening it. Like a cornered animal, he went on the offense.

"I can't work for a man who doesn't trust me. This is your last chance, Walt. You either accept me at my word and send Amber back to the kitchen, or I'll walk. The choice is up to you."

Nina had heard people talk about a tension so thick they could cut it with a knife, but she'd never fully understood the phrase. Not till now. Her gaze shifted between Tobias's obstinate jaw and the look of pure dismay that colored Walt's expression.

"You'd do that?" the owner asked. "Leave in the middle of the dinner service? Without giving notice?"

"I'm not going to have you questioning my integrity every time I turn around. You either believe me, or you don't. You open that door, I'll take it as a sign that you don't. In that case, I'm outta here." The smirk on Tobias's face told everyone in the room he was certain he had the owner over a barrel. "Without a head chef, it'll be interesting to see how long you can keep this place afloat," he added, just in case Walt hadn't understood what was at stake.

Tobias was probably counting on the owner to be more interested in the bottom line than in ferreting out the truth. But Nina thought the other chef had seriously underestimated his boss. She wrested her gaze from Tobias and fixed it on Walt. He'd grown up in Sugar Sand Beach. He knew better than she did how deep the sense of camaraderie ran in the small town. His own mother was well past retirement age, yet she still flipped the sign on the door of Polly's Posies from Closed to Open promptly at ten each morning. She served on the town council and had her finger in every pie that had ever been baked in their little patch of sand and seagrass. Why? Because it would make her rich? Nope. Because she cared deeply for the people around her, and she didn't suffer fools lightly. Unless Nina was seriously mistaken, Polly had instilled those same values in her son.

"So be it," Walt said, reaching a decision at last. The tension that had carved harsh lines in his face faded. His shoulders relaxed, but when he spoke, his voice was firm, even, decisive. "Open the door, Tobias," he commanded.

A heady mix of shock and disbelief drained all the color from Tobias's face, leaving it nearly as white as his chef's coat. As the full weight of the mistake he'd made started to sink in, he did as he was told with a shaky hand.

"Out of my way," he snarled.

A slim figure in white stepped aside as he barreled past.

"Tobias?" The woman called after him. The chef didn't slow his headlong march down the hall. Moments later, a door slammed.

Was that it?

Nina shook her head. Tobias's hasty departure sure looked like guilty admission, but she still had questions. Like, how had he gotten his grubby hands on her recipes? And how was all this going to help clear her name?

"Look!" Erin jabbed her with an elbow.

She followed her friend's pointed glance to the doorway, where Tobias's second-in-command stood. Nina blinked and rubbed her eyes. Was she seeing things?

"Krystal? What are you doing here?" Before the words were even out of her mouth, all the puzzle pieces slid into place. She spared a quick look at Erin, who wore a knowing smile.

Still perched on the corner of his desk, Walt looked confused. "Who's Krystal?"

"She is." Nina pointed a finger at the young brunette who'd failed to show up for work on the Monday following the craft fair. "She's been working as my part-time assistant for the past month. I assume she rushed straight here from the inn each day and spilled all my secrets to Toby." A new thought crystalized. "Or texted them to him."

Walt's mouth gaped open. "Amber? Is this true?"

Whatever her name was, the young cook

stared at the floor. To his credit, Walt didn't hesitate. "You're fired," he said, pointing a finger at the woman who looked like she might dissolve in a puddle of tears at any moment. "Clear out your locker and leave. If I were you, I wouldn't try to find work within a hundred miles of here. That goes double for your boyfriend." He leaned forward. "He is your boyfriend, right?"

"Well." Krystal/Amber's voice hitched. "He was." Her uncertain glance down the hall said that particular matter was up for debate.

Nina wavered on the verge of letting the young chef walk out the door. The girl had done a horrible, despicable thing, and she deserved to lose her job over it. But once upon a time, she'd stood in the woman's kitchen clogs. She knew how it felt to be blinded by love. In her case, it had cost her dearly. It nearly had this time, too. But she wanted Krystal to know there could be a light at the end of the tunnel.

"You can come back from this," she said softly. "If you want it bad enough, you can learn from your mistakes, start over. It'll take hard work and dedication, but you can…"

"No, thanks." Krystal/Amber reached up and pulled a few pens from her head. Her pale hair fell around her shoulders. "I've decided restaurant work is not for me. It's too hot and too messy, and it ruins my manicure. My daddy owns a big real estate company in Indiana. I'll give that a try. I'll get to wear nice clothes and makeup and get my nails done every week." With that, she flounced out of the office.

"Oh. My. Word," Nina gasped. Laughter bubbled up from her midsection.

Erin clasped her arm. "Have you ever...?" She dissolved into giggles.

Walt's hearty laughter joined theirs. For the next few minutes, they replayed the scene.

"It ruins my manicure," Erin cackled and laughed some more.

"Makeup and nice clothes?" Nina chortled.

Walt sobered first. "I don't know why I'm laughing." He wiped his eyes. "The good Lord only knows what's going on in the kitchen now that both my two top people have left." He caught his breath. "Not that I'm sad to see them go in the least. I won't abide cheaters and liars in my restaurant." He cast a pleading look at Nina.

"Chef Nina, I know it's a huge ask, but if you could see your way clear to taking over my kitchen, I'd be forever in your debt."

Nina slowly considered the pros and cons. Other than taking time away from the cafe—which wasn't opening anytime soon—she couldn't think of a single reason why she shouldn't lend a hand. It was the neighborly thing to do. Plus, building a good relationship with the restaurant owner couldn't hurt, to say nothing of the boost it would give her own reputation.

"I can give you a week. Two at the most," she offered. "I'll help you find someone who can take over on a permanent basis, too. I know a lot of chefs who'd jump at the chance to move here from Virginia." She could think of one in particular.

"That's more than generous of you." Walt bobbed his head. "And frankly, more than I deserve after the trick Tobias and Amber pulled."

Nina shrugged. "Not your fault. We both had the wool pulled over our eyes by those two. Tobias fooled you. Amber or Krystal or whatever her name is, she fooled me, too. Besides, this'll be a piece of cake." She lifted one eyebrow. A sly smile worked its way across her lips. "After all, I already know all the recipes."

Nineteen

Erin

E rin plumped the cushions on the porch furniture. Choosing her favorite—a high-back chair with a skosh more room than the others, she sank onto it with a contented sigh. A single serving of Nina's Gulf Coast Sunset stood at her elbow on the glass-topped table. It wasn't often she had the house all to herself, and she intended to make the most of it. She propped her feet up, ready to enjoy a cool evening breeze to the melodic accompaniment of waves rushing to the shore.

This week's copy of the *Sugar Sand Beach Gazette* lay, folded, on the table. She usually read the paper from the front page to the comics as soon as it arrived. Not for the hard-hitting national coverage, of which there was absolutely none, but for the human interest stories that detailed the comings and goings of her neighbors and friends, their losses and their celebrations.

Two weeks ago, articles covering every aspect of the town's Fourth of July celebrations had filled the entire paper. From a full-color photograph of fireworks on the beach above the front page fold to an editorial note thanking the organizers and committee members who'd put together another successful weekend, no detail had been considered too small to mention. Pictures of the van she and her friends had donated made the bottom half of the front page. A sidebar listed all the businesses and individuals who'd filled the vehicle to overflowing with gifts. The rest of the eight-page weekly had covered everything from descriptions of the homemade floats in the parade to a story about the wreath-maker whose booth won a blue ribbon in the craft fair.

Erin sipped her drink and picked up this week's Gazette. It wasn't actually the copy she'd retrieved from the end of their driveway earlier. Nina had snatched that one out of her hands and taken it straight to her room. Erin didn't blame her, even though she'd had to make a special trip to the grocery store to get another copy. Or copies—she'd bought up every one she could get her hands on. Now she paged past all the other small-town news and went straight for the Dine In Sugar Sand column near the back.

She refolded the paper so only that section showed. Leaning back in her chair, she smoothed the creases and settled in to read about the night a reviewer from the Gazette had ventured all the way to Panama City to check out a relatively new restaurant.

...On my recent visit to the Happy Dolphin in nearby Panama City, this reporter got more than she'd bargained for in the form of ringside entertainment when the restaurant's head chef, Tobias, went on a rant. The object of the angry cook's diatribe was none other than Sugar Sand Beach's very own Nina Gray, an excellent chef in her own right, as anyone who attended this year's festivities on the Fourth of July can attest. There was quite the flare-up over the ownership of certain recipes, and diners worried that the dueling chefs might come to blows until owner Walt Denton intervened.

Unlike Chef Tobias's prime rib—which this reviewer deemed as dry as the proverbial bone—this story gets juicier and juicier. According to an unnamed source, in his hunt for new recipes, Chef Tobias allegedly planted his assistant, Krystal, undercover as Chef Nina's assistant. The conniving Krystal then made copies of Chef Nina's recipes (including the one for those tasty meatballs we all enjoyed at the inn's open house) and handed them off to her boss. At which point Chef Tobias claimed he'd created them all by himself.

When Chef Nina uncovered the diabolical plot, she had no option but to confront the thief, who then defended himself quite stringently in full view of diners and staff. Things got dicey for a bit while the owner dug deep into the competing chefs' stories, not giving up until he uncovered the truth. Word is Walt Denton fired Chef Tobias and his ne'er-do-well assistant on the spot.

But that's not all. In a move that was far more than gracious considering how the ex-chef had wronged her, Chef Nina has temporarily taken over the kitchen at the Happy Dolphin while Walt, one of Sugar Sand's favorite sons, searches for a new head chef.

Bravo for Chef Nina and her Sugar Sand Cafe! Be sure to visit the restaurant when it opens in the fall. This intrepid reviewer definitely will.

Chuckling, Erin let the newsprint slide onto her lap. Planning to someday frame the article and hang it on the wall, she flapped the pages open. While she smoothed out the creases, she spotted an ad for the hardware store right next to a small article about a tropical wave that had formed off the coast of Africa. She shook her head in wonder at a paper that didn't cover national news but fretted over a storm on the other side of the Atlantic. She stretched her arms over her head and yawned.

A pair of headlights caught her attention as a vehicle turned off the main road. Curious, she tracked the car's movement up the driveway to the house. She tilted her head. It was too early for Reggie and Michelle to return from the movie they'd gone to see in Destin. They'd invited her to join them, of course, but she'd begged off. She and Megan planned to check out a new fishing spot in the morning, and she'd learned long ago that late nights and early wake-ups didn't mix.

It wasn't Nina, either. This was the chef's final week at the Happy Dolphin. Though they'd all agreed that taking over Walt's kitchen presented a rare and wonderful opportunity, no one—not even the chef herself—thought making the hour-long drive home from Panama City in the middle of the night on her own was a good idea. So while Erin and her friends took turns ferrying Nina to her temporary job each day, Zeke had made it his mission to give the chef a ride back after the Dolphin closed each night.

But that would come to an end soon. A grill master Nina had worked with in Virginia had accepted the position as Walt's new head chef. Charlie and his family would arrive this weekend. By Monday, Nina would be back at work in her own kitchen, preparing for the grand opening, which was getting closer every day. As for her relationship with Zeke, Erin suspected they'd all be seeing a lot more of the handsome carpenter in the coming months.

But if Michelle and Reggie or Zeke and Nina weren't coming up the driveway, who was?

The unexpected visitor slowly drove into the graveled parking area and stopped. A rusty hinge squeaked as the new arrival stepped out of an older Land Rover. Hampered by the deepening twilight, Erin studied the approaching figure. Should she head inside and lock the doors? She laughed at the thought. What kind of innkeeper greeted potential guests with locked doors and barred windows? Besides, there was something oddly comforting in the outline of the man who had headed up the walkway toward the porch where she sat. As he emerged out of the shadows, she recognized the square set of wide shoulders that angled to a narrow waist above muscular thighs. Warmth spread through her chest.

"R-Ron." Her tongue tripped over the name she'd once uttered a dozen times a day. When he stepped into the light that spilled from the porch, she asked, "What brings you to the Sugar Sand Inn?"

Thank you for reading
The Cafe At Sugar Sand Inn!

If you loved this book and want to help the series
continue,
take a moment to leave a review!

Want to know what happens next in
Sugar Sand Beach?

Sign up for Leigh's newsletter to get the latest
news
about upcoming releases, excerpts, and more!
https://leighduncan.com/newsletter/

Acknowledgements

Every book takes a team effort. I want to give special thanks to those who made The Gift at Sugar Sand Inn possible.

Cover design
Chris Kridler at
Sky Diary Productions

House photo used in cover illustration
Taken by Jerrye and Roy Klotz via Wikipedia,
licensed under Creative Commons
(link: https://creativecommons.org/licenses/by-sa/4.0/deed.en)

Editing Services
Chris Kridler at
Sky Diary Productions

Interior formatting
Amy Atwell and Team
Author E.M.S.

About the Author

Leigh Duncan is the award-winning author of more than two dozen novels, novellas and short stories. Though she started writing fiction at the tender age of six, she didn't get serious about writing a novel until her 40th birthday, and she offers all would-be authors this piece of advice: Don't wait so long!

Leigh sold her first, full-length novel in 2010. In 2017, she was thrilled when Hallmark Publishing chose her as the lead author for their new line of romances and cozy mysteries. A National Readers' Choice Award winner, an Amazon best-selling author and recently named a National Best-Selling author by Publisher's Weekly, Leigh lives on Florida's East Coast where she writes women's fiction and sweet, contemporary romance with a dash of Southern sass.

Want to get in touch with Leigh? She loves to hear from readers and fans. Visit leighduncan.com to send her a note. Join Leigh on Facebook, and don't forget to sign up for her newsletter so you get the latest news about fun giveaways, special offers or her next book!

About the Cover

The minute I came up with the idea of writing about four best friends who open a beach-side inn, I knew exactly which house I wanted to put on the covers of these books. With its gingerbread trim and Queen Anne-style architecture, the Wood/Spann house is easily one of the most beautiful homes I've ever seen. Built in 1895 by F.S. Wood, the house is a part of Troy, Alabama's College Street Historical District and is listed in the National Registry of Historic Places. Best of all, it belongs to a member of my very own family!

Aunt Betty, thank you so much for letting me feature your incredible home on the covers of the books in the Sugar Sand Beach series!

Made in United States
North Haven, CT
20 April 2024

51543291R00211